HUNT
THEM
DOWN

ALSO BY SIMON GERVAIS

MIKE WALTON SERIES

The Thin Black Line
A Long Gray Line
A Red Dotted Line
A Thick Crimson Line

HUNT THEM DOWN

A PIERCE HUNT THRILLER

SIMON GERVAIS

 THOMAS & MERCER

Text copyright © 2019 by Simon Gervais
All rights reserved.

Published by Thomas & Mercer, Seattle

www.apub.com

Amazon, the Amazon logo, and Thomas & Mercer are trademarks of Amazon.com, Inc., or its affiliates.

ISBN-13: 9781503903210 (hardcover)
ISBN-10: 1503903214 (hardcover)
ISBN-13: 9781503904507 (paperback)
ISBN-10: 1503904504 (paperback)

Cover design by Jae Song

Printed in the United States of America

First Edition

To my wife, Lisane, for making everything possible

CHAPTER ONE

Chicago, Illinois

Special Agent Pierce Hunt was pissed. Whoever at headquarters had the bright idea to embed a big shot reporter like Luke Moore in his team was an idiot. He had enough on his mind without the additional chore of babysitting a prima donna. He shook his head in frustration.

"We're two minutes out," Hunt said into the microphone of his PRC-126 as his driver cranked the wheel of the Dodge Durango and accelerated out of the final turn.

Hunt and the rest of his rapid response team—RRT—had flown in from Stafford, Virginia, the night before. They were about to hit the stash of Ramón Figueroa, a midlevel associate of Valentina Mieles— also known as the Black Tosca—who controlled the heroin trade in the Albany Park neighborhood of Chicago. Intelligence indicated they would find over a quarter of a ton of pure heroin hidden in the warehouse. It was an incredible amount. In the last few years, the Black Tosca's cartel had gone from being a low-quality heroin producer to becoming the dominant Mexican drug cartel by refining opium paste into high-grade heroin that sold for much less than it used to. The other cartels quickly embraced the method, and in no time, unwitting people addicted to painkillers were switching to heroin because the prices were now lower than prescription pills.

Chicago—one of the United States' largest interior cargo ports and the world's third-largest handler of shipping containers—had become a huge drug distribution center. With over one billion square feet of warehouse property, it offered the traffickers plenty of space to hide their products.

"Are you nervous, Agent Hunt?" Moore asked.

Hunt ignored him. The man was a real pain in the ass.

"Agent Hunt, I asked you if you were—"

"Stop talking now, or I'll tape your mouth shut," Hunt warned him. When the reporter didn't reply, Hunt continued, "You stay in the truck. You don't move until I tell you to. Understood?"

A quick look over his shoulder told Hunt the reporter wasn't used to being talked to like that. Still, the man nodded, which was the smart thing to do when flanked by two massive DEA special agents dressed in combat gear.

There were three other agents in the Dodge Durango and another thirty in seven similar vehicles. Hunt knew them well and trusted them to do their jobs and to watch each other's backs. Six snipers were already in position and had been trained on the target for the last three hours. Hunt checked on them one last time.

"Sierra One from Alpha One."

"Go ahead for Sierra One."

"Sitrep, over."

"Site is green. Traffic is light. No movement in and out of the building. The two panel vans are still parked in the open drive-in doors. Sierra Two is ready to cut the power on your order."

"Ten-four, Sierra One."

The protocol for operations such as this required linking with city officials in order to turn off the power grid in the area. There were approvals to receive, board meetings to attend, but Hunt didn't trust anyone outside his team and his chain of command to keep their mouths shut, so he hadn't mentioned anything about cutting power in the operational plan he had submitted to the brass. They'd do it manu-ally. He was more than happy to get a reprimand if straying from the plan kept his men safe.

Built in the midfifties, the warehouse was located on Lawrence Avenue and was made of reinforced concrete. It had two drive-in doors with eighteen-foot clearances, a total square footage of just under twenty-five thousand, two floors, and two six-thousand-pound-capacity elevators. Hunt and his team had studied the blueprints and practiced their assault on a replica at their headquarters in Virginia. The ware-house's office occupied less than 5 percent of the total square footage, so they were confident that the two floors would be large open spaces and not a cluster of small individual storage rooms. That didn't mean it would be left undefended—hence the high number of RRT operators taking part in the raid.

A quarter of a ton of heroin—226 kilograms—represented a sig-nificant amount of money. The wholesale price of a single kilogram was $60,000. Cutting the heroin with vitamin B and other substances pro-vided enough powder to fill twenty-five thousand single-dose envelopes that would be sold at $5 to street-level dealers, who in turn would sell them for between $10 and $15 to their customers. The DEA had done the math: each kilo brought in a $70,000 profit to the mill operator.

That's over $15 million in heroin. Hunt wasn't naive. To him and his men, $15 million was a fortune. But to the drug traffickers it was nothing, and it tortured Hunt not being able to hurt the damn cartels. He had seen firsthand the devastation and misery hard drugs left in their wake when his younger brother, Jake, had overdosed on the stuff fifteen years ago. Hunt might not be able to harm the cartels, but if his actions saved even just one life and spared a family the grief associated with the loss of one of their own, it was all worth it.

"Sierra One from Alpha One," Hunt said as the driver turned onto Lawrence Avenue.

"Go for Sierra One."

"We're one minute out."

"Copy that, Alpha One. You're one minute out. Standing by to cut power."

With the exception of the two drive-in bays, a standard-size windowless door was the only entrance. Hunt had no doubt the traffickers had reinforced the strike plate and the doorframe with a high-end dead bolt, so he had come prepared. A ram wouldn't do here, nor would a thermal option. He didn't want his two breachers to spend too much time exposed. Hunt was a fan of explosive breaching, and that was the method they'd be using today. One team would go through the door while his team would enter through one of the bays. With the power out, the simultaneous breaches would allow his team to deliver overwhelming force before any of the defenders could understand they'd been hit.

That was the plan, anyway. But how often did anything go according to plan?

CHAPTER TWO

Chicago, Illinois

Luke Moore of HJ-TV Chicago News wasn't at his first rodeo. He disliked the DEA agents, and he knew they despised him back. They were a bunch of bullies with guns, just like the local PD. *Dangerous bullies with guns.* And Luke would make sure they didn't break the law. If the big guy in the passenger seat thought Luke would stay inside the vehicle, he didn't know Luke's reputation very well. They might have guns, but Luke had his camera. He had started tweeting about the raid the moment they left the regional DEA office. The hundreds of likes and retweets coming in from his half a million followers melted his last barrier of intellectual resistance against sharing everything live on social media. Once at the warehouse and outside the SUV, he'd be in the perfect position to capture anything these bullies did. His bosses might slap him on the wrist since sharing live content of this operation was strictly forbidden, but he would be quickly forgiven if the ratings were there. And Luke knew they would be. They always were when he was bashing the police in the pursuit of justice.

———

Ramón Figueroa was eating a bag of barbecue potato chips when his phone rang. He licked his fingers clean before answering.

"Yes?"

"The DEA is on its way."

Figueroa sat straighter in his chair. "What? Are you sure?"

"You know that reporter, Luke Moore—"

"I know who he is!" Figueroa snapped back. Moore was a local reporter well known for his bias against the police.

"Moore is live tweeting about a raid he's part of. He mentioned a link to the Black Tosca's cartel."

Fuck.

"How long do we have?"

"About fifteen minutes. Tops."

Maldita. Figueroa banged his desk with the palm of his hand. He'd have to leave a lot of product behind. But that was the cost of doing business. It would set them back a month, no more.

"We'll move to site two. I'll call you when we get there." He hung up, removed the battery from the burner phone, and grabbed his suppressed AR-15.

Figueroa hurried down the stairs and jogged to the lab, where Edmundo and Juan—his two team leaders—were supervising the addition of cutting agents to the heroin.

Both men turned when they saw their boss barge in without a mask.

"DEA will be here in less than fifteen minutes," Figueroa whispered. "Get the rest of the guys, and pack everything you can in the trucks. I want to be out of here in five. Leave everything else behind."

Edmundo pointed at the dozen workers cutting the heroin. All of them were women between the ages of fifteen and twenty who had, in one way or another, fallen into the hands of the cartel. They were slaves, victims of human trafficking. As an added humiliation, they were forced to work naked.

"Them too?"

Figueroa shook his head. "No. We'll load the trucks ourselves."

"As you wish, boss." Juan raised his rifle.

Figueroa pushed the barrel back down. "Their blood will contaminate the heroin. Usher them into the corner. Do it there," he said, pointing to a space at the opposite end of the lab.

Edmundo approached the workers and barked orders in Spanish. The women looked nervously at Figueroa, knowing something awful was about to happen. But what could they do? They were naked and unarmed, but it was human nature to hold on to hope.

Maybe, just maybe, if they did what they were told, everything would be all right.

CHAPTER THREE

Chicago, Illinois

Hunt was less than half a mile from the warehouse when the lead sniper broke the air.

"Alpha One, Sierra One, over."

"Go for Alpha One."

"I have movement at the drive-ins. Six males of Hispanic origin climbed into the vans. One of them is Ramón Figueroa. Some of the men are armed with what seem to be AR-15s."

Hunt's hopes of a victimless raid evaporated quickly.

The intelligence provided to his team hadn't indicated any other commercial operations going on at the warehouse. It made his next tactical decision much easier.

"Sierra One, you're clear to engage on your authority. Don't let the vans get away."

"Sierra One copies. All Sierra elements are clear to engage on my authority."

———

Figueroa closed the door and started the diesel engine. Site two was another warehouse ten miles away. Two of his men would ride with him. He had ordered Juan, Edmundo, and a third man to take a separate route. It had been his decision to have only five men with him on Lawrence Avenue. By keeping a low profile, he had hoped to extend his stay longer than the ninety days he usually remained at a given place.

He wished he could have brought the girls, but fifteen minutes wasn't enough time to get them dressed and to secure them in the back of each truck. And they were cheap anyway. Much cheaper than heroin. His associates would have no problem sending more girls his way. He knew the drill.

Born thirty years ago in a lower-middle-class family near Reynosa, Mexico, a city about eleven miles south of McAllen, Texas, on the southern bank of the Rio Grande, Figueroa had watched his parents work for an American-owned aluminum vents factory. It hadn't taken long for him to figure out that the Americans were doing business in his hometown because of the low labor rates the hardworking Mexicans were willing to accept. Not Figueroa. In town, he'd seen men who lived a far easier lifestyle, had more money, and drove shiny black cars. That was what he wanted for himself too. His initial job working for the local kingpin had been menial, but his loyalty and his willingness to do what he was told without asking questions had helped him work his way up the ladder. Within two years, he'd been tasked with accompanying shipments of young girls to the United States. Half a decade later, and with a shiny black Escalade parked in his underground garage, Figueroa was the Black Tosca's representative in Chicago.

In his side mirror, Figueroa saw Trevor exit the warehouse with Fernando. Trevor was the youngest in his crew, but he had already proven himself as a merciless street enforcer. He was passionate about his job, but maybe a little too ambitious for Figueroa's taste. He'd have to keep a close eye on him. Trust only went so far. Fernando, though, was a different animal. At twenty-six, he was five years Trevor's senior and a graduate of the accounting program at the University of Chicago. Fernando was incapable of violence; his forte was analyzing corporate balance sheets and keeping financial records.

"We're good to go, boss," Trevor said as he slammed the sliding door behind him.

Figueroa gently pressed the gas pedal, and the van moved forward. He cranked the steering wheel hard to the left to leave some space for the other van parked next to them. He felt the van shudder lightly, as if he had driven over a glass bottle. A millisecond later, bullets punched through the hood of the van.

Figueroa jammed his foot down on the gas pedal, and the tires spun before catching traction. The van leaped forward and onto the street outside the warehouse. He had to call site two to warn them and ask for backup. As he pulled his phone from his pocket, the van swerved into the opposite lane. An oncoming car blared its horn. Figueroa jerked the wheel to the right to avoid a head-on collision, and his phone fell in between the seats. He searched for it with his right hand. The tips of his fingers touched it, but that only pushed the phone farther down and out of reach.

"Call site two now," he shouted.

Before Trevor or Fernando could do so, the van jolted right. Figueroa attempted to recover, but the engine didn't respond. The steering wheel was heavy and sluggish, and the van came to a stop in the middle of the road, its left front and rear tires shot out.

"Out!"

Figueroa grabbed his AR-15 and jumped out of the van. Trevor did the same, but Fernando remained in his seat, too terrified to move.

"There." Figueroa pointed toward three SUVs approaching at high speed. Their emergency lights confirmed they were law enforcement.

Figueroa and Trevor opened fire on the lead SUV.

———

Hunt watched his snipers engage with the targets. This was a busier neighborhood than he would have liked. In an effort to avoid collateral damage and unintended civilian casualties, Hunt had wanted to box in the panel vans at the warehouse, but they'd been seconds too late. Two hundred yards away, two men exited the immobilized van and raised their rifles.

"Gun, gun, gun," Hunt warned, bringing his MP5 to bear.

Hunt fired through the Durango's windshield as bullets ripped apart its side mirror. Puffs of dirt and asphalt erupted to the left of his targets. He adjusted his aim but lost it before he could fire again when the driver braked hard.

Hunt was out of the Durango before it had fully stopped.

"Alpha One from Sierra One, you have two tangos behind the van. I have no shots," said the sniper leader.

"Copy. Two targets behind the panel van."

The rush of adrenaline enhanced all Hunt's senses. He was exactly where he was supposed to be, and it felt good. In his peripheral vision, he spotted his men taking their positions next to him. To his immediate left was Scott Miller, the youngest guy on the team and a man Hunt had taken under his wing. Miller's abilities and leadership skills left no doubt in Hunt's mind that Miller would one day lead his own team.

They were still fifty yards away from the van when he saw a head pop out from behind the rear bumper. Hunt aligned his sights and was about to squeeze the trigger when the head exploded.

Good shot, Scott.

———

Figueroa watched in horror as Trevor collapsed next to him. The back of his head was covered in blood. Loud cracks told him the other van had come under fire too, probably from snipers perched at key locations around the warehouse. The fact that he was still alive meant the snipers had no clear shot or were too busy dealing with the rest of his crew.

"Fernando, get your ass out of the van," Figueroa screamed.

Puta.

Figueroa had no illusions. He wasn't going to kill them all by himself. His options were limited to surrendering to the DEA—and being killed in prison for his cowardice—or making a stand and trying to take as many with him as he could in death.

Figueroa considered his options and quickly came up with a plan. The interior of the van would offer both concealment and a wide field of fire. With Fernando's help, he would make the DEA pay dearly for interfering with the Black Tosca's business.

As Fernando slowly made his way out of the van, Figueroa grabbed him by the collar and pulled him close. "Here's what I want you to do."

———

"Stay vigilant," Hunt said to his team. "There are at least two more tangos associated with this van."

"Alpha One, Sierra One."

"Go."

"Three tangos down on the other side of the warehouse."

"Copy."

The wailing of police sirens from throughout the city filled the crisp morning air. Within minutes, the local cops would be everywhere, adding to the confusion. Hunt saw an unarmed man slowly come out from behind the panel van. He didn't recognize him.

"Hands in the air!" Hunt yelled. "Step away from the van!"

Hunt's eyes scanned the man for weapons. The man was shaking, and there was a wet patch on his pants between his legs.

"Keep your hands up and turn around slowly."

The sound of a semiautomatic weapon startled Hunt. Rounds came from nowhere, and he dropped to the ground as one whizzed next to his head. Miller wasn't as fast, though, and was hit twice. Hunt heard him grunt as he fell to his knees, but before Hunt could render him assistance, the man who had come out from behind the van reached behind his back. Hunt shot him with a double tap to the chest. The man collapsed on the spot, but the bullets didn't stop. It took Hunt another half second to understand that someone was firing at them from inside the van.

Hunt opened up with three-round bursts. His team followed his lead and did the same.

"Cease fire! Cease fire!" Hunt ordered almost immediately. He stood up. "On me!"

They had peppered the van with so many bullets that Hunt doubted whoever had fired at them was still a threat. Two agents covered him on his left while Hunt approached the van. He opened the sliding door. Ramón Figueroa lay there, his body riddled with bullets; an AR-15 remained firmly in his grasp. Hunt cleared the weapon while the rest of his team secured the perimeter and tended to the suspect Hunt had shot in the chest.

"Pierce, over here!" one of his men called.

Hunt turned his head and saw that the suspect he'd shot had been holding a pistol. Hunt exhaled loudly. He had made the right call. But his relief was short-lived. As Hunt completed his visual inspection of the scene, he saw that Miller remained immobile in the middle of the road. Hunt ran to him.

"Officer down! Officer down!" Hunt said over the radio as he knelt next to his fallen comrade.

Fuck!

Miller's eyes were still open. A small puddle of blood had formed under him. At least one armor-piercing round had gone through his vest and another through his throat. Hunt removed his gloves and felt for a pulse, already knowing he'd find none.

CHAPTER FOUR

Chicago, Illinois

Moore couldn't believe his luck. He checked his live viewers. Ten thousand and climbing. *Amazing.* The likes were coming in faster than ever before. And so were the comments.

He had filmed everything, including when the lead special agent—*what was his name again? Oh yeah, Hunt*—had shot the man who had just surrendered. Moore's whole body was shaking—not from fear but from excitement. He quietly climbed out of the Durango and continued to film. The scene was surreal. The panel van had so many bullet holes that it looked like an infantry platoon had used it for target practice. Part of him wished innocent people had been inside the van when the DEA agents fired at it. *That* would've been the biggest law enforcement blunder in the history of Chicago. *Worth a Pulitzer, maybe?*

Moore aimed his phone at the lead agent, who was kneeling next to what appeared to be a dead DEA agent. *Oh my God. I can't believe this. The viewers will go crazy. This will be international news within the hour.*

He jogged toward them. "What's the name of the dead agent?" he asked.

———

Hunt turned his head and saw that damn reporter aiming his phone at his fallen comrade. Moore was grinning as if he had just won the lottery. *The man is a plague*, Hunt thought with revulsion. His pompous, entitled attitude exemplified everything that was wrong in today's society. At that moment in time, there was nothing Hunt wanted more than to punch the reporter in the face, to inflict physical pain on that poor excuse of a man as payback for his lack of respect. The desire to wipe the smirk off the reporter's face was almost overwhelming, but something deep inside Hunt held him back.

The promise.

A promise he had made to himself years ago while he was still an Army Ranger. A promise on which the seals were still unbroken. A promise entailing that he would never, ever, come what may, use gratuitous violence again. Pea-brained Luke Moore, as ignorant and idiotic as he was, wasn't worth breaking the promise over.

Hunt's earpiece crackled.

"Alpha One, Bravo Two."

"Go for Alpha One."

"Pierce, you better make your way in here. There's something you need to see."

"Copy. On my way."

But Moore wasn't done with him yet. The reporter's phone now pointed at Hunt.

"What's the dead agent's name?" Moore repeated.

Hunt ignored him and started walking in the direction of the warehouse. Moore grabbed his elbow.

"I asked you a question," Moore spat. "You're on live—"

Hunt spun around and placed the palm of his left hand on Moore's chest.

"Get out of my face," Hunt warned. The ice in his voice was enough to make Moore step away, but neither man intended what happened next.

Moore tripped over his own feet and fell backward, managing to hit his head on the pavement in the process. After a stunned moment, he grimaced in pain and raised his hand to the back of his head. It came back bloody. To Hunt's surprise, he smiled.

"You're so fucked."

"Are you for real? I barely touched you, dickhead," Hunt said, regretting the words the moment they came out.

"You shoved me to the ground! That's assault, and I'm pressing charges."

CHAPTER FIVE

Chicago, Illinois

Hunt was still steaming over that idiot reporter, but he didn't have time to waste. He left Moore sitting on the pavement, still filming with his cell phone, and entered the warehouse. He might have been better off if he'd stayed outside.

Hunt wished anyone who said drug use was a victimless crime could see what was in front of him. The twelve young girls who had been slaughtered were all the proof the skeptics needed to see. The girls had never stood a chance.

Why had the cartel killed them? What had prompted them to depart the warehouse? Had they known the DEA was about to raid them? It certainly looked like it. But how?

Hunt's phone vibrated in his trouser pocket.

"Yes?"

"Pierce, this is Tom Hauer."

Hauer was the acting administrator of the DEA. He was a political appointee but a good guy nonetheless.

"Can I call you back, sir? We're still in the middle of the operation."

"No, you're not, I'm afraid. You're relieved of your command, and you're about to be placed under arrest by the Chicago Police Department."

"Say that again?" Hunt replied, his temper rising. This wasn't a good time to mess with him.

"You're relieved. I'm sorry, Pierce. It's all over the news. My hands are tied."

"What the hell are you talking about?"

"That reporter you pushed to the ground was filming. *Live*."

"For Christ's sake. I didn't push him to the ground. He tripped over his own feet."

"Doesn't matter." Hauer sighed. "He was tweeting during the whole goddamn operation, and when the shooting started, he switched to a live video feed. He's saying you shot an unarmed man. Tell me it isn't true."

"Moore's full of shit, sir. The man was armed," Hunt replied, his mind racing. Something Hauer had said had caught his attention. "Did you say Moore was tweeting? About the raid?"

"I'm on his Twitter feed now, and yes, he started tweeting the moment you left the office. How the hell did this happen?"

Shit! They knew we were coming because of Moore.

Hunt hung up on his boss.

"Follow me," he said to three of his team members. "I'm gonna strangle that journalist shitbag."

"Might not be a good idea, Pierce," Simon Carter told him. Carter was his second-in-command and a close friend.

Hunt stopped and looked Carter square in the eyes. "He screwed us. He publicly tweeted our location, Simon. Scott's death, and all of this, is on him."

Hunt saw his own fury reflected in Carter's eyes. Losing a teammate was bad enough, but they all knew the risks associated with the job. Being betrayed was a different story. Someone was about to pay dearly for his sins.

The moment Hunt stepped out of the warehouse, he was intercepted by a Chicago police lieutenant flanked by three other officers.

They had their hands on the butts of their pistols. Hunt was glad the guns were still holstered.

"Special Agent Pierce Hunt?" the lieutenant said.

"Not now, Lieutenant," Hunt said. "There's something we need to do. Give me five minutes."

For a moment, the officer looked confused. Then his eyes moved to the three DEA special agents in full combat gear standing behind the man he was supposed to take into custody. It didn't look as if they were going to allow their leader to be taken. At least not yet.

"All right," the lieutenant finally said, stepping aside.

Hunt nodded his thanks.

Outside, the sun was shining. Police vehicles and ambulances were everywhere. Someone had had the decency to cover Scott Miller's body with a sheet. There would be a time to mourn him, but now wasn't that time. Now was the time for revenge.

Hunt's gaze was fixed on Luke Moore, who was being treated by a paramedic in the back of an ambulance. A DEA special agent was standing next to him. The paramedic saw Hunt and took two steps back.

"Come with me," Hunt said, yanking Moore to his feet.

"I'm not going anywhere with you," Moore said and then started screaming. "Help me! This is police brutality!"

Hunt effortlessly lifted the reporter and slung him over his left shoulder.

"There's something I want to show you," Hunt said. "Your handiwork."

———

Moore didn't care that people were staring at him. It actually fit perfectly with his plan. In his mind, they were witnesses he would call upon to testify how unfairly the police had treated him.

He was already counting the millions he'd get from a civil lawsuit when his head bumped hard against a doorframe. Moore let out a whooshing sound and blinked back tears of pain.

He twisted his head to the other side and saw a bunch of Chicago police officers chatting together. "Hey, you saw that?" Moore screamed at them. "This guy is out of control. Do something!"

One of the officers pointed a finger toward him. "That's Luke Moore," he said.

"Who's he?" asked another.

"He's the cop hater I talked to you about."

One by one, the officers turned their backs.

———

Hunt lifted Moore off his shoulder and placed him on his feet, handling the journalist as though he was a wooden toy soldier. Moore had the good sense to remain quiet. Carter was standing guard next to the door leading into the laboratory.

"He needs to see what he's done," Hunt hissed.

Carter handed a gas mask to Hunt but didn't offer one to Moore.

"Him too," Hunt said reluctantly, and they waited for Moore to put a mask on.

Carter opened the door, and Hunt pushed Moore inside. The reporter stopped and tried to walk back out, but Hunt shoved him forward.

"What is this? Why are you bringing me here?" Moore demanded.

Hunt gripped Moore's neck and showed him the twelve naked bodies resting on the floor. "You did this," Hunt said.

Moore twisted, trying to turn his head away. "I had nothing to do with this. Who are they?"

"They were human slaves."

"Get me out of here! I had nothing to do with this!" Moore repeated, trying to get away. Hunt tightened his grip around the reporter's neck and kicked him behind the legs, forcing him onto his knees. In one swift motion, Hunt drew his firearm and placed the muzzle against the back of Moore's head.

———

Moore felt the pressure of the gun to his head. *Oh my God. I'm gonna die.* He had seen Hunt kill an unarmed man minutes ago. Hunt wouldn't hesitate to kill him here surrounded by his brutal and heartless peers. Moore wanted to cry for help, but he was too terrified. Beads of sweat had formed on his forehead, which made wearing the mask even less comfortable.

"Why are you doing this?" he asked.

"Did you tweet where we were going?"

Moore's gut became a knot. *Shit.*

Had he caused these deaths? Was he somehow responsible for this mayhem? Without warning, a terrible odor made its way to his olfactory sensory neurons. The stench was such that he gagged on it.

"What the hell?" he heard Hunt say.

It was then that Moore, on his knees and with a gun to his head, understood. The hot, wet weight that filled his underpants didn't lie. He had shit himself. Never in his life had he felt so humiliated and degraded. And for that, he'd make the DEA pay dearly.

CHAPTER SIX

Six months later

Miami, Florida

Pierce Hunt almost choked biting into the pizza slice. The watered-down tomato sauce did nothing to enhance the chemical taste of the seasoning or the soggy crust. Hunt was convinced the life expectancy of his fellow Americans would drop by a few years if this new recipe ever made it to the mainstream pizza chains.

"This is the best pizza ever," his fifteen-year-old daughter, Leila, said, already halfway through her second slice.

"Absolutely," Hunt lied between two emergency sips of Diet Coke. "Never tasted anything like this before."

Leila stopped chewing and cocked her head to one side. "You're such a bad liar," she said. "You really don't like it?"

"Why don't we try that new taco place next time?"

"Sure," Leila said without much enthusiasm. She took another bite and checked her phone.

"No phone while we eat, Leila," Hunt said. "This is our time."

"You checked yours, like, three times in the last five minutes."

Hunt wanted to say it was for work. That he had to. After all, it was his first day back on the job after a six-month suspension. But she was right; he couldn't ask her to do something if he wasn't willing to do the same.

She was growing so fast. Hunt remembered when she would fall asleep on his chest with her head tucked under his chin and her toes not even touching his belly button. She had been so little then. He missed those years. He craved having them back. Not just the years, but Jasmine too. She was a great mother to Leila, and she had been a good wife to him. He was the one who had pushed her—and Leila—out of his life. He hadn't done it intentionally, of course, but year after year, he had essentially let the DEA build a wall between him and his family.

Life was all about choices, and Hunt was wondering if he'd made the right ones. Looking at his daughter—now on her third pizza slice— he realized that his life was filled with bad choices. He'd left the army, joined the DEA, and immediately accepted the long undercover assignment that they'd offered him. If he had said no, maybe he, Leila, and Jasmine would still be a family.

His phone vibrated on the table, next to the pizza slice he had no intention of ever touching again.

"Dad?" Leila was looking at him, her disappointment evident. As he was about to take the call, her hand reached for his from across the table. "Please don't."

He had promised they'd go see a movie after lunch. His shift wasn't supposed to start until six. Taking the call might mean they wouldn't make it to the theater. She knew it. He knew it too. But he was who he was.

He took a deep breath and answered the call. "Special Agent Pierce Hunt."

———

"You know this is exactly why Mom left you, right?" Leila looked out the window of his four-year-old Ford F-150.

No, this isn't why your mom left me. But he was glad that was what she thought, because the truth would shatter the fragile relationship he was working so hard to rebuild with his only child.

"I'll make it up to you, Leila, I promise," Hunt said, slowing at a stop sign.

"You won't, Pierce, and you know it," she said, shifting her attention to her vibrating smartphone. "I'm not a child anymore."

He loathed being called Pierce by his daughter. That meant she was royally pissed. Maybe he shouldn't have taken the call. He glanced at her, and his eyes caught something he hadn't expected to see.

"What was that, Leila?"

"What?" she replied, clearly offended by his inquiry. She shut off her phone.

"The picture of a half-naked man I just saw," he said, his temper rising. "Who the hell was that?"

"It's nothing. It's just a picture," Leila replied. "It doesn't matter."

"It matters to me," Hunt said, doing his best to remain calm. He had recently started reading books on how to deal with teenage daughters. The authors were unanimous about one thing: it didn't serve anyone's interest to be either judgmental or hostile.

"You won't understand," Leila said, once again looking outside and away from him. "And Mom knows about it."

"She knows about what?" Hunt squeezed the steering wheel so hard his knuckles became white. He hated being kept in the dark. He wished he could put the blame on his ex-wife, but he knew who the real culprit was. He had lost the privilege of knowing what was going on in his daughter's life long ago.

"My boyfriend sent me a text. That's all. There's no need for you to fuss about it."

Boyfriend. Hunt's mind had shut off right there. He hadn't understood any other word. His baby girl was way too young to have a boyfriend.

And Jasmine *knows about this? She didn't care to tell me our fifteen-year-old daughter has a boyfriend?*

A boyfriend who had just sent Leila a picture of himself half-naked? Hunt didn't care anymore what the books said. He was going to find out where this young man lived and tell him to stay far away from his daughter.

Hunt was so lost in his own thoughts that he drove right through another stop sign and barely missed hitting an oncoming car.

"Dad!" Leila yelled at the top of her lungs. Her scream brought him back to the here and now.

Shit!

The red-and-blue lights of a police car appeared in his rearview mirror. Hunt sighed, ashamed he had nearly gotten into an accident while driving with his daughter. He definitely wouldn't try to badge his way out of this one. He deserved to pay every dollar of the fine.

"Sorry, Leila," he said. "I really am."

"You scared the hell out of me."

Hunt parallel parked and turned off the vehicle. He opened his window and removed the key from the ignition. Through his side mirror he saw the Miami-Dade police officer climb out of his cruiser. Hunt placed his hands on the steering wheel, making sure they were in plain sight.

The officer touched the taillight of Hunt's pickup truck with his thumb. This safety precaution had been practiced by police officers for decades as a way to leave behind evidence of the encounter. That was a good move that told Hunt the officer took his job seriously. No doubt the officer had also called in the Ford's license plate and the location of the traffic stop.

"Good afternoon, sir," the officer said, his right hand on top of his firearm. "Do you know why I pulled you over?" His eyes scanned the rear seats before stopping on Hunt's daughter in the front passenger seat. "You're okay, young lady?"

"Thanks for saving my life, Officer," Leila said without missing a beat. "My father nearly killed us both."

The officer's eyes narrowed on Hunt. With the kind of statement Leila had just made, Hunt fully expected the officer to order him out of his vehicle. *Just what I need on my first day out of suspension*, Hunt thought. *I might have to flash my badge after all.*

Before the officer could reply to Leila, Hunt took the initiative and told him, "My driver's license is in my right-side suit jacket pocket, and the registration is in the glove box. I'm with the DEA."

The officer's demeanor relaxed ever so slightly.

Hunt handed over his driver's license and the registration before presenting his DEA credentials.

The officer looked at the driver's license, his eyes widening, and then at Hunt. "You're Pierce Hunt? *The* Pierce Hunt?"

"Depends what you mean by that." Hunt shifted uncomfortably in his seat.

"You're the DEA agent who shoved that asshole reporter to the ground—"

"He actually tripped over his own feet, but yeah, that's me," Hunt said, smiling nervously. He didn't want the conversation to go any further. Not with Leila next to him. She had made it abundantly clear that his actions toward the reporter hadn't impressed her.

"Shit. The guys back at the station won't believe it," the officer said, shaking his head.

Hunt smiled politely. Moore's video of the raid on the Black Tosca's cartel warehouse—and particularly, his confrontation with Hunt—had made headlines around the country and had amassed over five million views on YouTube.

"Did you really put your gun against his head in the warehouse?" the officer asked, clearly excited.

"Not my proudest moment," Hunt said.

"Way I heard it, the guy caused the deaths of those women and one of your agents. He deserved it, if you ask me."

"Still cost me six months' salary." *And he got a two-and-a-half-million-dollar confidential settlement from the DEA*, Hunt thought. *For tripping over his own damn feet!*

"Anyway, it's a real honor to meet you. Sorry for what happened to your guy."

"Same here, Officer, and thank you." Hunt shook the man's outstretched hand.

"Here you go," the officer said, handing the driver's license and registration back to Hunt. "Stay safe."

"All right, I will," Hunt promised.

Once they were on their way, Leila said, "So these officers think you're cool because you killed two drug dealers and beat up a reporter on live video?" She seemed disgusted.

"Listen, baby," he started, swearing to himself he wouldn't get upset. "First of all, I didn't beat up anyone. Second, I don't know what they teach you at school, but you need to understand that I didn't have any choice—"

"You always have a choice," Leila said, the emotion in her voice rising. "You taught me that, remember?"

Here we go. She was using his words—taken out of context—against him. There was so much of her mother in her. Jasmine had never liked what he did for a living. She loved him, but he always felt she never knew for sure if he was the good guy or not. Sometimes he wasn't so sure either.

Especially after what he'd done in Gaza.

"Not this time, I'm afraid," he said, careful about his word choice. "It was either them or us."

Leila started to sob. "Do you know what it feels like to watch your father kill two men in cold blood?"

It wasn't in cold blood, he wanted to say. But he didn't. Instead he said, "No, I don't. Tell me."

"It's awful, Pierce, okay? It's, it's . . ." She looked for the right word. Tears rolled down her cheeks.

"Horrific? Sickening?" Hunt did his very best to offer a sympathetic ear to his daughter's plea. "I know, and I'm sorry."

"And I can't even talk about it to anyone but Mom because you're some kind of spy or whatever," she continued.

"I'm no spy. I'm a DEA agent," he tried to explain, knowing this wasn't what his daughter needed to hear. *God, I wish I was better at this.* "I know it's unfair that you can't talk about it, but, believe me, it's for your own security."

"Whatever."

It broke his heart to see her cry. A father's job was to protect his daughter. And clearly he had failed.

"I have nightmares. Did Mom tell you? Did she tell you how I still wet my bed like a two-year-old?"

Hunt stopped in a parking lot. He unbuckled his seat belt and walked around the truck. He opened the passenger door and pulled his daughter close to him. Her defenses faded away. He wrapped his arms around her, and she held him. He felt her warm tears on his neck.

"I'm sorry, Leila," he whispered. "I'm truly sorry you had to see that, but I can't apologize for doing the right thing. People trust me to protect their lives, and I took an oath to do just that. It's my job."

His daughter wiped her eyes with her sleeve. "You know what my nightmares are about?"

Hunt shook his head, angry he couldn't do more for his daughter.

"That it's you instead of them . . . that it's you who dies . . . who gets shot and bleeds out alone in the street," she said, fighting through her emotions. "Why couldn't you be a football player or something like that?"

"Like Chris?" he said, controlling his anger at the thought of Jasmine's new husband.

"Yeah, like Chris, Dad," she said, regaining control of herself. "And you don't have to say his name like that, you know."

Chris Moon was a Miami Dolphins player. Their star quarterback, to be exact. He and Hunt didn't get along too well. Moon was younger and taller, drove expensive cars, and had access to a one-hundred-foot Azimut yacht, but those weren't the things that bothered Hunt—or maybe they did just a tiny bit. What truly pissed him off was that Moon spent more time with Leila than he did.

"I don't like the guy, Leila. I can't lie."

"Well, Mom does, and he's cool with me."

"Okay."

"Okay what?"

"I'll smile next time I say his name," Hunt said.

Leila looked doubtful.

"Look, Leila," he continued, "I'm glad he takes care of you and your mom. I really am. But it's hard for me too, you know?"

His daughter squeezed his arm. "I know."

"I wish I could stay with you this weekend and bring you camping or go to the shooting range."

"Like we used to when I was a kid?"

You're still a kid, Hunt thought. "Yes, like we used to."

Leila shrugged. "The last time I went camping, I came back with a bunch of mosquito bites. So no thanks."

"Maybe we could go to the range another time, then?"

She screwed up her face and pulled away from him. "Ugh. Weren't you listening, Dad? Guns kill people. Don't you watch the news? I never want to touch one again. And I'm certainly not interested in going to some outdoor range filled with . . ."

"With what?"

"People like you."

Her words slapped him in the face.

Before he could recover, his daughter shrugged. "Don't worry about this weekend. I have plans anyway."

Hunt wanted to ask what kind of plans, but his words balled up in his throat.

He tried to hug her again, but Leila was stiff and didn't hug him back. Instead, she patted him on the back.

"Don't worry, Dad. You and I will catch up another time."

CHAPTER SEVEN

DEA Miami Field Division
Weston, Florida

Hunt looked at the 130,000-square-foot building housing the Miami Field Division. The DEA had moved there in 2009 after being evicted from its Doral headquarters. Even though the DEA kept outposts in Miami and Fort Lauderdale, Weston was where decisions were made. The DEA had invested over $4 million to reconfigure the building, tucked between a small hotel and a medical center, with security features, evidence vaults, interrogation rooms, and holding cells.

Tom Hauer, the DEA acting administrator, had transferred Hunt back to Miami after the fiasco in Chicago. There was no way Hunt could have kept his position as a team leader with the RRT in Virginia. That was fine. He would miss kicking in doors, but he was confident he would see action in Miami. Plus, he had no choice. A six-month suspension wasn't something his bank account had counted on. Fortunately for him, he had money tucked away. Not a lot, and certainly not enough to go through another suspension, but enough to allow him to pay his bills. Jasmine had offered to help, but it felt wrong to accept money from her knowing it came from her new husband.

But money was just one thing and not the main reason he was pleased to start working again. He missed the job, the camaraderie. He loved the adrenaline rush. He was addicted to it. Unfortunately for him, his suspension had included the strict interdiction against using any DEA facilities, including the shooting ranges. That didn't mean Hunt had been out of options during the past six months. He'd called his former platoon commander, Martin Riese, now a major and the executive officer for the Airborne and Ranger Training Brigade, headquartered at Fort Benning, Georgia, to ask if Riese could find him something useful to do.

Civilians, even DEA agents, weren't usually welcome in the close-knit community that was the Seventy-Fifth Ranger Regiment. But not only had Hunt served with the Rangers, he had also earned the Silver Star for valor in combat during the battle for the Haditha Dam in 2003. So it had been with genuine pleasure that Riese invited him to spend a few weeks at Fort Benning. It had been a win-win situation. In exchange for lecturing about the geopolitical implications of the war on drugs that the American government was waging within and outside its borders, Riese had allowed him to join a group of future Rangers during the mountain and swamp phases of Ranger school. Hunt had had a blast and had been pleased to see he still had the stamina necessary to keep up with the younger Rangers. He wondered where he'd be in life if he had decided to stay in the military.

Hunt took a deep breath and entered the building. He nodded to the security guards and swiped his identification card through the card reader. The light blinked red.

"Can I see your ID, sir?" one of the guards said.

Hunt handed him his credentials. "I'm Special Agent Pierce Hunt. It's my first day here."

The guard examined Hunt's ID. "Who are you here to see?"

"Daniel McMaster, the special agent in charge," Hunt replied.

"One moment." The guard placed a call, then turned his back to him. "Yes, sir," Hunt heard him say, then, "No, sir, the system indicates he's been dismissed."

What?

The guard hung up. "You'll have to wait here, Mr. Hunt. Someone will come down shortly. Please have a seat."

There was no point arguing with the guard. He was only doing his job. The DEA was a big organization, and Hunt wasn't surprised his status hadn't been updated. Still, *dismissed*?

Ten minutes later, two men wearing security uniforms appeared and signaled Hunt to follow them. They didn't say anything, not even a greeting.

They took the elevator to the third floor. The elevator door opened to a sea of cubicles occupied by DEA agents. One of the guards took the lead, and Hunt followed, an uneasy feeling nagging at him. He tried to make eye contact with some of the agents, but none of them looked away from their screens. It was weird. No one was talking, which was unusual. Typically, the bull pen was a noisy place where one sometimes had to yell to be heard by a colleague a few desks away.

He was in the middle of the room when someone shouted, "Ladies and gentlemen, Pierce Hunt!"

The room burst into earsplitting cheers and applause. For a brief moment, Hunt wondered what was going on. Agents were clapping and smiling, some shouting words he didn't understand. A few walked up to him and shook his hand, thanking him for what he had done to the reporter whose actions had contributed to the death of one of their own.

"I guess you weren't expecting such a welcome, Special Agent Hunt," said Daniel McMaster.

Hunt turned to face him. McMaster was tall—over six feet, maybe six two—with broad shoulders and dark brown hair starting to gray at the temples. A huge smile beneath his thick—and somewhat distracting—mustache put Hunt at ease. The two men shook hands.

"I certainly wasn't, sir," Hunt said.

"Glad to have you with us."

"Thanks. Happy to be here."

"Let's talk in my office." McMaster led the way.

McMaster's office wasn't decorated to impress or entertain. The focal point was a dark wood government-issue desk with two large American flags at either end. On the wall behind the desk was a massive DEA seal. A large glass wall separated his space from the bull pen, and Hunt imagined it gave the impression he had his finger on the pulse of his agents.

"Please have a seat, Pierce," McMaster said. "Coffee?"

"No thanks." Hunt sat in one of the chairs facing McMaster's desk. He looked through the glass wall and saw that most of the agents had resumed their seats.

"I'd like to start by telling you that I know you didn't request this transfer," McMaster began. "You might not realize it now, Pierce, but you've become a legend."

A legend? For killing two drug dealers and pointing my gun at an unarmed reporter's head? Oh boy, Leila wouldn't be impressed.

"I'm not sure this is a good—" Hunt started to reply, but McMaster raised his hand.

"Yes, it is, Pierce. These guys learned about your transfer late last week, and morale has never been higher. Do you realize that you've done something many of us have only dreamed about?"

Hunt couldn't help but smile, wondering if McMaster knew about the cash settlement Moore had received. "Yeah, I'm not naive, sir. But I was almost kicked out for it."

"But you weren't. And here you are."

"And I'm looking forward to starting work."

McMaster opened his desk drawer and removed a red folder to which Hunt's picture was stapled. He opened it.

"You served with the Seventy-Fifth Rangers?" McMaster said.

"From '95 to '07."

"Tell me—why did you really leave the army?" In a heartbeat, McMaster's eyes had grown cold. Gone was the warmth and sincere welcome Hunt had felt only a minute ago.

Hunt was taken aback. McMaster had drawn him in with flattery and small talk and then fired the question without preamble. *Does he know?* No, that was impossible. Nobody outside his unit knew. Nobody knew what he had done to save his teammate, his best friend.

"I'm not here to judge," McMaster said, his voice somewhat softer. "But after what I've seen you do in Chicago, I can't help but wonder if it's a good idea to send you into the field again."

"I'm not sure I'm following you."

"Do you know who I had over to dinner yesterday?" McMaster said. Before Hunt had a chance to answer, McMaster continued, "Cole Egan."

Hunt felt the blood drain from his face. *Cole Egan. So McMaster does know.*

"You look like you've seen a ghost, Pierce," McMaster said.

"How's Cole doing?" Hunt managed to say, still in shock that his new boss knew the man he had saved in Gaza.

"He's doing well, thanks to you."

"How do you—"

"He married my daughter three years ago." McMaster grinned. "She's the happiest she's ever been. Cole travels a lot for work—he's an international sales rep for a dental equipment company—but he takes good care of her. They're expecting."

Cole—about to be a father. Hunt was glad to hear that. But one of the best operators he had ever served with was earning his living by selling toothpaste? War changed people's ideas about life, and it was entirely possible that Cole had simply decided to walk away from it all and settle down with someone he loved. Cole had been through a lot, and he deserved to be happy.

And what about Hunt? Did he deserve happiness? In 2007, he and Cole had been part of a small contingent of Rangers and Delta Force operators sent to Gaza to train and assist President Abbas's Palestinian security forces in their underground fight against Hamas terrorists. But all hell had broken loose when two members of Hunt's team were killed and Cole Egan was taken prisoner. Their team had been ordered not to intervene, but within two hours of Cole's capture, Hunt, three other Rangers, and one Delta operator had mounted a rescue operation with intelligence Hunt had gathered through methods some might describe as unorthodox. The rescue had been deemed a military success, but the psychological scars of what he'd done—how far he'd gone to save a teammate—were still there, forever scorched in his mind.

"From what he told me, he owes you his life," McMaster continued. "I wanted to know a little more about the man who'd apparently saved my daughter's husband, you know? But Cole wouldn't say more, and when I reached out to my contact at the Department of Defense, I was told to back off. The only thing I was able to figure out was that you left the army a week after you shipped home. Why?"

"It's complicated," Hunt said. He was certainly not about to volunteer any information.

"Things often are. I've heard rumors about what happened in Gaza."

Hunt remained silent.

"I wasn't there. I don't have all the facts. But if the stories are true, and I'm not saying they are, someone lost control over there and left carnage behind him. Whatever the reasons, a lot of people died. I don't want to see that happen in the streets of Miami, Pierce."

"It won't."

"You threatened to kill that reporter," McMaster reminded him.

"Not my interpretation of what happened, sir. I wanted to scare him, to make him understand that his actions had consequences."

"It wasn't your job to do so."

"I know," Hunt admitted. "And I paid for my sins."

McMaster thought this over. For a full minute, neither man spoke. It was McMaster who broke the silence.

"Vicente Garcia."

Hunt nodded, happy to change the subject to one of his success stories. "What about him?"

"Seems like your friend Vicente was recently transferred to FDC Miami."

Hunt sighed. Infiltrating the Garcia crime family had been his first and most important undercover stint and the real reason why Jasmine had left him. The assignment had lasted over two years and was recognized as one of the biggest DEA busts of the past decade. Thanks to Hunt's work, they'd been able to arrest Vicente Garcia, the head of the crime syndicate. He was presently serving a life sentence in a maximum security prison—or at least he had been until recently. The federal detention center in downtown Miami was home to approximately fifteen hundred male and female inmates, but it wasn't a maximum security prison. Hunt wondered whom Garcia had blackmailed to get transferred there.

"That makes no sense whatsoever," Hunt said angrily. "Vicente's sphere of influence is right here in Miami. Why would anyone agree to transfer him?"

"Because he agreed to tell us everything he knows about the Black Tosca," McMaster said with a smile. "And once we have her in custody, he'll testify against her."

Hunt nearly fell off his chair. Valentina Mieles—a.k.a. the Black Tosca—was the most powerful woman in the drug world. She was originally from Colombia, but her influence reached way beyond Latin America. The Black Tosca was allegedly responsible for the kidnappings and murders of at least thirty Americans in the past year alone. Scott Miller's murderer, Ramón Figueroa, had been her man in Chicago. Having someone like Vicente Garcia testify against her was a big deal. But it also raised questions.

"I wasn't expecting this," Hunt said, scratching his head. "What did you promise him? Vicente isn't the kind of guy to betray his own."

"We didn't have to promise him anything. The Black Tosca is making a move on Garcia's entire network."

Since the DEA had put Vicente behind bars, his son, Tony, had taken over the reins. Under his leadership, the Garcia family had done very well and was raking in money like never before. Because of this, they had become a prime acquisition target for the Black Tosca.

"So this is a defensive move on his part," Hunt said.

"Kind of. He wants us to do his dirty work for him."

"And we'll just go along with this?"

"For now," McMaster said. "We need a win, Pierce. The DEA needs a win. Damn, the White House needs a win. People are looking at us and wondering what the DEA is doing to stop that fucking drug from coming into our country."

Hunt nodded. This was a difficult subject for him; it always brought up memories of his brother.

McMaster continued, "Heroin is everywhere. People are able to get a huge high for less than ten dollars. Do you know who the new heroin addicts are?"

Hunt's thoughts drifted back in time to the night he had discovered Jake dead in the basement of his family's house, a moment that had forever altered the direction of his life. He knew very well who the new addicts were.

"Teenagers," he answered.

"Heroin used to be confined to hard-core drug users, but not anymore," McMaster said. "The use of heroin among teenagers has risen one hundred percent in the last five years. More than fifty-five thousand people died from overdoses last year, and over sixty percent of those deaths involved an opioid."

Hunt was aware of that fact. More people were dying from drug overdoses than from guns and car accidents.

"We've been fighting this war for too long," McMaster said. "And we've been on the losing side. As I said, we need a win."

Hunt had heard this speech before, but the higher-ups always seemed to get cold feet when the time came to strike a huge blow.

"And, of course, a catch like the Black Tosca would look really good on your résumé," Hunt said.

A flash of anger appeared in McMaster's eyes, but it was quickly extinguished.

"It would look good on *everybody's* résumé. You need a win too, Pierce."

Hunt couldn't fault the DEA for wanting to arrest and prosecute the Black Tosca. She was dangerous. She had ruined the lives of too many families by providing a dirt-cheap product that even kids working for minimum wages could afford to shoot up their arms.

"What's my role?" Hunt asked.

"We want you in on Vicente Garcia's interrogation. You know him, and he knows you. You're almost family, right?"

Hunt shifted uncomfortably in his chair. He didn't appreciate the jab. Anna Garcia—Vicente's daughter—had been his way inside the Garcia crime family. The DEA had specifically targeted her, using Hunt as their weapon of choice. Truth was he had fallen hard for her, and she for him. It had been a mistake. A grave mistake that had cost Hunt his family. Still, it was true that Hunt and Vicente had, through Anna, shared a powerful bond for almost two years.

"He hates my guts. He won't talk to me." Which was also true. When Hunt had put the handcuffs around Vicente's wrists, Vicente had promised to one day kill him. And it wouldn't be for the arrest but for breaking his daughter's heart.

"You won't be handling the interrogation," McMaster replied. "We just want you to listen in and steer our partners from Mexico in the right direction. You'll know if Garcia lies."

Partners from Mexico? "So this isn't an American operation?"

"If the intelligence we get from Garcia pans out, we'll need the Mexicans' help if we are to conduct an operation within Mexico."

"I see." Hunt wasn't a fan of the Mexican police. The DEA had lost too many good agents due to the Mexican authorities' inability to root out the corrupt officers within their ranks.

"On that note, I'd like you to meet someone," McMaster said, before turning on the intercom and instructing his secretary to let his guest in. "Play nice, Pierce. We need the Mexicans on this," his new boss reminded him.

A medium-size man dressed in a dark gray suit entered the office. He was in his late forties with thinning black hair. He smiled at Hunt and offered his hand. He had perfectly white teeth.

"Special Agent Hunt, this is Chief Inspector Julio Zorita of the Mexican Federal Police."

"Nice to meet you," Hunt said, forcing a smile he hoped looked genuine.

"The pleasure is all mine," Zorita said. His grip was strong and sincere.

"The chief inspector—"

"Please, call me Julio."

"Julio is the head of the General Directorate of Strategic Operations within the National Gendarmerie Division," continued McMaster. "He'll be our liaison with the Mexican government."

"I'm to be the eyes and ears of the general commissioner," Zorita added.

Hunt nodded. "What's the time frame for Garcia's transfer?"

"It's tomorrow," Zorita said. "We've planned so it falls on a Sunday afternoon. Traffic should be much lighter."

"Indeed," McMaster confirmed. "The US Marshals Special Operations Group will move Garcia to a safe house, where he'll stay until we catch the Black Tosca."

That was a smart move. With the Black Tosca in play, even men like Vicente Garcia weren't immune to her wrath. Starting tomorrow, solitary confinement or not, Garcia would have a huge target painted on his back. No one was naive enough to believe Garcia's treachery would remain a secret.

"I want in on Garcia's transfer," Hunt said.

McMaster raised an eyebrow and looked at Zorita.

"I don't see why you couldn't," the Mexican said.

McMaster didn't look convinced, and Hunt thought he was about to veto his request, but instead he picked up his phone. "Let me call the deputy US marshal supervising tomorrow's move. We'll see what he says."

McMaster dialed the number by heart and gave the marshal a quick summary of Hunt's RRT and Ranger qualifications. He listened for half a minute before he said, "Thanks, John. I'll let him know."

"So?" Hunt asked once McMaster had hung up.

"You owe me one."

But Hunt had a feeling that getting involved with the Garcias again was something he'd come to regret.

CHAPTER EIGHT

2010
Miami, Florida

As the security officer signaled him to enter the courtroom, Hunt knew his life was about to take a turn for the worse. He had dedicated the past two years to the biggest undercover DEA operation of the decade. The arrest of Vicente Garcia had generated a tremendous amount of good publicity for the agency and had, albeit briefly, disrupted the flow of opioids coming through South Florida.

But at what cost? Hunt asked himself as he looked up at the ceiling of the Wilkie D. Ferguson Jr. Courthouse.

What ended up being a big victory for the DEA was nothing but a tremendous waste to Hunt. He was on the verge of losing everything. Hunt had no doubt he was about to get grilled on the stand. That was fine. Lawyers didn't scare him. He was, after all, the main witness against Vicente Garcia, so it was normal they'd go at him with everything they could find in an attempt to destroy his character. It wouldn't matter. The evidence against Garcia was solid. What terrified him, though, was that within the next few hours, his wife—whom he had seen only a handful of times during the past two years—would learn of his infidelity. That scared him to death.

Anna Garcia, Vicente's daughter, had been Hunt's mark from the get-go. She'd been his way into the organization. The analysts had chosen her not only because she was smart but also because she didn't seem to possess the criminal mind that was rampant within her family. And they'd been right. Her role within the Garcia crime family was trivial, and Hunt hadn't bothered digging too deep because the focus of the investigation had always been her father. At least that was how he justified his decision not to prod too aggressively. The fact that he'd fallen for Anna within minutes of seeing her certainly had nothing to do with it, right?

He'd been such a fool. He had played a dangerous game, and now he was about to pay the price.

Hunt could feel Anna's eyes on him. He didn't dare to look in her direction, afraid of what he might see. His heart had never beaten so fast, and he couldn't quite breathe. The courtroom was packed, raising its temperature a few degrees. Film crews were barred from the courtroom and had to make do with waiting in the hallway. He couldn't even imagine the confusion Anna must have felt when he walked into the courtroom through the main door and not the one reserved for the accused. The last time she'd seen him was when the DEA had broken into their home and arrested him and Vicente, who'd stayed over after drinking too much wine during dinner. Unbeknownst to Anna, it was Hunt who had called in the cavalry. Vicente was well protected inside his own home. Not so much at the house Hunt had shared with Anna.

"Are you okay, sir? You're quite pale."

He looked at the prosecutor, an intelligent and stylish woman in her midthirties. Her form-fitting black dress showed off her slim figure as she made her way to the witness stand where he was seated.

"I'm fine. Thank you."

"Please say your name for the court record," the prosecutor requested.

Hunt couldn't resist. He looked in Anna's direction. She met his gaze from the gallery. There was no emotion on her face, but a multitude of questions hovered in her eyes. He closed his eyes and exhaled, wishing he was anywhere but in this courtroom.

"Sir, your name, please," the prosecutor insisted.

"My name is Pierce Hunt."

"Thank you, Mr. Hunt."

Mr. Hunt. There it was. His real name, out in the open. No longer a secret to the woman with whom he had shared everything for the last two years. *Almost everything*, Hunt reminded himself.

Hunt caught Vicente Garcia staring at him. The man's scowl made his intent crystal clear. Murder.

"And what is your profession, sir?" the prosecutor continued.

Hang on, Anna, this one is going to hurt.

"I'm a DEA agent."

There was a collective gasp in the courtroom.

"And is it true that for the last two years you infiltrated the Garcia family—"

Hunt barely registered the prosecutor's question. His attention was on Anna. The last hopeful gleam had finally vanished from her eyes. He had lost her, like he knew he would. Still, it tortured him to see her broken, utterly hopeless because of his actions. But the fact of the matter was that he had a job to do. People like Vicente Garcia thought the laws didn't apply to them. They were wrong. Drug dealers had taken Hunt's younger brother's life. The least he could do to avenge Jake's death was to send the Vicentes of this world behind bars. It was his sacred duty to do so. He owed it to Jake and to the thousands of families who had lost a loved one to illegal drugs. They were the true victims, not Anna Garcia.

"Would you like me to repeat the question, Agent Hunt?"

"Yes—"

A cry of rage interrupted him. In shock, he watched as Anna sprang out of her seat and jumped over the next one. She took three quick steps and lunged at him. The security officer to Hunt's left, taken by surprise, was slow to react, but the one standing next to the judge was quicker, and he intercepted Anna midflight. He slammed her to the ground.

The courtroom fell silent. Even the judge didn't seem to know what to do.

Anna turned her heard toward Hunt and yelled at the top of her lungs, "You fucking bastard! I trusted you! I trusted you!"

Then, quieter, as if all strength had left her, she said, "How could you do this to me? I loved you."

The agony and tears in her voice ripped at him. Her eyes, though, no longer held anger but pain. A pain that was so intense it sliced him open.

I loved you too.

CHAPTER NINE

Present day
San Miguel de Allende, Mexico

Valentina Mieles banged her fist on the table.

"The ungrateful son of a bitch!" Mieles raged. "After everything I've done for him and his entire goddamned family. This? This is how he repays me? By talking to the DEA?"

There were five other people seated around the opulent dining table. Anywhere else in Mexico, these men would be feared. But here, in the sanctuary of the Black Tosca's private residence, they were the ones bowing to a higher power. They worshipped her the way abused animals served their vicious owners, doing anything for even an illusion of approval. Her displeasure, she could tell, made them all nervous.

"Why am I just hearing about this now?"

Only one man was courageous enough to look at her and speak his mind. Hector Mieles. Her cousin.

"It was a mistake to think Tony Garcia would simply roll over and go quietly," Hector offered. He was her right-hand man. "As you know, over the years he and his father have built a solid distribution network. It would be wise for us to keep as much of it intact as we can. As for the reason why you're learning about it tonight, I myself just got word from our man in Florida."

The Black Tosca, dressed in an elegant nightgown, rose from the chair she had occupied at the end of the table. She looked at Hector. Even seated, he looked tall. He was her opposite. She was petite, barely five feet, and he was only four inches shy of seven feet. Over the years, most probably because of her physical appearance, many men had made the mistake of underestimating her. In several cases, it had cost them their lives. What she lacked in physical stature, she made up for tenfold in wit, determination, and a healthy dose of brutality. And what she couldn't do by herself, Hector did for her. Her cartel had its own intelligence division, and most of the intelligence assets in her network were sources she had developed personally. Some were former lovers she had blackmailed; others she had bought outright.

"Be that as it may, Vicente needs to be stopped. He knows too much about our operations. He's a threat to all of us." The Black Tosca looked around the table. "Don't think for a minute that you'll be safe if the Americans come after me. Because you'll be next."

They were all aware of the far-reaching hands of the American special forces and the DEA. The new American president didn't care much about his relationship with Mexico. He didn't mind rattling the cage, which made him a very dangerous man.

"Do you hear what I'm saying, Hector?"

"I've already seen to it. Don't worry, Valentina, I won't let him testify against you." Her cousin's voice was surprisingly shrill for such an imposing man. "Right after we're done here, I'm flying to Miami to oversee the operation. There will be no mistakes."

The Black Tosca nodded. When it came to human resources, Hector was her greatest asset. The rank and file respected him, and her enemies feared him. It was his ruthlessness and his efficiency at eliminating her enemies that had propelled him to her side, not their family bond.

47

"I want the whole Garcia family gone and their operations shut down, at least until we've replaced them with people loyal to us."

"That might be difficult," Hector said. "Tony Garcia is well protected."

"Maybe, but his daughter isn't. Do whatever it takes, Hector. I don't care. Just get the job done."

CHAPTER TEN

Pompano Beach, Florida

Cole Egan's lungs were burning as he sprinted the last quarter mile to his house. Egan embraced the pain. Thanks to Ranger school and countless missions in shitholes all over the world, it was a feeling he recognized well.

He was drenched in sweat by the time he reached the front door. In the kitchen he grabbed a bottle of water from the pantry and an apple from the fridge. He started the coffee machine and made his way to the master bedroom. Katherine was still sound asleep. He was fascinated by the way the early morning sun shined off her white, soft-as-silk skin. He stood for several minutes, watching her sleep before he silently walked to the en suite to shave and shower.

———

Katherine Egan knew her husband was staring at her. She couldn't even hear him breathe, but she felt his presence. It had always amazed her—and maybe scared her a bit too—how he could remain perfectly still for so long. A couple years ago, while catching a movie at the theater, she'd noticed that he hadn't moved once during the entire film. When she'd confronted him about it, he'd told her he had fallen asleep, which she'd known wasn't true.

They had met five years ago in Mexico City during a dental expo. Bonding over too many drinks in the lobby bar of the hotel hosting the conference, they had quickly gone from business contacts to lovers. She didn't remember if it was the wine or his rugged good looks and amazing physique, but bringing a complete stranger to her hotel room had been the craziest thing she had ever done. On the second night, he had invited her to his lush bachelor pad in Mexico City. Sharing a bottle of Dom Pérignon on the large balcony with the mind-blowing views had been so romantic that she still got goosebumps thinking about it. On that night, it hadn't been the wine that had gotten to her—it had been his thick mop of golden hair and his eyes, so deep and blue but also full of secrets. They had made love in his sumptuous bedroom, tenderly at first and then with full abandon. Exhausted but utterly fulfilled, they had fallen asleep tangled in each other's arms.

Over the course of the conference, she'd learned that Cole had been in the army and had served three tours in Afghanistan and Iraq. He was now a distributor of high-tech dental equipment and owned, in addition to his bachelor pad in Mexico City, a beautiful and very expensive house in Pompano Beach right on Lake Santa Barbara. She had moved in with him a week after the conference and never looked back, though a part of her wondered where the money to buy the house had come from. Dental reps earned a good living, but certainly not enough to afford a house like that.

One night, lying in bed next to him, she questioned him about it.

"You never asked me to contribute even a penny to the mortgage, baby—why's that?"

"You're my wife. What's mine is yours."

She had hoped he'd reveal a bit more, but he had remained silent. Cole didn't share much about his past, at least not voluntarily. She didn't mind. Everyone had secrets, right? And who knew, maybe his parents had left him a bit of money before they passed?

But even to her, it didn't ring true. An aura of mystery hovered over Cole, but one she actually found attractive. He was a kind man with a sharp edge. She had always been attracted to bad boys anyway. And seriously, how bad could he really be?

———

Egan dried himself and combed his hair back. The next few days would be busy. He had *clients* to meet in Mexico tomorrow night and wasn't sure when he'd be able to swing back to Florida to spend a couple days with Katherine before leaving again. Truth was, in his line of work, he never was quite sure if he'd actually *be* back. He had made his fair share of enemies over the years, and the very real possibility of never seeing his wife again made him feel queasy.

He pushed the negative thoughts aside and stepped out of the en suite, wearing only a white towel around his waist. His wife was standing next to their bed, waiting for him, naked. She held her belly in that proud and protective gesture only pregnant women could do. Her breasts were larger now, rounder and fuller. Her sheer beauty mesmerized him.

Even though the studies Egan had read about pregnancy implied that most women had reduced sexual desire and activity during the early weeks of a pregnancy, this didn't hold true for Katherine. On the contrary, it was as if her pregnancy hormones had supercharged her libido.

She took tentative steps toward him and placed her hands on his bare chest, her fingers running along the raised scar tissue crisscrossing his abdomen. His pulse spiked.

"How long will you be gone?"

He honestly didn't know. He never did. "A few days."

"Can I come with you?" she asked with a raised eyebrow.

"Not this time, baby, I'm sorry." He cupped her head in his hands. "Mexico City isn't the nicest place to travel to when you're pregnant. Because of the pollution, you know? And aren't your days filled with patients who need their teeth removed?"

She sighed but tugged on his towel nonetheless. It fell at his feet. "I'm gonna miss this."

CHAPTER ELEVEN

Federal Detention Center
Miami, Florida

While he waited for the US marshals to get Vicente Garcia, Hunt adjusted the waist straps of his soft body armor, remembering the morning before the start of Vicente Garcia's trial when Leila had asked him how a soft piece of clothing could stop bullets. Hunt had found the question fascinating, and even though he was running late for court, he'd decided to answer her query, not knowing that the very next day, Jasmine—with his precious Leila in tow—would walk away from him after he told her what had happened in the courtroom. Kneeling next to Leila, he had taken her hand and placed it against the fabric of his body armor.

"Think of it as a soccer net," he'd told her. "What happens to the net when you kick the ball into it?"

"It moves!"

"You're correct, sweetie; it does. When the ball hits the net, it pushes back against the tethers at that specific point, dispersing the energy all around it, so no matter where the soccer ball hits the net, the whole net absorbs the impact."

His daughter thought about what he had said for a second, then said, "But bullets are much faster than a soccer ball, Dad."

"That's very true. Bullets fly superfast, but you know what?"

Simon Gervais

"What?"

"My body armor is also much stronger than a soccer net."

Hunt had guided his daughter's hand over his soft body armor and continued, "This material is five times stronger than a piece of metal."

"No way!" his daughter had cried out. "It's so soft."

Hunt was brought back to reality by a crackling in his earpiece: "They're on their way. Be ready."

Hunt drank half of the water in his water bottle. He wasn't exactly nervous, but it would have been a lie not to admit he was anxious about seeing Garcia again. Hunt was seated next to Chief Inspector Zorita in the third row of the second Suburban; two members of the US Marshals Special Operations Group occupied the front passenger and driver seats. John Robbins, the highest-ranking deputy US marshal in the motorcade, was in the second row so he could be next to Garcia.

Earlier that morning, Robbins had shown Hunt the route they'd take to the safe house. With traffic, he didn't expect the travel time to take more than an hour.

Eager to draw as little attention to the motorcade as he could, Robbins had ordered the three-vehicle convoy to park inside the underground garage of the federal detention building.

"Here they come," the driver said.

Hunt couldn't take his eyes off Garcia as he approached the Suburban. Garcia was six feet tall but had gained a few pounds since Hunt had last seen him. His hair was still black, but his stubble bore flecks of white. Even in handcuffs and sporting an orange jumpsuit, Vicente Garcia was a man to be reckoned with. His green eyes didn't miss much, and his natural charm easily masked the cruelty he was capable of inflicting on his adversaries. To his right, Hunt felt Zorita stiffen.

Two US marshals wearing green combat fatigues and armed with automatic weapons flanked Garcia. One of them opened the door and helped him climb aboard.

Garcia spotted Hunt right away and smiled at him before taking his seat next to Robbins.

"What a pleasant surprise, Terrance. Or do you go by Pierce now?"

"Nice to see you too, Vicente."

"You know you broke my daughter's heart, don't you?"

Hunt bit his lip.

"She really cared about you," Garcia said while Robbins fastened his seat belt. Garcia sounded sincere, but Hunt knew better than to fall for it.

"You smell good, Vicente. Someone splash some cologne on your neck? Is it for me, or do you have a special someone in prison?"

Garcia twisted in his seat but didn't reply directly.

"And who are you again?" Garcia asked, looking straight at Zorita. "I've seen you before, yes?"

"No, I'd remember if we'd met before."

Garcia sat with his back straight, his eyes fixed on the front of the vehicle. "I wouldn't trust this one if I were you, Pierce."

Garcia was a narcissist and a master at pitting people against each other. Nonetheless, Hunt glanced at Zorita, who simply shook his head and rolled his eyes, not even bothering to reply to Garcia.

"Enough, Vicente," Robbins said, poking Garcia with his elbow.

The motorcade started rolling, and Hunt had the uneasy feeling he had just boarded his own funeral hearse.

CHAPTER TWELVE

Miami, Florida

Hector Mieles's phone chirped in his pocket. He looked at the screen. His lookout in the vicinity of FDC Miami had just confirmed that the convoy was en route. He had also attached a picture of the three-vehicle motorcade. Hector and fifteen other members of the Black Tosca's cartel had taken position on the first and fourth floors of two construction sites. As it was Sunday, the sites were vacant except for four security officers the builders had contracted to patrol the perimeter. All four of them were now in the bed of their pickup truck, their throats cut.

Hector had one more phone call to make before he could focus exclusively on the upcoming ambush.

Someone picked up on the first ring.

"What's the girl's status?" Hector asked.

"She's mobile with her regular driver and a new bodyguard."

"Is she alone?"

The man hesitated. "No, she isn't," he finally said. He sounded disappointed. "She's with another girl."

Hector shook his head. That was unfortunate. Sophia—Tony Garcia's fifteen-year-old daughter and the granddaughter of Vicente Garcia—rarely had friends with her. Hector, himself a father of two, wouldn't take any pleasure in what was coming next, but he had his orders.

"Execute," he said.

"Understood." This time, his interlocutor seemed relieved. "I'll call you back once it is done."

With that out of the way, Hector switched his focus back to the operation at hand.

"It's time," he said to his men over the radio. "Take your positions."

Most of his men were either like him, former *Infantería de Marina*—the Mexican Marines—or ex-members of the *Brigada de Fusileros Paracaidistas*—the Parachute Rifle Brigade. They didn't need to be told twice what to do. The plan was simple and made even easier by the fact that they weren't going to worry about collateral damage. Hector tapped the magazine of his FX-05 assault rifle to make sure it was well inserted while the man next to him checked on his RPG launcher. One after the other, his men confirmed they were in position.

It was going to be a bloodbath.

CHAPTER THIRTEEN

Miami, Florida

The first half mile went without a hitch. The motorcade had just turned north on Second Avenue when Hunt caught a puff of light gray-blue smoke coming from a construction building ahead of them. He could have easily missed it, but his eyes were at the right place at the right time. Not that it made any difference. Hunt recognized the situation for what it was—an ambush—only an instant before the rocket-propelled grenade's rocket motor ignited.

"RPG!"

Traveling at close to three hundred yards per second, it took the high-explosive round less than a second to reach the lead Suburban. The warhead went through the windshield and exploded inside the SUV, killing all its occupants instantly. The explosion momentarily blinded Hunt, and a millisecond later he felt the Suburban ram the rear of the lead SUV. Fortunately, the driver of the Suburban providing rear security was able to brake in time and was initiating an evasive maneuver. He didn't get far, as scared motorists on the road were leaving their cars and running in all directions. The US marshal in the passenger seat was already on the radio calling in the ambush and requesting immediate assistance. A second RPG hit a car to their left, flipping it to its side. The deflagration rocked the Suburban.

"Everybody okay?" Robbins shouted.

Hunt looked to his right at Zorita to check whether the Mexican chief inspector was all right. His head was slumped over his chest.

"Zorita?" Hunt said, unbuckling his seat belt so he could reach the injured man.

Zorita raised his head and slammed his left elbow into Hunt's face. Hunt was flung backward. Through his blurred vision, he saw Zorita pull out his pistol, aiming it at Garcia's head. Hunt shouted a warning and lunged at Zorita just as he pulled the trigger.

CHAPTER FOURTEEN

Hallandale Beach, Florida

Leila DeGray couldn't stop thinking about her father. She knew he wanted back in her life, but after what he'd done to her mother, how could she let him in? Still, it couldn't hurt to see him for a few hours every second Saturday, right? He wasn't a bad man per se, just different. He didn't live the same kind of life she did. His was filled with violence and pain, hers with nonalcoholic piña coladas and days at the beach with her friends. And homework. Tons of homework.

Maybe one day she'd open up to him, but for now, she was happy she didn't share the same last name.

She would have loved to have a father like Sophia's. He was the nicest guy ever. For her fifteenth birthday, Sophia's dad had bought her a monkey. How cool was that? A monkey! And he had drivers and bodyguards and really, really expensive cars. But Sophia didn't have a mother. Which was sad. Sophia's mom had died in a freak skiing accident many years ago.

Truth was, Leila couldn't complain too much. Since her mom had moved in with Chris five years ago, she was living the high life too. She attended the best private school money could buy, she vacationed in the most exotic spots on the planet—her favorite was Tahiti—and Chris had even bought her a WaveRunner for Christmas. So yeah, she had it good.

Chris had dropped her at Sophia's for lunch. Since Monday was a day off from school, the plan was to pick her up again tomorrow right after breakfast. Leila loved sleepovers, especially at Sophia's colossal mansion. Plus, Tony, Sophia's dad, was a great cook, and he had promised the girls he'd bake them fresh blueberry muffins. But for now, it was movie time.

"What are you thinking about?" Sophia asked her, bringing her back to reality.

"Nothing," Leila replied. "I'm just looking forward to watching that movie."

"Me too! And the popcorn. Don't forget the popcorn!"

"With a ton of butter," Leila added.

"You bet, girl! Are you gonna have popcorn too, Charlie?" Sophia asked her bodyguard, who was seated in the front passenger seat of the huge Mercedes SUV.

Even though Leila had only recently become close friends with Sophia, she'd been around her long enough to know she was only teasing him. Charlie was a new guy, but Leila was pretty sure he'd say no. Sophia's previous bodyguard had once explained his job was to protect her, and in order to do so to the best of his ability, he needed to have his hands free. Leila loved traveling with Sophia and her bodyguards. It made her feel important, especially when people tried to take pictures of them.

Charlie twisted in his seat to look at Sophia. "Of course I will. But no butter for me," he said without a hint of a smile. Then he asked the driver. "What about you, Antonio?"

"Same thing."

Sophia looked puzzled. By Charlie's tone of voice, Leila knew he was joking, but Sophia had no idea her leg was being pulled.

"I'm joking, kiddo," Charlie said, this time with a smile.

A quick look outside the SUV told Leila they were less than five minutes away from the theater. The traffic light in front of them turned red, and the driver stopped just behind a silver Hummer H2. To their left and right, two identical Dodge Caravans abruptly stopped, even though they both had room to move forward another three car lengths.

Leila saw Antonio take a look in the rearview mirror. Charlie wasn't smiling anymore.

"What the hell?" Antonio said.

Leila turned around. There was another black Dodge Caravan. It was so close to the Mercedes's rear bumper that Leila couldn't see its headlights.

"Shit!" Charlie said.

Alarmed, Leila turned her attention back to the front, only to see the hatchback of the Hummer open. Two men dressed in black and wearing balaclavas were holding guns in their hands.

Sophia screamed.

To Leila, everything happened in slow motion. Charlie reached for something inside his jacket while Antonio tried to shift the Mercedes into reverse. A pistol appeared in Charlie's hands. He briefly looked at Leila and yelled something she didn't understand. Then white and red sparkles appeared at the end of the big guns the men in black were holding. Leila wanted to close her eyes but couldn't. She was mesmerized by what was going on.

Holes appeared in the windshield. Two at first. One in front of Charlie, another in front of Antonio. Leila was surprised how forcefully Charlie was shoved back in his seat. It was as if someone had punched him hard in the stomach. Charlie screamed. He raised his pistol in front of him, and two more holes appeared in the windshield. He dropped his pistol.

Men climbed out of the black Dodge Caravan. One of them had something that looked like a hammer, a kind Leila had never seen before. The driver's side window exploded, a hand reached inside the vehicle, and suddenly her door opened. Leila felt Sophia's hand grabbing her forearm. Men were taking her friend away.

She had to stop them.

The gun. Charlie's gun.

Leila leaped forward, her hands searching for the pistol she knew was there. Strong hands grasped her ankles. Her heart jumped. She was being pulled backward.

No!

Dad, I need you!

Her fingers touched metal.

The gun.

It was much heavier than she thought it would be. She tried to twist to face the man who was pulling her, but it was too late. They had already dragged her outside the Mercedes. Her arms were pinned to her side. Someone was holding her tight. She screamed and pulled the trigger. Again and again. Chips of concrete cut through her pants, slicing her skin.

Someone swore. Her arms were released. She pointed the gun toward one of her aggressors, but something hit her hard on the back of the head.

Everything went black.

CHAPTER FIFTEEN

Miami, Florida

Hector Mieles didn't lose any time. The moment he confirmed the motorcade was immobilized, he ordered the men he had in flanking positions to attack. The first phase of the ambush had gone well, but he was a hardened combat veteran who knew he needed to press his advantage.

Their first objective was to get to Vicente Garcia and to make sure he was dead in case Chief Inspector Zorita failed to do his job in the opening seconds of the engagement. Their secondary objective, almost as important as the first, was to secure and evacuate the chief inspector. As much as the Black Tosca could be merciless and cold-blooded toward her enemies, she was loyal to those who served her well. And Zorita had served her valiantly for close to two decades. The intelligence Zorita had provided had allowed them to enact numerous takeovers of rival cartels. Knowing when and whom to strike had given her an edge over her adversaries.

Hector had no problem risking his men's lives—even his own if it came to that—to help a fellow warrior. That was exactly what Julio Zorita was, a warrior. It didn't matter for which cause they fought. As long as they were on the same side, Hector considered him a brother. The cartel members were his family. He had handpicked all the men with him today. What he wanted most was to get the job done and then head home to his family and the relative safety of San Miguel de Allende.

Hector watched as his men converged on the burning motorcade while the rest of his group, perched on the fourth floor of the construction site, covered them with a steady barrage of gunfire. Hector spotted a US marshal climbing out of the rear SUV and fired two shots in his direction. He missed, but his rounds landed close enough that the deputy marshal had to seek refuge behind the SUV's engine block, allowing Hector's men to cover more ground before they were fired upon.

Hector had switched his aim back to the rear Suburban when bullets struck the barricade to his left. Pablo—the man operating the RPG—yelled in pain as he dropped the launcher and collapsed to his knees, blood spurting from a neck wound. Hector dashed to Pablo and caught him as he fell to his side. Rounds continued to pepper their position, but Pablo, his eyes half-glazed, hardly seemed to notice.

"Sir, there's a chopper hovering above us," said Oscar, the man charged with their air defense.

Hector had known the US marshals would be using air support. He had planned for this eventuality.

"Take it out."

"Yes, sir. Also, our men across the street are pinned down," Oscar continued.

"We need to get moving, then," Hector said matter-of-factly. "But get that chopper down first. The moment one aircraft goes down, this will be a no-fly zone, and it will make our lives much easier when it's time to withdraw."

Once Oscar had left, Hector looked down at Pablo. There was nothing he could do for him. Pulling his knife from his sheath, he plunged it into Pablo's ear. Pablo's body stiffened. With his other hand, Hector closed Pablo's eyes.

"Follow me," Hector ordered the rest of his men as he grabbed the launcher left behind by Pablo. "Let's get the job done."

CHAPTER SIXTEEN

Miami, Florida

Hunt's ears were ringing as he fought Zorita for control of the pistol. The shot had missed Garcia but hit the driver in the shoulder. Robbins was yelling something, but Hunt was too busy to care what it was. Both his hands were locked on Zorita's right wrist as he angled the weapon up and away. A second shot rang out, and the bullet punched a hole through the roof. Hunt, who was now on top of Zorita, kneed him once in the solar plexus and again in the head as Zorita pitched forward. Zorita's head snapped back as blood erupted from his broken nose. Zorita's eyes became unfocused, and Hunt seized the moment to strike two vicious punches to the man's jaw before he wrestled the gun away. But Zorita wasn't done yet. Out of nowhere, a knife appeared in his hand. Hunt reacted instinctively and fired twice point-blank into Zorita's upper chest. Zorita jerked backward, and his eyes rolled into his head, his body slumping sideways on the leather seat of the SUV.

Damn it! Hunt would have loved to have a nice long chat with the treacherous son of a bitch to find out who had turned him.

The fight had lasted less than twenty seconds, but the tactical situation outside the Suburban had changed drastically. A burning car blocked the left lane, and a concrete barrier prevented any movement to the right. They were sitting ducks. Men dressed in black combat gear were approaching from the construction site to their right, while supporting gunfire coming from their front kept the US marshals pinned down. They needed to get out of the vehicles. The closest safe house was the detention center. That was where they had to go.

Robbins had reached the same conclusion because he ordered everyone out of the SUVs.

The US marshals didn't need to be told twice. The five deputies riding in the rear vehicle rushed out, took positions around the Suburban carrying Garcia, and started to return effective fire.

"Take the handcuffs off," Garcia pleaded.

"Shut up," Robbins replied. "As far as I'm concerned, this is a rescue attempt."

"What? Are you crazy? They want me dead."

It wasn't Hunt's place to speak his mind, but this didn't look like a rescue to him. Not after Zorita had tried to take Garcia out.

"Out, out, out!" Robbins yelled.

The injured driver was the first to successfully exit the vehicle, and he opened Garcia's door. There seemed to be a break in the supportive fire coming from across the street. Hunt climbed over the second-row seats and squeezed past Garcia. He yanked on Garcia's handcuffs and dragged him out.

Chaos waited for them outside the vehicle. Sirens wailed. Some civilians, struck by fragments from the burning vehicles, were bleeding out on the street. The only saving graces were the deputies who still stood their ground and returned fire.

"Let's leapfrog back to Fifth Street," Hunt suggested, keeping his pistol in the low-ready position.

"You heard the man," Robbins said. "Let's go."

"Contact right!" one of the deputy US marshals yelled. A volley of gunfire forced them to take cover behind the Suburban.

"Contact front!" shouted another one.

Shit! That wasn't good. Two separate supporting forces were approaching their position. Hunt looked around for another weapon. His pistol wasn't going to cut it against automatic weapons.

"We need to move," Robbins said. "Hunt, you go with Garcia. We'll cover your retreat. Go!"

Hunt looked at Garcia. To his credit, the drug lord didn't look frightened. On the contrary, he seemed to be quite comfortable amid the chaos.

"You're ready?" Hunt asked him.

Garcia nodded. "We can't stay here, anyway."

Hunt searched for a safe spot to run to. They couldn't just leave their cover without knowing where they were going. A white minivan was parked fifty yards away. It was a hell of a long distance to run without cover, but they had to move.

"You see the white minivan? Run to it. I'm right behind you."

Without hesitation, and with a speed that surprised Hunt, Garcia got up and sprinted toward the minivan. Hunt was right on his heels. True to their word, the US marshals covered him with a sustained barrage of gunfire.

To his left, Hunt saw a black figure raise his rifle toward Garcia. Hunt fired on the run, his bullets missing the mark but close enough to force the man to fire before he had taken careful aim. Hunt's sixth shot hit his rifle, and the man transitioned to his pistol. Hunt stopped, knelt down, and pulled the trigger three more times in quick succession. The man fell, fatally wounded. Hunt changed his magazine and scanned for more threats. He saw other assailants, but they were too far for him to engage with his Glock. He looked to his right to check on Garcia and found him lying on the ground ten yards short of the white minivan. He was crawling toward the minivan, leaving a thick crimson line in his wake.

Damn it! Hunt got back to his feet and ran toward him. He had to bring Garcia to safety. Without him, they had nothing on the Black Tosca. Garcia's testimony was key.

Hunt hadn't covered even half the distance when a tremendous explosion from behind propelled him forward.

———

Hector Mieles had had enough. He had seen two of his men cut down by the marshals. All the deputies had taken cover behind the remaining Suburban. Local police reinforcements were on their way. He needed to finish this quickly. If he could hit the SUV with an RPG, it would shift the momentum back to his camp. But in order to reach a firing position, he'd have to run in the open for twenty yards.

"Ernesto!" he shouted to the man closest to him. "In ten seconds, I want you to empty a full magazine!"

Ernesto changed his magazine and gave him the thumbs-up. Hector took a deep breath and focused on what he had to do. He counted to three and broke cover. He ran as fast as he could, half expecting to get hit. Behind him, he could hear Ernesto's FX-05 firing on full automatic. Hector slid to safety behind a blue mailbox just as Ernesto's rifle fell silent. A quick look in Ernesto's direction told Hector his man had been hit.

Hector peeked around the mailbox. The Suburban was sixty yards away. From his position he could see at least five deputies firing their weapons at the rest of his men. It was time to end this. He came out from behind the mailbox and crouched into a stable firing position. One of the deputies saw him, but Hector fired before the deputy could bring his weapon around.

The RPG hit the Suburban just above the left rear tire. The car exploded in a ball of fire, sending razor-sharp metal blasting throughout the area.

———

Hunt opened his eyes. A terrible headache threatened to send him back into darkness. He was on his back, staring at the blue sky. Somewhere, a machine gun chattered.

Garcia? Where was Vicente Garcia?

Hunt patted himself down for any signs of injury. He had none, except for the headache. He sat up and searched for Garcia. The drug lord had made it to the white minivan. He was clutching his right leg with both hands. Hunt turned his head, and what he saw made him sick. The deputies, who had all been much closer to the Suburban, were down. Some had been cut to pieces by the exploding SUV. Others were still alive, slowly crawling away from the burning vehicle.

Men in black fatigues approached the downed agents. Hunt frantically searched for his gun. It was a few feet away. He crawled on his knees, pieces of glass embedding themselves in his hands. A single shot was fired. Then another. Behind him, good men were being executed. Hunt reached his pistol, grabbed it with both hands, and winced in pain as the shards of glass cut deeper into his skin. There were too many attackers. He'd never kill them all. He could play dead and hope they would leave. He thought about his daughter, Leila, and about all the missed opportunities. Then, from his peripheral vision, he spotted John Robbins slowly making his way toward him. A black-clad man had spotted him too and was raising his rifle.

Hunt fired. Once. Twice. Three times. The black-clad man fell.

Hunt swung his pistol left and brought his sights upon his next target. The man fired first, but his rounds went high. Hunt pulled the trigger and hit the man below his right eye. Behind him was another man. Hunt hesitated a fraction of a second. This man was also dressed in black fatigues, but he was by far the tallest of the bunch. He was built like a bulldozer. His pistol, which was pointed directly at Hunt, looked like a toy gun in his hands.

Both men fired at the same time.

CHAPTER SEVENTEEN

Miami, Florida

With most of the surviving US marshals too stunned to return fire, Hector ordered his remaining men to advance. He pulled his pistol out of its holster and leapfrogged toward the burning Suburban. None of the marshals had escaped the explosion unscathed. Their clothes were shredded, their exposed skin scorched. Some were hunched over on their knees in apparent agony; others were moaning, their pleas animal-like. They were easy prey, and his men took them out with merciful single shots to the head. One marshal who had managed to crawl away from the Suburban was about to be put down when a bullet whizzed past Hector. The man next to him fell. Hector spun around only to see another of his men crumple, shot in the head.

There! A man had his pistol trained on him. He was thirty-five yards away, dressed in blue jeans and black soft body armor. Behind him, Vicente Garcia was resting his back against the front tire of a parked minivan. Hector fired once and then rolled to his right. A bullet grazed his left arm, just below the elbow. He ignored the burning sensation and dashed across the street while zigzagging left and right. He jumped over a concrete barricade as more rounds impacted around him. He landed on the other side and took in his surroundings. The sirens were getting closer by the second, sending waves of sound off the adjoining buildings. Not wanting to appear where he was last seen, Hector duckwalked along the barricade. Vicente Garcia was less than twenty-five yards away. The marshal, the one who had grazed him, had to expect Hector would pop his head out from cover to check on Vicente Garcia. The trick was to do it quickly.

Up, he sees me, I'm down.

Two rounds zipped past where his head had been a quarter of a second before.

This guy's good, Hector thought. Even though his peek had lasted less than three full seconds, Hector had gotten the info he wanted. Vicente Garcia hadn't moved much, but to Hector's dismay, he had shifted to the opposite side of the minivan, making him much harder to hit. Hector estimated he had less than half a minute to take out Garcia before law enforcement officers cornered him.

There was no easy way to do this, and his window of opportunity was almost shut. He duckwalked ten feet to his right before taking a deep breath.

Up, he sees me . . .

CHAPTER EIGHTEEN

Miami, Florida

The bullet hit the pavement an inch to his right before deflecting away. Hunt fired at his running target, but, for his size, the man was surprisingly quick and agile. He disappeared behind a concrete barrier. With a quick look behind him, Hunt confirmed Vicente Garcia had made it to the minivan.

A head popped up from behind the barricade, and Hunt let go two shots. The head disappeared. Hunt shuffled backward, keeping his pistol up and pointed toward the barricade. Garcia had his back against the rear tire of the minivan. His hands, dark with blood, were covering a large wound on his leg.

"Put pressure on it," Hunt said.

"What do you think I'm doing?"

Hunt used his left hand to remove his belt. He threw it on Garcia's lap.

"Tighten the belt above the bullet wound. You need to stop the bleeding."

"You have to do it. I can't let go. I think the bullet nicked an artery."

For the first time, Hunt noticed a panicked look on Garcia's face. Blood squirted from beneath his hands. Hunt had seen enough wounds in Afghanistan to understand Garcia didn't stand a chance if he didn't stop the bleeding. He was about to holster his pistol to help Garcia when the rear window of the minivan exploded, spraying chips of glass all around him.

Bullets pinged off the sheet metal of the minivan. The shooter was making his move. Hunt chanced a peek, allowing only two inches of his body to emerge from behind the van. What he saw startled him, if only for a moment. The shooter was charging his position and was already halfway there. Hunt tried to duck back but caught a round on the right side of his ribs. The bulletproof vest saved his life and spread the impact, but the round packed enough punch to spin him around and out of cover. Another bullet hit him square in the back, knocking him to the ground and squeezing all the air out of his lungs. His pistol flew out of his hand and skittered out of reach under the minivan.

Hunt forced himself onto his back and frantically scooted backward to position himself between the oncoming shooter and Vicente Garcia.

———

Hector saw his target fall flat on his stomach but almost immediately move out of sight. He inserted a fresh magazine while continuing to close the distance. He was about to resume shooting to cover his advance when he heard running footsteps behind him. Hector turned to face the upcoming threat, but he was too late. A US marshal tackled him at full speed. Hector dropped his pistol as he was knocked off balance but managed to grab the agent's waist and throw him off by rotating his hips clockwise and using the marshal's momentum against him. The marshal lost his footing and fell, rolling a few times. Hector was on him in a flash and grabbed him by the throat. He squeezed hard, digging his thumbs and fingers deep into the man's neck. The marshal's eyes bulged, and his hands flailed in a futile attempt to break the viselike grip. Hector slammed the marshal's head against the pavement once, twice, and the third time, with a distinct cracking sound, he knew he had killed the man.

Hector hurried back to his feet and picked up the pistol he had dropped during the altercation. Fifty yards away, Garcia and the other marshal were escaping. Hector grunted in frustration. The flashing emergency lights of police cars reflected off the buildings. He was out of time. In ten seconds, he'd be surrounded.

He raised his pistol to eye level, aligned his sights on the fleeing men, steadied his breathing, and pulled the trigger.

———

They were almost there. Another ten yards and they'd be safe. The backups were arriving now. In a minute or two, the area would be secure. Garcia had lost so much blood that he was barely conscious.

"C'mon, old man," Hunt said, helping him forward.

Garcia's hair was slicked in sweat, his eyes wild and unseeing. His face was a mask of pain, but he pushed on.

Then Garcia pitched forward like a felled tree. Hunt tried to keep him going, but Garcia's legs folded beneath him. A round whizzed past and then another. Hunt hit the ground, angling his body so he could see where the shots were coming from.

The tall, bulldozer-like shooter was methodically firing his pistol at them. Another bullet zipped above Hunt's head, so close it made the hairs stand up on the back of his neck. Hunt crawled on top of Garcia's body and shielded it with his own.

———

As Hector made his escape, he wondered if Garcia was dead. He had struck him at least once, of that he was sure. He wished he could have put a few more rounds into Garcia before the surviving marshal had blocked him. There was no point in staying longer. Police were everywhere, but amid the chaos, they had no idea who was who. The trick was to slip through before they cordoned off the area.

"All elements, this is Bravo Zero-Six," he said over their comms system. "Retreat back to site three. I say again, retreat back to site three. Follow your personal exit protocols."

Only six men acknowledged. Not good.

Maybe some had equipment malfunctions? That was wishful thinking. Nothing about this mission had gone according to plan. The opposing force's response had been stronger and much more effective than he wanted it to be. The Black Tosca wouldn't mind the losses as long as the objective was achieved.

But he did.

If he managed to get out of this mess alive, he'd go back to his operational plan and review it entirely to look for things he could improve on. Maybe losses didn't bother his cousin, but they troubled him. Poor dead Pablo wouldn't let him sleep in peace for a while.

Now wasn't the time to worry about tomorrow, though. He had to get his men out of the area. Thankfully, they had preemptively stashed cars all over the neighborhood. All were filled with clothes, cash, hotel keys, and new sets of identities.

Hector's getaway car was a five-year-old gray Honda Civic. The key was where it was supposed to be, in the exhaust pipe. He was about to unlock the door when he felt a presence behind him. He tried to see a reflection in the window, but the angle was all wrong.

"Sir, please keep your hands where I can see them."

Damn it. A cop.

Hector had already disposed of his pistol and bulletproof vest, but since he was wearing a black T-shirt and a pair of black combat pants tucked in his boots, he couldn't blame the officer for being suspicious. He slowly turned toward the officer, making sure he kept his hands at his side. They were two streets away from where the ambush had taken place, and there were only a few pedestrians on the street.

The moment he made eye contact with the officer, Hector knew how he was going to play it.

"Please don't shoot me! Please don't shoot me," he pleaded, getting on his knees and raising his hands above his head. "I have five children. Please don't kill me!"

He closed his eyes like someone expecting to get hit.

"Sir, I won't shoot you," the officer replied. "But you need to tell me who you are and what you're doing here."

"Are you a real cop? Or are you one of *them*?" Hector asked.

"What? I'm with the Miami-Dade Police Department, sir. You have nothing to be afraid of."

"My name is Ramón Esposito, and I'm a security guard at the construction site," Hector explained, hoping it would justify how he was dressed. "I tried . . . I really did."

"Did you see what happened?"

"The . . . the people who shot at the black SUVs. Some . . . some of them were dressed just like you," Hector said, pointing to the officer. "They were wearing the same uniforms."

That got the officer's attention. "Are you sure?"

"Yes, I'm sure, Officer," Hector replied, looking shocked and a bit desperate. He pointed to where the marshal's bullet had grazed his arm. "They shot me."

"Shit!" the officer said out loud before turning to his radio. "This is Officer Mancusi. Please note shooters may be dressed in police uniforms."

Mancusi looked at Hector. "Do you know where they went?"

"I'm . . . I'm not sure. I'm sorry," Hector replied, grabbing his injured arm.

"Do you need medical assistance?"

"Yes, I think so, but some people are in worse shape than me. I can drive myself to the hospital."

"I appreciate this, sir," Mancusi said. "But before you go, I'll need to get your name and contact info. The detectives will want a statement from you."

That was a problem. The new set of IDs was in the Honda's trunk, sealed in a plastic bag next to another plastic bag containing a spare pistol and extra ammunition.

"Yes, yes, of course, I'll be happy to help," Hector replied, nodding. "Can I get up? My wallet is in my back pocket."

Officer Mancusi's demeanor had changed from suspicious to somewhat friendly. Hector guessed he had a foot and a hundred pounds on the officer. With the knife he had tucked against his belt, it would be an easy takedown. Hector almost felt sorry for the officer. He wouldn't go home tonight.

Hunt strained his neck to catch sight of the shooter. Bolts of pain ripped through his entire back and side as he commanded his body to get up. Police officers had flocked to the area, yelling conflicting orders to the poor citizens unlucky enough to have remained close by. The shooter was gone, had completely vanished, leaving nothing but death and destruction in his wake.

Hunt patted himself down but found no injuries. He did the same with Garcia, who hadn't moved an inch for the past minute. His hands quickly became drenched in blood. A gunshot wound in the upper right area of Garcia's back was bleeding profusely. There was no visible exit wound. Hunt gently turned Garcia on his back. Garcia's eyes stared back at him, lifeless.

One more look around confirmed there was no other immediate threat. Hector didn't so much as blink before he attacked, catching Officer Mancusi by surprise. The strike was swift and deadly. He faked left—not that it was necessary—but struck from the right. He plunged his knife into Mancusi's exposed neck. The blade penetrated the skin, and Hector felt it stick into something. He twisted the handle and pushed harder. The blade responded and tore in farther. The scraping of the serrated steel on bone was clearly audible. No sound escaped Mancusi's mouth as he died in Hector's arms.

Hector unlocked the Honda Civic and effortlessly dropped Mancusi's body on the back seat. A curtain moving in the window of an apartment building across the street caught his attention, but Hector decided against investigating further. He jumped in the driver's seat of the Civic, started the engine, and sped away just as five police officers dressed in tactical gear emerged from a side street between two condo towers. They were one hundred yards behind him, and Hector kept an eye on the officers in his rearview mirror. They made no attempt to stop him, and they were too far away to get the license plate number.

But even if they had, Hector wouldn't keep the car for long.

Not with a dead police officer in his back seat.

CHAPTER NINETEEN

Hallandale Beach, Florida

Leila woke with a splitting headache, but the memories of her kidnapping were vivid. Were the abductors watching her now? The thought of being watched sent a chill down her spine. She lay still, quietly listening for sounds that would betray someone else's presence.

Nothing.

Sophia. Oh my God. Sophia!

Leila opened her eyes. She was in a dimly lit room, handcuffed to a bed. Her wrists hurt. The handcuffs were too tight and cutting into her skin. There was a sink and a toilet on the opposite side of the room. A video camera poked from a corner of the ceiling. The faint odor of coffee and cigarettes reached her.

So she wasn't alone. Panic clawed at her. Were they going to rape her? Her lungs tightened, making it difficult to breathe.

The door next to her bed burst open, startling her. A very tall and very big man entered the room. She had never seen him before. She didn't know why, but even though he was good-looking, the man scared her to death. He sat down at the end of the bed. She recoiled at the thought of him touching her, but the handcuffs prohibited her from going very far.

She was helpless. Tears rushed to her eyes.

"I'm no danger to you, child," the man said. His English was impeccable but had a pronounced Spanish accent.

Leila was too terrified to reply and didn't dare look at him, afraid of what she might read in his eyes. She heard him sigh.

"What's your name?" he asked.

Her heart pounded in her chest, almost suffocating her with anxiety.

"My name is Hector," the man offered. "I have two daughters. One of them is fifteen years old. That's about your age, right?"

Leila nodded.

"That's what I thought. You're friends with Sophia, yes?"

She nodded again.

"You're hungry?"

She was. Her stomach growled. But the handcuffs squeezing her wrists pained her more than her hunger. "My wrists," she said, looking at her handcuffs. "You're, like, seven feet tall. I'm fifteen years old."

He laughed. *A sincere laugh*, she thought.

"You're right, Miss . . . ?"

She almost told him her name. But she didn't.

He shrugged. He stood up and pulled a small key from his black combat pants. He unlocked the handcuffs. She massaged her tender wrists and whispered a thank-you.

"As I said, I'm no threat to you, young lady. But I need to know who you are."

He waited a few seconds. When she didn't reply, he continued, "What about lunch? You like egg sandwiches? And potato chips?"

"You'll feed me if I give you my name, is that it?"

He laughed again. "Is that an offer? If so, I accept."

Now that she had seen him laugh twice in the past minute, she was a little bit less scared of him. Maybe this was just a big mistake, and once Hector learned who she was, he would let her go?

She was being optimistic. She knew that. But she preferred that to the alternative.

———

Hector left the room and closed the door behind him. It locked itself automatically.

"She's hungry," Hector said to the *sicario* standing guard outside the room. "Go make her a sandwich, and bring some potato chips and a soda, will you?"

"Yes, sir, right away." The *sicario*—a man named Emilio—scurried away. Like the men Hector had led during the ambush, Emilio was former military. He had been a military prison guard, so it was fitting that he was now running the Black Tosca's safe house in Hallandale Beach.

Hector took the stairs to the ground floor and walked to the covered porch facing the ocean. The view was spectacular, with the sun hung high in the pale blue sky and the water echoing its azure color. Back home in San Miguel de Allende, it was all about the majestic mountains and the lush green rolling hills, but, here in Florida, it was the ocean that took the prize. The ocean had always fascinated him. Sailing was in his blood, and he hoped that one day, God willing, he could retire on a nice yacht and cruise the Mediterranean with his family. Hector closed his eyes for a moment to let the liquid sunshine meet his face, but it was the sweet ocean breeze that came sweeping in, blowing cool air through his hair.

Today hadn't been an easy one. But it had been successful. In five minutes, he was due to call the Black Tosca and report on the day's operations. He hoped she'd be indulgent. He was unsure, though, about the young girl—Sophia's friend. Abducting her hadn't been part of the plan. What would the Black Tosca want to do with her? Hector suspected she wouldn't be spared, but who knew? It all depended on who she was.

And it was his job to find out.

CHAPTER TWENTY

Miami, Florida

Hunt tried to remove his bulletproof vest, but the muscles in his back screamed for him to stop. The round that had hit him in the back was embedded in the vest, and he could feel the dimple where it had struck. A paramedic—a young woman with dark brown hair—saw him struggle and offered her assistance. Hunt raised his hand and let the paramedic help him slip out of the vest.

The paramedic lifted his T-shirt and examined him. Her hands were soft and warm and probed gently over his muscular side and back.

"You'll have a severe bruise or two, but you'll be okay," she said. "The vest saved your life."

She walked away before Hunt could thank her. She had a lot to do.

The area around him looked like a war zone. Now that the shooting was over and the scene was secured by law enforcement officers, paramedics and firefighters were flooding the street. Their professionalism was apparent. They surveyed the scene and moved around to assess who could be helped and who couldn't.

Most couldn't.

Hunt walked the street and examined the shells of the still-burning Suburbans. Dead bodies were scattered around, a mix of civilians, US marshals, and black-clad assaulters. After a while, Hunt came to the conclusion that he was the only man to survive the ambush and that he owed his life to John Robbins, who had sacrificed himself to allow Hunt and Garcia the opportunity to escape.

"Special Agent Hunt?"

Hunt turned around. A uniformed police officer was doing his best to catch up to him. He had a cell phone in his hand.

"Are you Special Agent Pierce Hunt?" the officer asked.

"Yes."

"It's for you, sir." The officer handed him the cell phone.

Who would want to reach him via another man's phone? Hunt thanked the officer and said, "This is Pierce Hunt."

"Pierce, for God's sake, where are you? I tried to reach you on your cell."

Hunt recognized the voice instantly. McMaster.

"Still at the site of the ambush," he told his boss.

"Are you okay? I heard it's a real clusterfuck."

Hunt pinched his nose. He couldn't argue with that. Then he thought about Zorita, the Mexican federal agent. *The traitorous son of a bitch.*

"Julio Zorita, you know, your Mexican pal?" Hunt asked, his temper rising as his eyes settled on Robbins—whose body was being lifted into the back of an ambulance.

"Pierce—"

"He betrayed us. I'm not sure what the total body count will be, but these deaths, they're on him. Every single one of them."

"I . . . I didn't know. Shit."

"I'm the only one left, Daniel."

McMaster remained silent for the better part of a minute. When he spoke again, his voice was thick with emotion, which surprised Hunt. "Listen, Pierce, I—I don't know how to say this . . . I . . ."

A sick feeling settled in the bottom of Hunt's stomach. *What now?* "Just say it."

"Your daughter was kidnapped less than an hour ago."

Hunt was sure he hadn't heard McMaster correctly. Leila was with his ex-wife. Jasmine would have called him if anything had happened to her. Unless Jasmine had been taken too.

Didn't McMaster tell him he had tried to reach him on his cell? Hunt frantically searched his pockets for his phone.

Where is it? A cold fear crept over him. *Where is my damn phone?*

"Pierce? Pierce, you there?"

Hunt wasn't listening. Where was his phone?

My tactical vest. He had left it on the sidewalk where the paramedic had helped him. *Was it still there?* Still clutching the other officer's phone against his ear, Hunt jogged down the street. He found his bulletproof vest exactly where he had left it. His phone was in one of the front pockets. He had eleven missed calls.

He sagged on the sidewalk as if someone had cut him off at the knees.

Eleven missed calls. Two were from the DEA office; all the others came from Jasmine's cell. It took Hunt a while to find his voice, but when he did, it was low and hoarse.

"What about Jasmine?"

"She's shaken, but she wasn't with Leila when it happened."

That was the first good news of the day. He had to speak with her. He'd call her as soon as he was done with McMaster.

"Tell me what you know."

"Not much for now, I'm afraid," McMaster started. "It happened in Hallandale Beach, and it was a professional hit."

A professional hit? That didn't make one bit of sense. Very few people knew he had a daughter. He kept his work life separate from his personal one. His daughter didn't even carry his name. Could it be Garcia exacting some sort of revenge? Hunt doubted it. No one in Garcia's organization knew about Leila—or about Jasmine, for that matter. Could they have found out?

"How do you know it was done by professionals?" he asked.

"A motorist caught the whole thing on his dashcam. We'll have the footage within the hour."

"Who was she with?"

"Pierce, it's kind of . . . seriously, it's too soon to tell for sure."

Hunt didn't like McMaster's answer. "For God's sake, McMaster, don't mess with me."

At the other end of the line, McMaster cleared his throat. "We ran the plate of the vehicle that was carrying Leila, and we think she was with Sophia Garcia."

Sophia Garcia. The sound of Tony Garcia's fifteen-year-old daughter's name was like a punch to the stomach, a clean blow that took Hunt's breath away. What the hell was Leila doing with Sophia Garcia? Were they friends? That sounded improbable. Even if Vicente had somehow found out about Leila, he would have never ordered a hit on her. And with his own granddaughter in the vehicle? Impossible.

Could Leila have been in the wrong place at the wrong time? If that was the case, who in hell would dare order a hit against Tony Garcia's daughter? Then something clicked in Hunt's brain, and all at once he knew. Whoever had ambushed the motorcade had also ordered the hit on Sophia Garcia.

"I'll call you back," he said to McMaster.

Hunt made his way back to the ambush site, hoping at least one of the assaulters was still alive.

CHAPTER TWENTY-ONE

Miami, Florida

To say Jasmine DeGray was worried would be an understatement. She was terrified and rightfully so if she believed the detective seated on the other side of the large contemporary coffee table. She had stopped crying, but her swollen eyes couldn't seem to focus. She couldn't stop her imagination from running wild, envisioning all the horrific things the kidnappers could do to her beautiful Leila.

A pang of guilt rushed through her. Why had she said yes? If she had said no to the sleepover, Leila would still be here, not God knows where.

Oh my God! What have I done?

Chris's big arms around her shoulders did nothing to appease the monsters running loose in her head. She started sobbing again and buried her face in her husband's shirt.

"Can't you see she's had enough? Can't you come back later, Detective?" she heard him say.

"I wish I could, Mr. Moon. Believe me, I know how hard this is. But the first forty-eight hours are the most crucial. This is when the trail is freshest."

"I—" Moon started, but Jasmine squeezed his leg and sat straighter.

"It's okay, Chris," she said. "The detective's right."

She took a deep breath and wiped her eyes with the back of her hand. "Ask away."

"How long has Leila been friends with Sophia?"

"A year, maybe less. They got closer a couple months ago."

"What changed their relationship?"

Why was the officer probing in that direction? What did this have to do with anything? The detective must have sensed her concerns because he said, "Trust me, Ms. DeGray. This is important."

"Leila decided to invite her to a home game," she said.

"The Miami Dolphins, right?"

"Chris has ten tickets per game that he gives away to friends and family members," she explained.

The detective wrote something in his notebook and switched his attention to her husband. "Mr. Moon, did you ever invite Sophia's father to a game?"

"I did, once. Why?"

"Do you know who he is?"

"We aren't friends per se, but he seems like a nice guy. He always takes great care of Leila when she's there, you know?"

"Of course. Have you ever been to his residence?"

"Once or twice to pick up Leila," Moon replied.

"Mr. Moon, I have to ask, do you know who Tony Garcia is? I mean, do you know what he does for a living?"

Moon shook his head. "I never asked. But he's definitely wealthy."

"You never thought about Googling the guy before sending your daughter for a sleepover?"

Jasmine understood this wasn't a question, and she didn't appreciate the detective's tone. Her husband clearly didn't either because he bolted off the sofa and was almost on top of the detective when Jasmine yelled at him to stop.

"Chris!"

Her husband stopped, but he pointed a finger toward the detective. "Say what you have to say, and be done with it," he growled.

The detective had retreated deeper into the sofa. He raised his hands in surrender.

"I'm sorry," he said. "I didn't mean to be rude to you or your wife. But Tony Garcia? He's the head of the most influential crime syndicate in Florida. Didn't you know that?"

The detective's words echoed in Jasmine's head. *Tony Garcia. Crime syndicate.*

Suddenly, she became dizzy, and the air, like the hope of finding her daughter alive, seemed to have been sucked out of the room. How was she supposed to know that Sophia's father was *that* Tony Garcia? There were dozens of Tony Garcias in Miami alone.

Because you're her mom, and a good mom is supposed to protect her child.

Jasmine swallowed hard. She could feel the tears coming, clogging her throat and blurring her vision. A soft cry escaped her lips as guilt overwhelmed her. Then she thought of her ex-husband, and all the bad memories she associated with Pierce came back. The infidelities, the empty promises, the lies—his goddamn job was still ruining their lives all these years later.

She had understood his motive to join the DEA. Hell, she had even encouraged him to become a special agent. She knew how close Pierce had been to his younger brother, Jake. His death had shaken Pierce to his core. If joining the DEA could somehow help Pierce cope with his loss, then so be it. What she hadn't signed up for was the two years of undercover work he'd agreed to without discussing it with her. During those two years, she had seen her husband for a grand total of forty-two days. That hadn't been enough to maintain a healthy relationship, but she had never lost faith, hoping that once his assignment was over, he would return to her and they could once again be a family.

But Vicente Garcia's trial had shattered that dream.

The news of her husband's infidelity had been the ultimate betrayal. After everything she'd endured, everything she had sacrificed, she could stand no more. The morning after his first court appearance, she'd taken Leila. She had filed for divorce the same week. She hadn't exactly been happy that Pierce's moving back to southern Florida meant Leila would see more of him, and today's events had proved her right. Her precious daughter was gone.

No, not gone—kidnapped! Because of you, Pierce. I've lost her because of you! The dark world you live in has finally caught up to us. You bastard.

"Hon, you okay?" Moon asked. "The detective asked you a question."

Jasmine wiped her eyes with the back of her hands. "I'm sorry, Detective. What was that?" she asked.

"You've heard of him, Ms. DeGray? Vicente Garcia?" the detective asked.

She was about to reply when her cell phone rang. She looked at the call display.

Pierce Hunt.

CHAPTER TWENTY-TWO

Miami, Florida

Pierce Hunt punched Jasmine's number into his cell as he fought the anger roiling in his belly. He ground his teeth until his jaw hurt and cursed loudly when he dialed the wrong number. He did his best to get his heart rate back to normal, but it was easier said than done.

There had been no enemy survivors. Every single assaulter was dead. A search of their bodies and clothes had revealed little of interest. The FBI was now on the scene and collecting evidence, but since cooperation between the FBI and DEA was at an all-time low, Hunt didn't expect to receive any actionable intelligence from their investigation. That was why he had taken pictures of the dead assaulters. An application on his cell phone allowed him to collect their fingerprints too. He hadn't yet decided if he'd share the photos and fingerprints with McMaster. Despite his new boss's apparent surprise at Zorita's betrayal, McMaster's relationship with Zorita bothered him.

Hunt managed to dial Jasmine's number on his third try, and she picked up on the second ring.

"What do you want?"

Her tone caught him off guard.

"Are you safe?"

"They took Leila, Pierce. They took my girl! What have you done?"

"I—"

"Where are you?"

"Close by. Are you home?"

"Yes, I'm with Chris and a Miami police detective."

"I can be there in twenty minutes," he offered.

"No!" she shouted. "It's your damn fault, Pierce. Oh my God, this is so on you."

Her words were unexpected, crude, and spoken out of anger. But they nevertheless crushed him. His knuckles turned white, and he felt his phone crack under the pressure. He forced himself to relax. Jasmine didn't have all the facts, and if she needed someone to pin the blame on, he would assume that role.

"I really think we should talk, Jasmine," he said as gently as he could once he had regained his composure.

"Why would I care about anything you have to say?"

"Someone ambushed the motorcade I was in today. They killed Vicente Garcia. And they almost killed me."

He heard her gasp. His words had cut through the haze of her rage. "When? I mean how? Oh my God, Pierce . . . what the fuck's going on?"

"Wait for me. I'll be there in twenty."

CHAPTER TWENTY-THREE

San Miguel de Allende

Valentina Mieles tossed her flip phone to Nicolás, her main bodyguard and part-time lover. He caught it with his right hand and immediately started to dismantle it. It didn't matter that they'd had sex twice in the past hour. Her eyes remained glued to Nicolás. He was standing naked at the foot of her bed, his muscles glistening from his recent efforts. With his soft brown eyes and his high cheekbones, he seemed approachable, a kind man.

But she knew better. Nicolás was a killer.

He had done unspeakable things for her and would continue to do so to cement her power. But like all the other men who had played cameo roles in her life, Nicolás was expendable.

"Leave me," she ordered him, casting one last look at his naked body. She had some thinking to do and found herself incapable of focusing on the task at hand when Nicolás was naked in front of her.

Nicolás bowed, took two steps back, and vanished out of sight.

Her conversation with Hector had pleased her. The operation had been costly, but Vicente Garcia was dead. With his death, the United States government had lost its star witness. There was no doubt in her mind that her message had been heard loud and clear. People would think twice about crossing her in any way. Not that they didn't before, but some people needed a reminder once in a while.

The other operation had gone according to plan. One of her men had been injured by Sophia's girlfriend, but he would be fine. The two girls were now sequestered at her Hallandale Beach safe house. Hector wanted to call Tony Garcia to negotiate the terms of his daughter's release, but she had vetoed him. She would take care of it herself. She wanted Tony Garcia to understand there was only one way this would end.

His death.

The thought brought a smile to her lips. With Tony Garcia gone, her cartel would control over 80 percent of the drug trade in Florida, and, more importantly, she'd finally avenge the savage murder of her father. But it was of the utmost importance that Tony understood why this was happening to him and his family. Vicente had killed her father over a minor financial disagreement. For this, she was going to decimate their entire family and take over their business.

She got out of bed and walked to the bathroom just off the sitting area. The bathroom was as sumptuous as the rest of the house. The shower was all glass, bigger than most walk-in closets, and had twenty body jets. She turned on the overhead rain shower and let the hot water run over her thick black hair. She remained motionless for a minute to clear her mind before she hit the button for the wall jets. She tried to keep the images of her father's death from overriding her brain, but she couldn't.

She never could.

Anger built up rapidly inside her and turned to hatred.

How dare they burn him alive? In front of me? I was thirteen years old!

Suddenly his screams became her screams, his pain her pain. She slid down the slick marble wall until she was curled over her knees. She covered her ears with her hands and squeezed her eyes shut, hoping to drive out the sickening visions.

It didn't work. And the memories were driving her crazy.

How long she stayed there, crying, she had no idea, but by the time she got out of the shower, her fingers and toes were pruned. Never before had the images appeared so real. She had lost control over her emotions, and that couldn't stand. She vowed to never let it happen again. And she knew exactly what she needed to do to accomplish that.

She toweled herself dry, wrapped another towel around her wet hair, and walked back into her bedroom. She grabbed a new burner phone from her nightstand and called Hector.

He answered on the first ring. She spent the next two minutes explaining what she expected of him. She could tell he wasn't pleased, but, in the end, he would do as she said.

She was the Black Tosca after all, and she had just ordered another death.

CHAPTER TWENTY-FOUR

Miami, Florida

Hunt called McMaster to give him a situation report as he drove toward Jasmine and Chris Moon's opulent residence in La Gorce, an idyllic island located north of Indian Creek and along the shores of Biscayne Bay.

McMaster understood Hunt's need to go see his ex-wife but insisted he stop by the office for a debriefing afterward. The investigation into this afternoon's events—the media had already dubbed it the Garcia Fiasco—would be long and drawn out. The FBI would want to speak with Hunt sooner rather than later. Truth be told, he was surprised McMaster had given him permission to go to his ex-wife's first. *McMaster must have called in a few favors*, Hunt thought.

Though Hunt had been to the house many times before, he still couldn't believe some people had so much money—or were actually willing to part with so much cash to buy a property. The fact that Jasmine had been the listing agent when Chris bought it might have played a role. Hunt knew that was how they'd met.

A lucky break for her, Hunt thought.

He gave his name to the security guard manning the main entrance of the gated community. The security guard studied his driver's license and took down his plate number before letting him through. Hunt hated to admit it, but La Gorce was pretty nice. It was a short twenty-minute drive from Miami International Airport—very practical if you had a private jet—and offered international-grade tennis and cricket courts to its residents. Chris Moon's mansion sat facing southwest on an acre of land jutting into the Biscayne Bay. The gates were open, and Hunt drove his Ford into the circular driveway.

Jasmine was outside waiting for him. Her shoulders slumped. He could see she had been crying, something she almost never did. He wished there was something he could say to make her feel better, but he promised himself he wouldn't lie to her; there was nothing to gain by sugarcoating the situation.

"Hey," he said, climbing out of his truck.

She surprised him by running straight into his arms. She hugged him tight, and he wrapped his arms around her. She sobbed into his neck, and he let her release her pain in silence.

Stay strong. Keep it together, he willed himself. Not an easy thing to do when the mother of your child—and a woman you had once loved more than anything else in the world—wept in your arms because your daughter, the child you conceived together out of love, had been kidnapped.

"We should go in," she suggested after a moment. "Chris and the detective are in the backyard."

Hunt looked at his ex-wife, and even though her salty tears had washed away her usual blush, she still looked beautiful.

"Okay," he said, wiping her tears away with his thumbs.

"And, Pierce, I'm sorry about what I said."

"Don't worry about it, Jasmine, but thank you."

She led him into the house. There were lots of windows, lots of light coming in. Expensive paintings hung on the walls. Hunt didn't know much about art, but he felt that some of the pieces would be right at home in a museum or art gallery. They stopped by the kitchen, which was large, bright, and modern, and she asked him if he wanted a drink.

"I need one," she added.

"Sure. Okay."

With shaking hands, she pulled two crystal tumblers from a cabinet and poured a generous amount of whiskey into them. She threw her whiskey back in two gulps, and he did the same. The alcohol burned as it slid down his throat. He'd always enjoyed a good whiskey and the burn that came from it. But not today.

Jasmine left her empty glass on the quartz countertop and headed outside to the patio without another word. The moment he stepped foot outside, the scent of salt air teased his nose. The whole backyard, with its manicured grass, looked like a tropical oasis. It featured a massive in-ground pool with its own waterfall, perfectly hedged bushes, and a collection of flowerbeds filled with exotic flowers.

Chris Moon and a man whom Hunt presumed to be the detective Jasmine had talked about were standing next to the pool. Moon saw him first and nodded. He looked miserable. As much as Hunt resented him, Hunt knew he adored Leila, and for that he was grateful.

They shook hands, and Moon introduced him to Detective Milburne.

Their eyes met, and Hunt thought he saw a brief smile of recognition on the detective's face. "Nice to make your acquaintance, Special Agent Hunt. I'm sorry we meet under such unfortunate circumstances."

"What can you tell me, Detective Milburne?"

The detective cleared his throat. "We know that Tony Garcia's daughter was taken too. They were headed to a movie theater—"

"How do you know this?" Hunt asked.

"My partner spoke with Mr. Garcia. She relayed what she learned to me. May I continue?"

"Of course."

"Their SUV was attacked—ambushed, really—by four vehicles. Men came out of the vehicles and killed Sophia's driver and bodyguard with automatic weapons before taking Sophia and Leila away."

My God. Hunt could see the whole incident play out in his head.

"One more thing I should add, Agent Hunt," Milburne said. "Your daughter didn't go down quietly."

"What do you mean?"

"Somehow she managed to gain access to a gun—"

"A gun?" he asked incredulously. "How's that even possible?"

"We think she took it from the dead bodyguard."

"And you know that how?"

"A motorist captured the event on his dashcam."

"I want to see that video," Hunt said. "When can I watch it?"

"I don't think that will be possible, but please let me finish. Your daughter fired the gun numerous times and injured one of her kidnappers."

Hunt didn't know if he should be proud or terrified at the news.

"She shot one of them?" he asked, exchanging a look with Moon. The big footballer seemed lost for words.

"I'm told our forensic team found traces of blood," Milburne said, but he added quickly, "We're not sure who it belongs to."

Hunt's gut tightened. He wasn't afraid of much. As an Army Ranger, and now as a DEA special agent, he'd seen plenty of terrifying shit. He'd been shot, stabbed, hunted, and tortured, but he'd never been as scared as he was now.

My baby girl. My Leila. Injured. Gone.

A feeling of anger started to bubble up from within, a kind of anger he usually reserved for people trying to kill him. Whoever had done this was going to pay. He didn't care who they were. He didn't care whom they worked for. He didn't care if it cost him everything he had, even his life. He'd find the people responsible. Not just the ones who had snatched his little girl but also the ones who had ordered the hit.

And he would crush them.

Detective Milburne was still speaking, but Hunt had tuned him out, his mind already planning his next move. He needed access to the dashcam footage.

"I need to see the video," Hunt said, interrupting Milburne midsentence.

"What?"

"The dashcam video. I want it."

Milburne shook his head, and Hunt knew that whatever the detective was about to say wasn't what he wanted to hear. In a flash, Hunt grabbed him by the collar and pulled him close.

"Listen to me, Detective," he growled. "That video you talked about, I want to see it now. My daughter has been taken, and I'll get her back. And this starts with me watching this video. Got it?"

Milburne's face had turned red, and, for a moment, Hunt wondered if he had gone too far. He released his grip and pushed off the detective. Moon, who had been too stunned to intervene, was still standing next to Hunt, his mouth agape.

"I'd feel the same way if I were in your shoes," Milburne said a moment later, massaging his throat. "The video is evidence, Agent Hunt. You know that."

Hunt had to give the detective credit for keeping his cool. Still, Hunt's gaze narrowed on the detective, willing him to agree to show him the video.

"But since you're a colleague, and my boss is a fan of yours, I'll make a couple of phone calls and see what I can do about that footage."

CHAPTER TWENTY-FIVE

Coral Gables, Florida

Anna Garcia had deep worry lines carved in her face. The kidnapping of her niece and the murder of her father had been part of a series of violent events across the city. Her brother, Tony, and his men were shaking down their contacts, hoping to find clues as to who was responsible. Anna's associates within the police force had told her there was a video of Sophia and her friend's abduction. Anna had offered $10,000 to the first cop to bring that tape to her or her brother.

The living room of Tony's eight-thousand-square-foot classic Spanish two-story home had been transformed into an operation center. A bay of computers and sophisticated phone-tapping equipment were set up on a folding table, and a large corkboard was filled with neatly organized photos and other pieces of intelligence Tony's men were calling in.

So far, with the exception of the dashcam video, there had been no solid leads. It was driving Anna nuts. Their failure to find Sophia was digging into her heart and soul, leaving her feeling helpless and vulnerable.

Vulnerable. Not a sensation she enjoyed. Her family's betrayal by Terrance Davis—a.k.a. Pierce Hunt—had transformed her. She had fallen in love with the man. Hard. She had given him everything and introduced him to her family. When she'd realized she had fallen for a lie, she'd started questioning her own self-worth. Hunt's treachery had stolen her pride and her heart, had put her father in jail, and had now gotten him killed. There was no man on earth she hated more than Pierce Hunt.

But that's not true anymore, is it? Whoever had kidnapped Sophia and Leila had taken the prize. It wasn't a stretch to link the attack on her father's motorcade to the girls' kidnapping—all of it a ripple effect from Hunt's betrayal.

After her father's arrest, she had tried to track Hunt down, but like a ghost he had disappeared, helped by the all-powerful DEA. She had never seen or heard from him again.

Until Chicago.

At first she hadn't been able to believe it. Was it really him? Then the media had reported his name.

Pierce Hunt.

Dios mío.

Hunt had almost killed a reporter, they'd said. Pointed a gun right at his head. That had surprised her. Hunt was an impulsive man, yes, but very protective of the ones he loved. He could be a meticulous son of a bitch too. How else could he have played her for two years? The man was like a chameleon, and for him to lose his cool, the reporter must have done something stupid.

Hunt used to be protective of her once, which was why his treason wounded her so much. After her father's trial, she had begged her brother to send a hit team after him, but he had refused, saying it was too dangerous, that it would start another war with the DEA. They had enough on their hands as it was. She understood why her brother had been reluctant, but that didn't mean she wouldn't pursue him on her own, like a ferocious tigress.

She would get her revenge. One way or the other, Pierce Hunt would pay for his sins. But first things first. They needed to find Sophia and her friend.

Then it would be Hunt's turn.

———

When Tony came home an hour later, he was pissed. Anna had seen him in a bad mood before, and it was always best to keep a distance when he was like that. Tony was a loving father, but he was a different man when it came to the family business. He was prone to using violence when things didn't go his way. There was a reason his men feared him. Anna wasn't scared of her brother, but with Sophia's kidnapping, all bets were off.

Tony's eyes were just visible beneath the brim of his Miami Dolphins cap as he entered the living room. His lips were pressed together so tightly that Anna could barely see them, and the seething anger in his eyes sent shivers down her spine.

Anna's heart rate soared, and she felt weak at the knees.

Oh no. Please God. Not Sophia. I'll give my life for hers.

"What's wrong?" she asked shakily, fearing the worst. "Is Sophia—"

"It's the Black Tosca," he spat. "That double-crossing, backstabbing cockroach."

The Black Tosca? Valentina Mieles?

"Why would—" she started to ask, but her brother cut her off with a wave of his hand.

"There are things you don't know, Anna," he said curtly.

She wasn't about to let her brother walk all over her, so she held his glare. Sophia was her blood too. "Then tell me."

He looked at her, his face a mask of rage.

"You're the best dad I know, Tony, but you're also a controlling, manipulative asshole," she added. "I have a right to know."

Her scolding seemed to surprise him. All of a sudden, it was as if all his strength left him. Tony slumped onto the sofa, his face haggard, worry clouding his eyes. Anna put her hand on his arm and gave it a little squeeze before kneeling next to him.

"Let me help you, Tony. We're family."

"You can't help me, little sister," he said, blinking back tears, all trace of anger gone.

"What happened out there? Where are the men?"

He sighed. "We're under attack, Anna. I've ordered the men to patrol the property."

Tony's property was huge. His house was nestled on a two-and-a-half-acre lot at the end of a cul-de-sac in the prestigious gated community of Journey's End. In addition to the eight-thousand-square-foot house, the exterior included a large separate guesthouse, a five-car garage, staff quarters, and a grand private driveway surrounded by lush tropical trees. His security system was the best money could buy, but it didn't mean a clever kill team couldn't breach it.

"By the Black Tosca? Why?" Anna pressed him.

"Because Father was about to testify against her."

She stared at Tony blankly. "What?"

His words had left a sickening sensation in the pit of her stomach.

"Don't look so shocked, Anna. With Dad in prison, someone had to lead the family. Under my leadership, we became the de facto organization for anyone wanting to move product in and out of Miami and along the Florida coast."

Anna didn't know all the operational details, but she knew the family money came from the drug trade. She understood this and was a willing participant in the family business. Nonetheless, her father and brother had always been the ones making the hard decisions. Her job was to keep the books straight and to perform computer-generated trend analysis. Tony had developed some legitimate businesses—mostly in construction—but most of the family's activities revolved around the illegal drug trade. She hadn't chosen any of this, but it was her family, and loyalty to her clan was central to her identity. Family first.

Always.

"Correct me if I'm wrong, but didn't Father have an arrangement with the Black Tosca?"

Tony chuckled derisively. "She's the Black Tosca, Anna. Valentina Mieles does what she wants, when she wants."

Anna didn't respond, so her brother continued. "She approached me some time ago. In fact, she sent her cousin Hector to make me an offer to buy out the business. I refused. The terms weren't satisfactory."

"And?"

"Hector left, and I thought that was it."

"But it wasn't it."

"No," Tony admitted. "A couple weeks later, our shipments started to get confiscated at the port, and one of our eighteen-wheelers was stopped on the highway. We lost a lot of money, and six of our men are now in jail."

"You think the Black Tosca is responsible?"

"I know so, and Father did too."

"That's why he decided to go against her?"

Tony nodded. "But someone betrayed him, and the only explanation I can come up with is that the Black Tosca had someone inside the DEA feeding her intel."

"Why the hit on Sophia, then?"

Tony hesitated. "I don't know, Anna. To show me we're all vulnerable?" He seemed as though he wanted to add something else but didn't.

"What is it that you're not telling me, Tony?"

Her brother didn't reply. His face had turned pale, and there was a wild grief in his eyes. She could only imagine the agony he was in and how guilty he must feel that his actions had gotten his daughter kidnapped. But she couldn't shake the feeling that there was something else. Whatever it was, her brother wasn't ready to share it with her.

"What do we do next?" she asked.

Tony pinched the bridge of his nose between his thumb and forefinger. He bowed his head and closed his eyes. "She called me," he said.

"Who? The Black Tosca?"

"She wants my head, Anna. She literally wants my head," he said, his voice cracking. "If my severed head isn't in her possession in forty-eight hours, she'll burn Sophia alive. And she'll stream it live."

Tears flooded Anna's eyes. *This isn't happening.* "And what about the other girl, Leila?"

"They'll burn her too," he whispered. "I can't allow this to happen."

Her brain went into overdrive, dark images crowding out her thoughts. She tried to push them away, but they became more insistent.

"What will you do?"

"Do I really have a choice? I'll cut my own head off if it means—"

Anna slapped him so hard the crack of her palm against his cheek echoed in the living room. "Shut up!" she yelled. "Don't say shit like that, Tony."

Tony looked stunned, but his voice was flat. "What do you want me to do, Anna? The Black Tosca has my balls in a vise, and she's tightening the fucking screws."

Anna knew he was right. The family had taken painful hits from their enemies. But they had to fight back. Somehow, they needed to turn the tables and go on the offensive.

But how?

Then an idea came to her, and she almost dismissed it right off the bat. How could she think about him now? He had betrayed her trust and broken her heart. He had lied about who he was.

Pierce Hunt.

If she was right, Hunt's quick mind—the one he had used to trick her—his tactical prowess, and his sheer determination could be exactly what she needed.

Would he answer her call? Deep down, she knew the answer to that question. It hadn't all been a lie between them. It couldn't have been. She had seen him struggle with his emotions while on the witness stand during her father's trial. The passion they'd shared—nobody could fake such intensity.

She'd never dialed the contact number written on the small piece of paper he had left on her desk the night before the DEA had barged in and arrested him and her father. Even after the trial, when she'd needed answers, she had resisted the urge to call and had even thought about burning the damn thing. But she had held on to it. She could recite its message from memory.

Just know you'll always have a home in my heart. If something happens, call this number. I'll always be there for you.

Chances were he'd tell her to fuck off, but it was worth a try.

CHAPTER TWENTY-SIX

Miami, Florida

In the formal living room, Hunt had settled into an uncomfortable silence with Jasmine. Moon was in the kitchen fixing everyone a drink, and Detective Milburne was on the phone in the adjacent room. The more Hunt thought about what had happened to his daughter, the more irritated he became. His heart wanted to blame Jasmine and Moon for the situation Leila found herself in, but his brain told him he was as guilty as they were. There was nothing to gain by playing the blaming game.

Hunt also had to concede that it was hard to control whom your child hung out with at school. Sophia Garcia seemed to be a great kid—if a little bit spoiled—and, knowing Jasmine, he was sure she tried as hard as she could to permit Leila to hang out only with peers who would be good influences. He couldn't fault her for not knowing that Sophia's father was *the* Tony Garcia. She had never talked to the man—only Moon had—and it was clear to Hunt that the football star hadn't known about Tony's ties to the drug trade. Hunt believed Moon when he told him that as far as he was concerned, Tony Garcia was a legitimate business owner.

Hunt's thoughts moved to the last time he'd spoken to his daughter. They had argued about her boyfriend.

A boyfriend.

It seemed so trivial now. Had he been too harsh with Leila about it?

Moon came back to the formal living room carrying several drinks on a tray. Hunt's cell phone rang before he could take his Diet Coke, and he excused himself and stepped into the hallway to answer.

McMaster said, "Heads up, Pierce. The FBI just issued a warrant for your arrest."

The words were so unexpected that Hunt froze.

A warrant? What in hell for?

He didn't have time to deal with this bullshit. "On what charge?"

"I'm not exactly sure, to be honest. I got a tip from one of my contacts at the MDPD. He said it's about today's ambush."

None of this was making any sense. He had done nothing wrong.

McMaster continued, "The moment I'm officially notified about the warrant, I'll have to disclose your location to the investigators. If I were you, I'd ditch that phone of yours."

Clearly, his boss was trying to help him. Getting a new phone was easy, but what was he supposed to do with the fingerprints he'd taken from the assaulters? He didn't have the freedom to wait any longer to decide whether he could trust McMaster. He had to.

"Can you do me a favor?" Hunt asked.

"I just did," McMaster replied before hanging up.

Damn!

Could he really blame McMaster? He barely knew the guy, and McMaster had put his neck out for him by telling him about the warrant. But that didn't explain why a warrant had been issued in the first place.

It's about the ambush, McMaster had said.

Hunt's phone chirped again, this time with an automatic alert from the call center he used to monitor his former undercover phone numbers. There was a message waiting for him. He entered his nine-digit personal identification number and listened. His heart skipped a beat when he recognized Anna's voice.

109

I'm not even sure you'll get this. But if you do, please reach out to me. You know how. If what we shared ever meant anything to you, I beg you to make contact. I need your help.

Did she know Leila was his daughter? No, it was impossible. She had no way of finding out, unless Leila had said something. *Highly unlikely.* His daughter barely talked to him, and their relationship was touch-and-go. Plus, Leila was using her mother's maiden name.

Should he call Anna back? What guarantee did he have that she wouldn't try to kill him for what he'd done to her? And what about her brother, Tony? He wasn't the forgiving type, and, with the warrant, Hunt certainly didn't need any more trouble at this point.

Hunt sensed a presence behind him, the same way a blind man might sense the position of the sun from its warmth. He didn't have to turn around to guess who it was. If McMaster's contact at the Miami-Dade Police Department knew about the warrant, so did Detective Milburne.

"Do you have the dashcam video of my daughter's kidnapping, Detective?" Hunt asked, keeping his back to the detective and turning off his phone.

"I'm afraid the camera disappeared from the evidence locker, Mr. Hunt," Milburne replied. "I'm sure someone misplaced it—that's all."

Hunt cursed. *Like things aren't bad enough already.*

"There's another delicate matter we need to discuss, Mr. Hunt," Milburne said, his voice strained. Hunt noticed the detective had used the word *mister*, not *agent*.

Yes, I know. My arrest, Hunt thought.

Hunt turned to face him. The detective was standing a safe distance away, his right hand on the butt of his pistol. No doubt Milburne had called for backup. The idyllic island of La Gorce would soon be cordoned off.

"What is it?" Hunt said, letting things play out. He hoped to learn who had authorized the arrest warrant and why.

"I know this isn't a good time, and I'm sure this will be cleared the moment you speak with the FBI, but they've issued a warrant for your arrest."

Hunt made an effort to appear surprised and docile. "Really? On what grounds?"

"I don't know," Milburne replied, but Hunt sensed the detective was lying.

"Stop the bullshit, and tell me what's really going on."

"Aggravated battery."

Hunt frowned. "What are you taking about?"

"One of your rounds hit a bystander," Milburne said, his voice sincere and apologetic. "I'm truly sorry."

Hunt's right knee buckled, and he had to hold on to the wall to remain standing. Could it be true? Harming an innocent bystander was a law enforcement officer's worst nightmare.

"Is the person okay?" Hunt managed to mumble.

"I'm told he's in surgery. The bullet missed his shinbone by a fraction of an inch and tore through his calf," Milburne explained, using his fingers to show by how much the round had missed the bone.

Hunt breathed a sigh of relief, but the respite was short-lived.

"You'll have to come with me," Milburne said, pulling out his handcuffs. "I'm sorry, but I have no choice. Someone caught the whole scene from an adjacent building. The person you shot is pressing charges."

Hunt grunted. He felt terrible for the bystander, and his sense of duty told him to follow the detective. But now that his daughter had been taken, he couldn't.

"Can I send a quick message?" he asked the detective.

"More cars are headed here," Milburne warned, "so make it quick."

"I need your lighter."

Milburne gave him a quizzical look but lobbed it to him anyway.

Hunt caught it with his left hand and typed a quick message to his friend Simon Carter—who was now leading the rapid response team since the events in Chicago. He attached the fingerprints he had lifted from the assaulters to his email before sending it. Carter was someone he trusted. He'd know what to do with those.

Hunt powered down his phone and quickly removed its back cover. He took out the SIM card and held it in the flame of Milburne's cigarette lighter until it had melted beyond salvage. He threw the lighter back to Milburne. For a second, Milburne took his eyes off Hunt to search for his lighter. Hunt made his move and closed the gap. With a powerful sweep of his right leg, he kicked the detective's feet from under him, and Milburne crashed down hard on his side in the hallway. Hunt grabbed his arm and flipped him over onto his stomach. Hunt used Milburne's own handcuffs to secure his hands behind his back. Milburne didn't resist or fight back. It was as if he understood perfectly what Hunt was doing and why. Was that why he had told him more cars were on the way?

Jasmine and Moon suddenly appeared around the corner from the living room, and if they were surprised or shocked by what they saw, they didn't show it. Jasmine asked, "What will you do?"

"I'm gonna get our daughter back."

She nodded to Chris in an *I told you so* manner.

"If you need money, anything, please let me know," Moon offered.

Hunt straightened. "As a matter of fact, can I borrow your new Blackwater?"

CHAPTER TWENTY-SEVEN

Miami, Florida

The quad Mercury Verado 350 engines roared to life, filling the air with a loud throbbing that pulsated through the entire boat. To Hunt, who had always dreamed of owning such a beast, the sound was intoxicating. He removed the lines holding the Blackwater to the dock before taking his position at the helm. He put the engines in gear and motored slowly out of the dredged channel leading to Biscayne Bay. He didn't know where he was going, just that he needed to get out of Dodge before more MDPD officers—presumably much less cooperative than Detective Milburne—stormed Moon's residence to arrest him.

Hunt headed due south toward Government Cut Inlet, a man-made shipping channel between Miami Beach and Fisher Island used by pleasure and commercial craft alike. The moment he exited the channel, he pushed the throttle forward, and the engines gurgled louder. The bow rose slightly before settling back down once the Blackwater 43 was out of the hole. A stiff breeze was picking up from the west, but the boat's twenty-thousand-pound hull carved through the waves with ease. Once he was a mile offshore, he put the gear in neutral and reached for his bag. He pulled out one of the two prepaid phones he carried and dialed a number he had never expected to call again.

Anna Garcia picked up on the third ring. "Is it you?"

"Yes," he replied.

"We need to talk. Where are you?"

Right to the point. No small talk. Her voice, usually so smooth and gentle, sounded choked with emotion. Or was it despair? Hunt could only imagine how difficult it must be for her to talk with him. He had betrayed her in the worst way a man could betray a woman. Through her heart. And he had used her to bring down her father.

"It's a bit complicated," he said. "Tell me where you want to meet."

"I know about the arrest warrant," she said.

"Why am I not surprised?"

The Garcia crime family was well connected and had a lot of sources in law enforcement. Still, he wouldn't be shocked if his face made the evening news today. The media across the country hated him for what he had done to Luke Moore. It didn't mean anything to them that the guy was an asshole and had been responsible for the death of a DEA special agent; Moore was one of them, and they'd do everything in their power to bury Hunt.

"Meet me at my brother's house," Anna said.

"The boat dock is still there, I presume?"

"The dock? Yes, why? You're on a boat?"

"As I said, it's complicated. See you in a few."

CHAPTER TWENTY-EIGHT

Hallandale Beach, Florida

Nothing his cousin had ever asked him to do had troubled Hector before. There were a few things he'd done that he wasn't proud of, like killing two priests who had betrayed the Black Tosca's confidence, but nothing worth losing a night's sleep over. Hector prided himself on his ability to put nasty memories away and move on to the next job. But this was different. Kids were his soft spot, and he didn't believe they should suffer because they'd been born into the wrong family. He had never intentionally hurt a child before.

There was a chance Tony Garcia would cooperate and give his life for his daughter's. If the roles were reversed, Hector would exchange his life for his kid's. Still, Hector had argued against giving Garcia forty-eight hours. Tony was a powerful man with a lot of resources. Why give him the chance to attempt a rescue? While the Black Tosca's network in Florida was solid, they weren't as safe here as they would be in Mexico. But his cousin, in all her wisdom, had decided that she wanted Garcia to suffer, to feel the same pain she'd endured when she was forced to watch her father be burned alive in front of her. Hector had warned her against such a drastic show of force, had explained to her that she would lose the fragile sympathy of the good people of San Miguel de Allende, who had until now largely closed their eyes to her illegal activities. There was an immense difference between looking the other way when it came to the drug-trafficking business—it was Mexico, after all—and forgiving the murder of two teenage girls broadcast live on the internet. The San Miguel de Allende population wouldn't want to be seen as accomplices to the sadistic slaughter his cousin had in mind.

Hector stared at the door across the hallway. In the end, he had failed to make her understand. The Black Tosca was interested in only one thing—revenge.

———

The door to her room opened, and, despite her fatigue, Leila jumped to her feet. Hector stood under the lintel, his head almost touching it. Notwithstanding his kindness and impeccable courtesy toward her, the man radiated the sort of authority that couldn't be denied. And it scared her.

"You owe me something," he said.

She swallowed a sob and thrust her chin out defiantly. "I already told you my name. It's your turn to tell me what I want to know."

Hector gave a little laugh. "Is that so?"

"Where's Sophia?"

Hector cracked his fingers, then folded his arms across his chest. "Nearby," he finally said. "Don't worry about your friend. As long as you continue cooperating with me, she'll be fine."

"You promise?" she asked, knowing how desperate that sounded.

He nodded. "Your parents, Leila. What are their names?"

That hadn't been part of the deal. Why did he need her parents' names? Then it came to her. It was just like in the movies. The bad guys wanted to get paid. That's why they had kidnapped her and Sophia. Their families were rich!

They want a ransom. Oh God! That was good news. Chris would pay anything for her release.

"My mom's name is Jasmine DeGray," she volunteered and then hesitated for a second when it came time to name her father. Maybe the kidnappers would back off if she mentioned her real dad. A quick Google search would tell them he was a federal agent who had almost shot a reporter in the head. Would that be enough to scare them? Probably not, since Hector's friends had killed Sophia's driver and bodyguard. If she was right and the kidnappers wanted money, she was better off telling them her father was Chris Moon. Everyone knew who he was.

"And your father's name?"

"Chris Moon," she said. Then she added, "The football player, you know?"

"Miami Dolphins, right?"

"Yes, yes, that's right," she said enthusiastically. "He has a lot of money. He's gonna pay you."

———

Hector closed the door behind him. The situation had just gotten more complicated. He had kept an eye on the news channels, but none had mentioned the kidnapping of Sophia and Leila. He was stunned at the lack of coverage. In a way, it was good for them. However, it also worried him. Why wasn't the media covering the public kidnapping of two young, pretty, rich teenagers? And one of them Chris Moon's daughter? Heck, the kidnapping should be the only thing the media was talking about.

Was he missing something? A press conference is the best way to ask for the public's help. So why weren't the police doing that?

He sat down at the computer in the office and pulled up Google. In 2009, the Miami Dolphins had drafted Chris Moon in the first round. Since then, they had won the Super Bowl, and Moon had become a record-setting quarterback. The man could perform miracles, if Hector was to believe the local newspapers. Last season, Moon had thrown a staggering fifty-four touchdown passes.

Hector couldn't care less about Moon's exploits on the field. What he was interested in was his personal life. Unfortunately, Chris Moon zealously guarded his personal life. Hector ran a search for Jasmine Moon but didn't have much success. A few pictures here and there, but that was it. He was about to close the browser when one of the photos grabbed his attention. The picture had been taken a year ago at the film festival in Cannes. In the photo, Moon had one arm around Jasmine, who was, in turn, affectionately holding Leila in front of her. The trio was smiling. White teeth all around.

The following line accompanied the picture:

Miami Dolphins quarterback Chris Moon with his wife, Jasmine, and her daughter, Leila.

Hector kicked himself for missing the obvious. She had said her name was Leila DeGray, not Leila Moon.

And her daughter, Leila . . . not *their* daughter, but *her* daughter. He didn't know why, instinct maybe, or just a distrust born of all these years living on the edge, but Hector knew this was something significant. Moon wasn't Leila's father. The girl had lied to him. It was possible she didn't know who her biological father was, but he quickly dismissed the idea. She had hesitated before giving him the name.

Why?

He was about to find out.

———

The door to her room flew open, and Hector barged in. He didn't shout or scream, but the kindness he'd shown her previously was gone. Something had changed. Leila noticed for the first time the destructive look in his eyes. Had he hurt Sophia? A long shiver wound down her spine as she thought of her friend.

"Chris Moon isn't your father, is he?"

Fear fluttered through her. She shook her head.

The slap to her face came as a complete surprise. She gasped at the sting, and her hand shot to her cheek. The tears she had been fighting came rolling down.

"Answer me, child," Hector hissed, his hand half-raised and ready to strike again.

Her whole body was shaking, and her legs were trembling so uncontrollably that it was as if they belonged to someone else.

"No, he isn't," she said, terrified he was going to hit her again.

"Why did you lie?"

"I live with him and Mom now," she explained, her eyes pleading with Hector to believe her. "My real father has no money. He couldn't pay you. The ransom, I mean."

Hector nodded.

"What's your father's name?"

"Pierce Hunt."

"And where does he live?"

"Right here in Florida."

"What does he do?"

"He works with the DEA."

———

A ransom. Hector believed her. He didn't think she had lied to hide her real father's identity. She thought her survival depended on someone paying a ransom. Chris Moon was wealthy; Pierce Hunt wasn't. It was as simple as that.

But the fact that her father was a federal agent changed things a bit. It wasn't cause for alarm yet, but he needed to check a few things out.

Pierce Hunt. The name rang a bell he couldn't quite place, and it bothered him. Google was a big help once again. An in-depth article about an incident involving a DEA agent named Pierce Hunt and Luke Moore, a Chicago reporter, darkened Hector's mood. Hunt wasn't a typical federal agent. He had served with the Army Rangers before joining the DEA. When the incident with the reporter happened, Hunt was an RRT team leader. Hector clicked on the images tab.

Unbelievable. A chuckle escaped his lips. Not that there was anything funny about the situation. It was more like a nervous laugh.

He knew who Pierce Hunt was after all. Hector touched the bloodstained bandage on his left arm. He had exchanged a few shots with the man today. And he had the distinct impression he and Hunt would see each other again very soon.

CHAPTER TWENTY-NINE

Miami, Florida

Hunt eased off the throttle and turned on the boat's remote-controlled spotlight. A powerful beam immediately reflected off the water. Hunt used a joystick mounted on the dash to direct the beam. He quickly found the two long poles indicating the entrance to the narrow channel leading to Tony Garcia's house and steered the boat in that direction. The house was hard to miss. Not only was it huge—at least by Hunt's standards—but spotlights were also aimed at the surrounding grounds. Hunt knew the residence was protected by an elaborate security system. As he got closer, he noted the armed men waiting for him on the dock.

Hunt used the joystick to back the boat into one of the slips. Hunt killed the engines, and one of the men threw a couple of lines to secure the boat.

"Leave your weapons in the boat, Mr. Hunt," he said.

Hunt didn't need to look up to recognize whom the voice belonged to. Mauricio Tasis, Tony Garcia's most brutal and loyal enforcer. Out of necessity, to strengthen his cover, Hunt had once forged a friendship with Tasis. His method of intelligence gathering was crude but highly effective. He wasn't afraid of breaking a bone or two, if needed.

"I'm not armed," Hunt lied. If Tasis thought Hunt was going to face Tony and Anna Garcia weaponless, he was badly mistaken. His pistol would remain in the boat's cabin, but his ceramic knife, which he could draw at a moment's notice, was secured to the underside of his left forearm. It wasn't much against the submachine guns Garcia's men were carrying, but it beat the hell out of having to count on one's fists to kill a man.

Tasis gestured for him to join him on the dock. Hunt obeyed and stepped out of the boat. One man pressed a gun into his back and used it to push him toward the edge of the dock. They were going to search him. Hunt had expected this and didn't complain. The handheld metal detector they used let out a low humming noise but didn't beep when it went over the ceramic knife. Still not satisfied even though the wand hadn't beeped, one man started to pat him down. That, though, Hunt wouldn't allow.

He pivoted 180 degrees and grabbed the man's left wrist, then twisted it to lock the elbow. The man's eyes opened wide in pain and shock. Hunt drove his left hand into the locked elbow, dislocating the man's arm. He then slammed his right elbow into the man's face, breaking his nose, before pushing him off the dock and into the water. The man's partner was quick to react and lashed out at Hunt with a knife while Tasis yelled at his man to stand down. Hunt stepped clear as the tip of the knife swung wildly past his chest. Before the man could try again, Hunt buried his knee deep into his abdomen, doubling him over and dropping him to his knees before easily wrenching the knife out of his hand. Hunt threw the knife into the ocean and then kneed the man again, this time under the chin, knocking him out. Hunt looked at Tasis. He hadn't moved an inch. He was still standing twenty feet away, a smile on his lips with his MP5 hanging from a sling on his neck.

"You haven't changed at all," Tasis said.

"We're still friends?"

The smile vanished, replaced by a sidelong look of disgust.

"You betrayed everyone I care for, Mr. Hunt, and not stopping you is my biggest failure."

"They kept you around nonetheless."

"Because I promised I'd kill you one day."

"So why don't you shoot me?" Hunt said, tapping his finger on his forehead. "This is your chance."

"Don't tempt me," Tasis replied, his voice cold as ice. "There's nothing I'd like to do more than put you down like the dog you are."

Hunt didn't doubt the man's seriousness. He'd feel exactly the same if he was in Tasis's shoes. Still, time was of the essence, and they had already lost enough of it bullshitting each other.

"Can I see her now?"

Tasis headed toward the residence, leaving Hunt to follow. "I pray to God your meeting doesn't go well."

"And why's that?"

"So I can put a bullet in your thick head."

CHAPTER THIRTY

Pompano Beach, Florida

One of his phones buzzed him awake. Cole Egan reluctantly rolled away from his wife and reached for it on the nightstand. He had a new text message: 9738184537120.

Damn it!

There was no way he was going back to sleep now. To anyone reading it—Katherine in particular—these numbers would look random. But Egan knew better. If he subtracted one from each number, he'd get a Chinese cell phone number. Protocols negotiated a little less than a decade ago stipulated he had fifteen minutes to call back. It was a simple code but an efficient one.

Egan quietly climbed out of bed. The night was pitch-black, and Katherine's soft breath was the only sound. He closed the bedroom door behind him and went to his office to make the call. He unlocked the filing cabinet in which he kept his biometric safe. From the safe, he grabbed one of many burner phones and dialed the Chinese number.

"I hope I didn't wake you," the voice on the other end said.

"We both know you couldn't care less."

"Very true. It makes me wonder why I try to make small talk with you."

"I was wondering the same thing," Egan said. "What can I do for you?"

"Hector will call you within the next five minutes at this number. He'll tell you what needs to be done."

That was unusual. Hector Mieles was a capable man and an exceptional leader. But Egan didn't work for him. He worked for only one person. That, too, had been negotiated.

Since Egan hadn't replied, the person at the other end decided to add an explanation. "This is a onetime deal, and I'll double your fee."

This was getting interesting. His normal fee was $200,000. The bonus would go a long way toward paying for his future kid's education. If his boss was ready to pony up such a large amount of money for a single target, there was a catch. So he asked what the catch was.

"He's a federal agent."

That wasn't a big deal. He had killed more than his share of DEA and ATF agents. Why the higher fee, then? As if his interlocutor had read his thoughts, the next statement offered somewhat of an explanation.

"In case you wonder why I'm offering a premium, the target is a highly trained DEA agent. He's also a veteran, just like you, Mr. Granger."

Mr. Granger had been his code name for the past ten years. In some circles, the name was both feared and respected. It was said Mr. Granger had never failed to kill his target and that his smile was the last thing you'd ever see.

"Five hundred thousand."

He heard his employer take a deep breath.

"I'm told you're expecting a child," the voice said. "Congratulations to you and Katherine. A boy or a girl?"

Even though the words were spoken quietly, Egan took them as the threat they were meant to be. It was also a clear message: *Don't push it, or I'll squish you.*

"What are the rules of engagement?"

"Get it done, but don't get caught. You're precious to me. Am I clear?"

"Yes."

Even Mr. Granger couldn't say no to the Black Tosca. Not if he wanted his family to keep breathing.

———

After relaying the caller's phone number to Hector, Valentina tossed the mobile phone into the roaring fireplace. If her cousin was the general of her army, Cole Egan—a.k.a. Mr. Granger—was her scalpel on American soil. He was meticulous and precise and had never failed to accomplish the missions she'd given him. And he was great in bed too. It had been a while since she had shared something intimate with him, but Egan wasn't the type of lover a woman forgot easily. She felt a tad jealous toward Katherine. Then she laughed at her own silliness. Maybe Egan could fake playing family for a while, but in the end, he was just like her—a sociopath.

———

Egan let his mind wander while he waited for Hector's call.

A decade ago, he had come back from Gaza shattered in mind and body. He spent ten months in a military hospital recovering from his wounds and undergoing numerous operations. His body healed, but his mind remained plagued by what the terrorists had done to him. After countless sessions with numerous army shrinks, they threw in the towel and discharged him.

Thank you for your service. Here's the door. Good luck with the rest of your life.

He had given them everything in exchange for what? Recurring nightmares and a derisory medical pension? At first glance, it looked that way, but that was shortsighted. In fact, the army had given him much more than that. It had given him the ability to dehumanize his enemies. And to kill them. And he was pretty damn good at it.

A French private military company, impressed with his résumé, had hired him and sent him to Venezuela to train future members of the Venezuelan president's protective detail. Not only did he love the job, but they'd paid him exponentially more than the United States military had. His new position gave him access to powerful men within the Venezuelan government. These powerful men, Egan quickly learned, were more than happy to part with large sums of money in exchange for the assassination of the antigovernment movement leaders who threatened to topple the president. It was a lucrative market, albeit a dangerous one. But Egan was a professional, and word spread around Caracas that a new, infallible assassin was in town. Soon after, he quit the PMC and started working solo, locally at first and then all over South America.

One day, after a successful assignment in Mexico, he woke up tied to a bed, naked. It was evident the bartender had slipped a narcotic into his drink. He recognized the woman standing next to him the moment he opened his eyes. The Black Tosca wasn't only the most stunning woman he had ever had the pleasure to share a room with, but she was also known as the most lethal bitch in the drug world. And here she was, staring at him, a black whip in her hand.

"What are you gonna do with that?" he asked in Spanish.

"I don't know yet. It depends," she replied in Spanish-inflected English he found irresistible.

"On what?"

"Do you know who I am?"

"Miss Universe?"

The whip came down hard on his right nipple. It hurt. Kind of.

"Do you know who I am?" she repeated.

"The Black Tosca."

She nodded and removed her pants. Her legs were gorgeous in shimmering thigh-high stockings.

"Would you like to work for me?"

"What if I say—"

That time the whip came down much harder on his nipple. It drew blood.

"Would you like to work for me?"

"I'd love to."

The Black Tosca smiled. "I'm glad you said that, because the next reprimand was a bullet in your pretty face, and that would have been a real shame. I kind of like you," she said, sitting on top of him.

The next morning, an understanding had been reached. She was going to pay him handsomely to operate in the United States. Once in a while, there would be an odd job for him in Mexico or in Europe. He would work for and report to only her.

His life changed six months later when she summoned him to a beautiful bachelor pad in Mexico City. After they had sex, she gave him a photo of Katherine McMaster.

"I want you to seduce this lovely girl."

"What for?"

"Because I fucking asked you to, and I pay you so much money that you'll do whatever I want."

He couldn't argue with her logic. Plus, the girl was pretty.

"What's her name?"

"Katherine McMaster. Her father is Daniel McMaster, the special agent in charge of the DEA's Weston field office."

"I see."

"This will be a long-term operation."

"Can you describe 'long term'?"

"Until I tell you to stop."

The phone chirped in Egan's hand. He had fallen asleep for a minute.

"Yes."

"Were you told I'd be calling?"

Hector.

"I was."

"We need you to take care of someone for us."

Of course you do, Hector, Egan thought. "Please send all pertinent information—"

"It's already in your draft folder."

That was quick.

To communicate electronically without leaving a trace, Egan and the Black Tosca would write messages and leave them in the draft folder. So instead of sending the messages, they would read each other's drafts and delete them the moment they were done with them.

Egan logged in to the account and clicked to open the draft email. Seeing a name from the past shocked him to the core.

Pierce Hunt.

How in hell did Hunt get involved with the Black Tosca? Then he remembered Hunt had joined the DEA right after he left the army. After Gaza, they hadn't kept in touch much. A few phone calls while he was working with the French PMC to let Hunt know he was back on his feet, but nothing once he started working solo. He doubted Hunt would approve of his career choice.

"So?" Hector asked after a minute had passed. "Any issues?"

"I know the man," Egan said.

"What? How?" Hector seemed to be genuinely intrigued.

"We served together."

"I see," Hector replied, disappointment evident in his voice. "Will it be a problem?"

Hector was worried. *And he should be*, Egan thought. Hunt wasn't someone you wanted to tangle with.

Even though they hadn't talked in a few years, Hunt was the one person he trusted with his life. They were still brothers, forever linked by the blood they'd shed together fighting in the desert. What if he refused the contract? Would the Black Tosca turn on him? She would be foolish to. Because of him, she had remote access to Daniel McMaster's two laptops, mobile phone, and desktop. He was her entry into the DEA's database. Five months ago, he would have taken his chances and turned down the assignment. But that was before Katherine had gotten pregnant.

"This man is a trained operator," Egan said. "He's not an easy mark."

"This is why my cousin doubled your fee," Hector reminded him.

"How did he come up on your radar?"

It took a few seconds for Hector to reply. "By mistake, really. We kidnapped his daughter when—"

"You kidnapped his daughter?" *How stupid were they?* "Are you out of your fucking mind? Pierce is a warrior. When confronted, he attacks."

"I said it was a mistake. I didn't—"

"You think he gives a shit if it was a mistake or not?" Egan was doing his absolute best not to yell into the phone. Hector seemed to have no idea of the gravity of the situation.

"We were supposed to grab only Tony Garcia's daughter," Hector explained. "We didn't know who Leila was."

"He won't rest before he kills everyone involved," Egan warned him.

"He's only one man."

"Maybe, but you have no idea what he's capable of, my friend. He's relentless, and he has nothing to lose. Please tell me his daughter is still alive."

"She is."

You're a lucky man, then, Hector. He'll kill you quickly.

"My suggestion to you is this," Egan said. "Put a bag over her head, then drop her at a busy street corner. Then leave and never come back."

He wondered if Hector would be clever enough to follow his advice. He wasn't.

"Enough talking. The instructions are in the draft folder. Do your job, Mr. Granger," Hector said, putting an end to the conversation. "And you'd better do it well."

The line went dead. *Shit!*

He could try to leave. Go to Thailand or something. He had just over $4 million stashed away in a safe deposit box in the Bahamas and another half mil stashed in his house. Not a huge amount, but enough to live comfortably in Asia with Katherine and the kid. If it was him alone, he was confident they wouldn't be able to track him down. But with Katherine and the kid in tow? Not so sure.

Was he ready to pay the ultimate price to find out?

CHAPTER THIRTY-ONE

Miami, Florida

Hunt followed Tasis into the main house. The faint smell of onions and cumin that came rolling out of the kitchen triggered a rush of emotions and memories. Some terrible ones, of course, but they weren't all bad. He had shared some good laughs here with Tony and Anna.

Tasis's voice reminded him things had changed since the last giggles.

"I'll be here, watching. Please do something stupid," Tasis whispered as Hunt walked past him and entered the living room, where Tony and Anna were seated.

Hunt didn't bother to reply and instead scanned the living room to make sure there wasn't anyone else waiting with a gun pointed at his head.

There was no one. Tasis closed the door behind him, and Hunt was left alone with Tony and Anna Garcia. Anna was seated next to her brother, and neither of them bothered to stand up. Anna's arms were folded, and her face was an impassive mask that Hunt couldn't read. But damned if she wasn't the most beautiful woman he'd ever laid eyes on. The thought of her ripe curves beneath her summer dress still stirred his blood. Her brother, on the other hand, looked like he wanted to skin him alive.

It was Anna who broke the silence. She placed a reassuring hand on Tony's arm and said, "Thanks for coming."

Hunt nodded but didn't say anything. It was kind of surreal to be in the same room as Anna and Tony. Twenty-four hours ago, that wouldn't have been possible. But now they all had to face the incredible and delicate situation in which they found themselves.

"So you kept the note I gave you," Hunt said.

"I wasn't sure you'd call back."

"I'm here, and I think that if we can help it at all, we shouldn't let our emotions get in the way."

Tony was looking at him with the most awful contempt.

"I'm sorry about your father, Anna," Hunt added.

His words seemed to reverberate in the living room. Before Anna could stop her brother, Tony jumped out of his seat and came at him. Hunt ducked the first punch, blocked the second, and jabbed Tony in the chest before he could throw another one.

"Back off, Tony," Hunt warned, feeling the adrenaline flowing through his body. He was getting mad too. He was here so that they could come up with a plan to find their daughters. If Tony needed to be knocked on his ass to realize they had to work together, Hunt was happy to oblige. But before this could happen, he had to let them know Leila was his daughter. He had no idea how they would react.

Tony's face was red with anger, the veins in his neck bulging. His fists were clenched, and Hunt guessed he wasn't about to back off despite his warning.

"How dare you talk about my father?" Tony roared. "He's dead because of you."

Tony telegraphed his next move and swung his fist toward Hunt's chin. Hunt stepped back, and the fist missed by a couple of inches.

"Stop it, Tony!" Anna yelled, but to no avail. Tony grunted and threw a hook that Hunt parried with his forearm and countered with a pistonlike jab, catching Tony flush on the chin; he followed with a right hook that slammed into Tony's cheek. The sound of bone against bone, with flesh caught in the middle, echoed off the living room's windows. Tony took three steps back, a dazed look on his face.

"Goddamn it! Stop it, you two!" Anna screamed.

The commotion prompted Tasis to barge into the room with his MP5 swinging. Hunt raised his hands.

"We're fine, Mauricio," Anna said.

Tasis looked at Tony. For a moment, Hunt wondered if Tony was about to ask Tasis to execute him. But a subtle nod from Tony sent his enforcer back into the corridor with a loud sigh. It was obvious to Hunt that this wasn't the outcome Tasis had hoped for.

"Have a seat, Tony, please," Hunt pleaded. "Can we focus on the reason why I'm here?"

"This thing between us," Tony replied as he sat, his eyes glinting with a fury Hunt had rarely seen, "it isn't over."

———

Anna questioned whether she'd done the right thing contacting Pierce. Clearly her brother wasn't ready to see him; she wasn't sure she was ready either. What she truly wanted to do was hide in a corner. The humiliation she had suffered at the hands of this man, especially at the trial, continued to weigh heavily on her shoulders.

Terrance Davis, the man she had fallen in love with, was ruthless but tender and compassionate at the same time. Pierce Hunt, on the other hand, was a mystery to her. She didn't know him at all, and certainly anything resembling trust between them had gone out the window when he betrayed her. For months after his treachery, she had been a total emotional wreck. Her appetite gone, she had lost ten pounds within a few short weeks. She thought all this was behind her, but seeing him again, here in her brother's house, brought back painful memories. A ton of questions popped into her head. Was any of the intimacy they had once shared genuine? Did he really love her? If so, how could he have been so cruel? For her, it would have been impossible to fake the craving she had felt for him.

Good God, I was such a fool.

She wished, in a quieter, more secret part of her mind, that he had truly loved her. That would mean that he would have at least suffered a little when everything fell apart. Not that any of that mattered. Anna took a deep breath and pushed aside her needs and uncertainties. "Can we talk?" she asked.

"I'd like to say something," Hunt said, "but you'll have to keep your cool. Especially you, Tony."

Tony opened his mouth, but Anna beat him to it.

"We're listening."

"I was with your father when he died."

"How—" Tony barked but stopped when Hunt raised his hand.

"Let me finish, then I'll answer your questions."

That shut Tony up, but Anna knew there was a fight raging inside him.

"Your father was being transferred to a safe house when his motorcade got ambushed this morning. I was part of his protective detail."

"The newspapers said you were suspended after what happened in Chicago," Anna said. She didn't know what to think anymore.

"Today was my first official day back on duty."

"You're DEA scum," Tony hissed. "Why were you part of his protection detail?"

"Vicente agreed to testify against Valentina Mieles, also known as the—"

"We know who she is," Tony cut in. "She's the bitch who kidnapped my daughter—"

"And mine," Hunt said softly.

"What are you talking about?" Anna asked, confused.

"Leila's my daughter."

Anna felt a massive jolt of electricity shoot through her body. For a moment, she forgot how to inhale. Hunt's words were so shocking that they froze her frame but thawed her heart. Could it be true?

She studied his face for any sign of deceit but didn't find any. His jaw was set, but his eyes revealed his vulnerability.

I'll be damned. He's telling the truth.

———

Hunt watched the color drain from Anna's cheeks.

"Un-fucking-believable," Tony said from the sofa, even though his tone betrayed the fact that he did believe it.

"So, as unreal as it sounds, Leila is Sophia's best friend," Anna said.

Everybody fell silent as they realized how awkward this was.

"I was supposed to bake them blueberry muffins, for God's sake," Tony said, his voice choked with tears as he raked his fingers through his thick black hair.

Hunt could see Anna had a thousand questions for him, so he said, "Leila's mother, Jasmine, is my ex-wife. She left me after I testified at your father's trial. She's married to Chris Moon now."

Anna nodded but didn't say anything for a long minute.

"You had a family while we were together." It wasn't a question, more like a statement of fact.

Still, Hunt replied, "I did, and for what it's worth—"

"I don't want to know, and frankly, I don't care," Anna said, even though they both knew it wasn't true. "Can we focus on getting our girls back?"

Sensing they had reached some kind of uneasy truce, Hunt sat down in an armchair facing Tony. "If the Black Tosca kidnapped our daughters, it makes sense she's the one who ordered the hit on the motorcade too."

Tony rubbed his face and said, "She called me half an hour ago."

Why didn't you lead with that instead of picking a fight? Hunt wanted to physically shake some sense into Tony, but he willed himself not to give in to his frustration. That would be counterproductive, to say the least. Instead he asked, "What did she say?"

Tony hesitated.

"Tell him, or I will," Anna prompted.

By the tense look Tony gave Hunt, it was obvious that whatever the Black Tosca had told him made him nervous.

"She wants my head," Tony finally said, making a cutting gesture across his neck.

"So your head for both our daughters?" That didn't seem like a bad trade to Hunt. Tony probably disagreed. Or maybe not.

"As much as I fucking hate you, Hunt," Tony said with a disarming sincerity, "I'd be willing to do it to save them."

For some reason, Hunt believed him.

"But you don't think she'll hold her end of the bargain."

"Do you?"

Hunt shook his head. There was a chance she would, but it would be stupid to bet his daughter's life on it.

"There's more," added Anna, looking at her brother.

The bulging vein in Tony's neck was now throbbing at a frantic rate. "If someone doesn't deliver my severed head to her within the next forty-five hours, our daughters will be burned alive."

Our. Daughters. Will. Be. Burned. Alive.

Tony's words were like a sledgehammer, beating him down with every syllable. Hunt's mind whirled. Images flicked at him with tantalizing clarity. He could see Leila, savagely beaten, with a tire full of gasoline around her neck. Only once before had he felt anything like the intensity of the fury now erupting deep inside his gut.

Gaza, 2007. The kidnapping of Cole Egan.

Hunt remembered vividly the events that followed his friend's abduction. McMaster had been right: to find his friend, he had left carnage in his wake. In fact, he had committed some truly atrocious acts in order to reach Cole before the Hamas terrorists could kill him. In order to make peace with his past, with the things he had done, he'd sworn to himself he would never kill or torture another person in cold blood again.

The promise.

This was why he had left the military and joined a federal law enforcement agency. With the DEA, the rules of engagement were better defined. It was also his hope that conducting antidrug operations in the United States would be less chaotic than hunting down terrorists overseas. On the contrary, the moral and ethical dilemmas he faced almost every day as a DEA special agent were often tougher than the challenges he had faced fighting terrorists abroad.

The delicate touch of Anna's hand on his knee brought him back to the present.

"We need your help, Pierce, and I think you need ours."

He slowly lifted his head to look at her. She must have seen something in his expression because her eyes widened, and she froze. A frown appeared, drawing her eyebrows together. She removed her hand from his knee and sat straighter.

"What?" he asked her.

He saw her shiver. "There's darkness in you that scares me."

Hunt felt it too, and he embraced it. Whatever the cost, he would find Leila and Sophia.

"Sometimes you need darkness to see the light," he said, knowing the next forty hours would be pitch-black.

CHAPTER THIRTY-TWO

Stafford, Virginia

Pierce Hunt. Text message.

Simon Carter recognized the ringtone; he would have ignored it otherwise. He opened his eyes and blinked at the naked woman sleeping beside him. With the exception of the few smile lines around her eyes, his wife hadn't changed at all since he had first fallen in love with her fifteen years ago. A glimmer of moonlight streamed in through a couple of broken blinds, highlighting the side of her face and the top of her shoulder. He kissed her lightly on her forehead and got out of bed without disturbing her. He picked up his phone from the charging station and went down to the kitchen. He foraged through the fridge and found a pot of leftover chicken à la king. He prepared himself a plate and put it in the microwave. While it heated, he poured a tall glass of ice water and gulped half of it down.

The last time Hunt had contacted him was to let him know he had been transferred to the Miami field division in Weston. Carter was happy for him. Hunt was a good man, well respected by his peers. True, his decisions in the field were highly intuitive, often very rash, and his complete lack of political correctness offended the higher-ups, but no one could argue about the results. Hunt always led from the front, and Carter had learned many important lessons from him. If Carter had become a good team leader, it was mainly due to Hunt's mentoring.

Simon Gervais

Carter opened Hunt's text message and saw it contained a multitude of attachments, all of them fingerprints. Hunt's message was short, direct, and to the point.

Carter read the text message twice. The ambush in Miami had made national news. The US marshals had lost good men in the attack, but there had been no mention of Hunt's involvement. His friend was in deep shit and needed his help. Hunt had left instructions on how to contact him.

The microwave beeped, but Carter ignored it. He wasn't hungry anymore.

"It's getting close to midnight, baby," his wife said from behind him. "Are you coming up?"

She was three-quarters of the way down the stairs. There was nothing he wanted more than to cuddle up with her under a pile of blankets, but Hunt's message meant he needed to head back to the office.

"I'm sorry, Emma; I need to go," he said, brandishing his phone.

Her worry was apparent. "Be careful, okay?" She had been a close friend of Scott Miller's wife, and Scott's death during the Chicago drug raid had shaken her, made her aware of just how dangerous Carter's job was.

"Always," he said, scooping her up in his arms.

Emma wrapped her arms around his neck and let him cradle her against his chest. His lips trailed across her hair and down to her neck.

"I love you," he whispered in her ear. "I'll be back in no time."

———

Though Carter drove with his habitual care, his mind was preoccupied. Rumors that Tom Hauer—the current acting administrator of the DEA—wanted to shut down the RRT program and replace it with regional special response teams—SRTs—bothered him. If that were to happen, each major domestic office would be required to maintain its own operational SRT, and chances were he'd be asked to relocate. He and Emma were happy in Stafford. She had found a job at one of the local schools, and they were less than an hour's drive from her parents. Carter loved his in-laws—both former CIA case officers—and he knew how much his wife cherished her time with them. If his team were disbanded, where would the DEA send him? Since he was the main breadwinner, he and his family wouldn't have any choice but to go where the DEA wanted him to go.

The other thing that troubled him was Hunt's email. A quick check into the DEA's network had indicated there was now an arrest warrant for Hunt. Apparently one of his rounds had hit a bystander during the ambush on Vicente Garcia's motorcade. If this was true, why the hell did Hunt refuse to turn himself in? Why had he run? Something was amiss. Running went against everything Hunt stood for.

He needed to speak to Hunt. And soon.

But, for now, he'd give his friend the benefit of the doubt and check those fingerprints.

CHAPTER THIRTY-THREE

Miami, Florida

Physically speaking, Anna knew everything about the man sitting next to her. The man she'd known as Terrance Davis wasn't classically pretty, but he was ruggedly sexy. His hard-to-look-away-from, piercing blue eyes were warm and understanding, but they could also become as hard as diamonds in the span of a second. He had dark brown hair that he liked to keep short. But what she remembered the most—and missed even more—were the tight bands of well-defined muscles layered across his flat stomach. Hunt had the body of an Olympic swimmer.

She used to know what Terrance Davis liked in bed, what worried him, and what made him happy. She knew what made him tick and what made him laugh. But what about Pierce Hunt? What did he like? What made him sad?

Pierce Hunt's eyes were different too. In his eyes burned an intensity she had never seen before. These were the eyes of an apex predator ready to do anything to get what he wanted. And since they all wanted the same thing, Hunt was exactly the type of man they needed to save the girls.

Three knocks on the door steered her attention away from her ex-lover.

———

This time Tasis was kind enough to announce his presence by knocking on the door before he entered. His MP5 was slung to his side and not pointed at Hunt's head, which, in Hunt's opinion, was a nice improvement. He was also carrying a sealed white envelope that he gave to Tony.

"From our friend at the MDPD," Tasis said before moving out of the room.

Tony glanced down at the envelope and took a deep breath.

"The video of our daughters' kidnapping," Tony explained.

The man was clearly shaken. His hands were unsteady as he tried to rip open the seal with his thumb. His fingers fumbled, and he dropped the envelope on the hardwood floor.

"Fuck!"

Before either Tony or Anna had time to pick up the envelope from the floor, Hunt had his ceramic knife in his hand. He flipped the blade so that the handle was presented first.

"Take this," he offered.

Tony's face hardened, his eyes traveling from the knife to Hunt's eyes. His lips parted, and it looked as if he wanted to say something, but after a long moment, he accepted the knife and used it to slice open the envelope. Tony pulled out a piece of paper and a thumb drive. He read the letter quickly and handed it to Anna, who read it, then gave it to Hunt.

Hunt glanced down at the note.

I'm very sorry, Mr. Garcia. Please know the whole department is actively searching for Sophia and her friend. Here's the video we talked about.

It didn't come as a surprise that Tony had men inside the department. What alarmed Hunt was the fact that he had access to someone high enough in the hierarchy to release a video that Detective Milburne had said was missing. But that was an issue he'd deal with later, if at all. For now, it served his purpose as much as Tony's.

In an unexpected gesture, Tony handed him back his knife and said, "I'll have to speak to Mauricio about this."

Hunt sheathed his knife and asked, "You gonna play the video?"

"I'll get my laptop," he said, leaving Hunt alone with Anna.

Hunt didn't mind the silence, but Anna was fidgeting in her chair. She looked at him, and he couldn't help but wonder if her thoughts mirrored his. He confirmed they did when she finally asked, "What chance do you think we have of finding them?"

He didn't want to lie to her, but he didn't want her to lose faith either. "The next forty hours or so are crucial. The police are doing everything—"

She cut him off sharply. "I couldn't care less about what the police are doing. What are *you* gonna do about it?"

He replied with total honesty. "I'll find the bastards who did this. I'll hunt them down. Then I'll give them one chance to tell me where the girls are before I start manipulating their bodies in ways they weren't meant to be manipulated."

His answer seemed to satisfy her because she gave him a slow nod, and the worry in her face lessened slightly.

Tony returned with his laptop. He set it up on the coffee table and angled it so that Anna and Hunt could see the screen. He pulled the thumb drive from his pocket and nervously twirled it before inserting it.

Hunt's body tensed in anticipation. It wasn't every day that you watched your daughter being kidnapped. When the video started, his heart was trip-hammering, and a nervous sweat pricked his forehead. At some point during the video, he heard Anna yelp with fright, and her hand gripped his arm. Hunt did his best to keep his cool and not let his temper get the best of him. It was as much for his own sake as Anna's. When the video ended, Anna looked as if she wanted to bolt out of the room. Tony simply sank deeper into the sofa and placed his head into his cupped hands.

Hunt was the first to compose himself. "I'll need to look at the video again."

When Tony didn't immediately react, Hunt clapped his hands to get his attention. "Wake up, Tony! Sophia needs you. Play the damn video again."

That did the trick. Tony came out of his trance and punched a key to restart the video.

"Now," Hunt said to Anna and Tony. "I know watching it over and over again is going to be difficult, but we need to pay attention and dissect the details in case they give us clues as to where they took our girls."

"This was done by professionals," Tony said.

Hunt concurred. He was glad Tony had regained his self-control.

"Let's watch it a couple of times, and then we'll compare notes, all right?" Hunt suggested.

And that's exactly what they did for the next fifteen minutes. Once Hunt was convinced he had learned everything there was to learn from the video, he looked at the two pages of notes he'd written.

"So?" Anna asked him, her voice still a bit shaky. "Anything you'd like to share?"

Before he could answer, his burner phone rang.

It was Simon Carter.

CHAPTER THIRTY-FOUR

Hallandale Beach, Florida

Hector Mieles wasn't one to slack off when it came to operational security. With the exception of what Mr. Granger had told him over the phone and what he had been able to find online, and also the couple of minutes they had spent shooting at each other, Hector didn't know much about Pierce Hunt. One thing was certain, though: the guy was bad news.

There was little doubt that Hunt was looking for them. Not only was the man dangerous, but he was a DEA agent too—and a former rapid response team leader at that. Hector didn't fear the DEA, but he respected their tenacity and how ruthless they were outside the United States. Friends who had fought in Afghanistan had told him about the DEA Foreign Advisory and Support Team—FAST. They were hardworking, dedicated, and also merciless toward Taliban kingpins and drug facilitators. He had no reason to believe Pierce Hunt would act differently with his team if he managed to pick up their trail. If this were Mexico, Hunt would never find them. Hector would leave a trail that would be impossible for Hunt to untangle. Here in the United States, they were in the lion's den. Treading carefully in this hostile environment was a necessity, not an option.

With that in mind, it only made sense to change location. The four vehicles his team had used to conduct the abductions of the two teenagers were inside the garage. Three more Mercedes SUVs were parked in front of the house. There were two additional safe houses available to him outside Miami. One was in Orlando, and the other one was in Hypoluxo. The one in Orlando was larger and had a significantly bigger weapons cache, but the distance was too far. The house in Hypoluxo was located in the Mediterranean-style gated community of the Hypoluxo Yacht Club. Although smaller in size, the three-bedroom, three-bath town house had two things going for it. First, a thirty-second walk from the house was the marina, where a Hydra-Sports 4200 Siesta, powered with quad Yamaha 350 engines, was fueled up and ready to go. With the Boynton Inlet a little less than half a mile away, and the Siesta's top speed of over sixty-five miles an hour, it would be difficult for the police or the Coast Guard to catch them if they had to flee by water. The boat couldn't outrace a helicopter, but they had a couple of RPG launchers on board for such an eventuality.

The second benefit of the Hypoluxo safe house was the proximity of the Palm Beach County Park Airport. It was a mere five minutes' drive away. The two pilots for the King Air 350 Hector had chartered were standing by at a nearby hotel.

A voice crackled in his earpiece.

"Hector, it's Antonio. Do you copy?"

Antonio was the leader of one of the two-man teams he had sent to do a recon of the safe house.

"You're five by five," Hector said.

"I-95 is light traffic only up to Boca Raton," Antonio said.

That was good to know. The other team was taking Highway 1. Both teams were to report to him every ten minutes with traffic updates, or sooner if they noticed anything unusual, like a police speed trap. Hector wanted to be gone within the hour. The only thing he had left to decide was how to proceed with the girls. Should he drug them? It would be the safest way to travel with them. So far they were cooperating with him and his men. Hector guessed they were too terrified to do otherwise. They were so young.

In Hector's mind, they were lucky he was the one in charge. He knew men—none of them on his team—who would have raped the girls by now, just to show them who was in charge. Hector had read about the history and evolution of human torture, and even though he never fully embraced its explicit usage, he also had no problem with it—or murder for that matter—when the situation called for it. But rape was another matter. It was wrong.

He made his way to the basement, where Emilio was faithfully babysitting the teenagers.

"Take a break," Hector said. "Go pack your gear. We're leaving soon."

Emilio stood up and stretched. "You want something to eat?"

Hector declined. "I just ate a protein bar."

"What will you do with them?" Emilio asked, his finger moving back and forth between Leila's and Sophia's doors.

Hector showed Emilio two syringes. "I'll put them to sleep."

———

Leila had an unsettled feeling in her chest, like a hard fist squeezed around her heart. She sensed that something bad was about to happen. She'd assumed that all of this was about a ransom. But what if it wasn't?

Hector's face had changed when she had told him about Pierce and the fact that he was a DEA agent. Could all of this be her father's fault? Could this be payback for some of the secret stuff he did?

Leila's thoughts moved to Sophia. Poor Sophia. She was the true victim here. Kidnapped because of Leila's father, a man she had never met, a man she didn't even know existed. How more unfair could this whole thing be? A deep sadness washed over her, and she suddenly felt an urgent need to throw up. She ran to the toilet but didn't make it. Vomit spurted out of her mouth and splashed against the cement floor.

The acidic taste was disgusting, making her retch again. Spasm after spasm racked her body, but only bile came out.

Fuck!

Her throat was wrecked, and her head ached like hell. She was one massive mess.

Sophia, what have I done to you? I'm so, so sorry.

She hated her father. She hated him for walking out on her mother. She hated him for working too much and for always making excuses. She hated him for thrusting himself back into her life. She hated him because he wasn't here. But most of all, she hated herself for feeling so helpless and for betraying her friend.

Then she heard the unmistakable sound of a key inside the lock.

Her tormentor was coming back.

The door opened, and Hector stepped in. For a moment, he hesitated.

At the sight of him, she felt adrenaline surge through her body, and all her pent-up rage and fury broke loose. With a feral scream of sheer anger, she attacked.

———

The pungent smell of vomit caught Hector off guard, and he recoiled. Startling him even more was Leila leaping at him as if she was possessed. She slammed into him, momentarily knocking him off balance, her screams echoing through the entire floor. Somehow, she managed to hold on to him with her legs and dug a finger deep into his right eye while scratching the other side of his face with her nails. His cheek throbbed where her nails had gouged deep cuts.

The little ungrateful bitch.

Hector backhanded her away with all his strength. She hit the ground hard and rolled several times before becoming still. Hector raised his hand to his right eye and cursed. Every time he blinked, a knifelike pain drove into his eye.

He sidestepped a fresh puddle of vomit and knelt down next to Leila. She was still motionless. Her chest wasn't falling or rising.

Mierda. Did I hit her too hard? Not that she didn't deserve it.

He pressed a finger on her neck to check for a pulse. He was relieved there was a strong one. He stuck his ear in her face and listened for a breath.

———

Leila's whole body hurt from landing on the floor. Every muscle. Her head was throbbing. She fought to remain conscious, afraid Hector would do unspeakable things to her if she didn't. She flinched when she heard his footsteps getting closer and closer. She kept her eyes closed and willed herself to lie still, but her heart was pounding.

Play dead, Leila. Maybe he'll leave you alone.

Her throat constricted when he touched her neck. A thick smell of sweat, shaving cream, and coffee made her nose burn. She opened her eyes a slit, only to realize he was right in her face, his ear less than two inches from her mouth.

She acted out of instinct more than anything else. She bit his ear. Hard. She felt a crunching between her teeth and wildly shook her head from left to right until a piece of Hector's ear tore away. The hot, salty, and metallic taste of his blood filled her mouth.

Hector, howling like a wild animal, grabbed her by the throat and squeezed, robbing her of oxygen. She tried to knock his arm away, but he was too strong. He gritted his teeth as his grip became even tighter. Leila frantically looked around for something, anything, that she could use to defend herself, but her strength was almost gone. She had only seconds to live, and the unfairness of it all crushed her. Her last thought was for Sophia. She hoped her best friend would fare better.

I'm sorry, Sophia.

Leila didn't feel the needle Hector jabbed into her neck. She had already passed out.

CHAPTER THIRTY-FIVE

Stafford, Virginia

Simon Carter punched in the number Hunt had given him and drummed his fingers on the table while he waited for his friend to pick up. Hunt picked up on the fourth ring.

"Thanks for doing this, brother," Hunt said by way of greeting.

"No worries, man. I'm here for you. Anything you need, you know that."

"I do. What do you have for me?"

Carter looked at the printout in front of him. "Listen, Pierce, most of the fingerprints you forwarded to me came back negative. But two of them scored a hit."

"What do we know?"

"That you're dealing with real professionals. The guys were former members of the Mexican navy, more specifically from the *Infantería de Marina*."

On the other end of the line, Hunt sighed.

"Their names are Eustacio Sarmiento and Juan Pablo Carballal," Carter added, his eyes still on the printout. "They spent seventy days at Camp Pendleton in California in 2010."

"Doing what?"

"Seems like they went through the Marine Corps's Basic Reconnaissance Course," Carter said. "That's how we got their fingerprints."

"Goddamn it! This makes me so sick."

Hunt's tone suggested he was beyond mad.

"You're telling me we trained those guys? And now they turned against us? This is fucking nuts!"

Carter didn't disagree with Hunt's assessment, but this was hardly the first time such things had happened. Rogue Afghan and Iraqi soldiers were increasingly turning their weapons against their American trainers. In fact, Carter had read somewhere that this was now the leading cause of death for NATO troops in Afghanistan. How sick was that for a statistic?

"I know," Carter replied.

"They killed all the marshals, Simon. All of them. I'm the only one who survived the ambush."

Carter clenched the receiver against his ear and swore under his breath. It pissed him off to no end that so many federal agents had lost their lives protecting a scumbag like Vicente Garcia.

"I'm sorry, Pierce."

"I don't think it's too far-fetched to assume the other assaulters were former members of the Mexican military too," Hunt said. "They knew what they were doing, Simon. They really did. They used the terrain for cover and concealment, and they exploited their superior firepower to cover their movements and to keep us pinned down. These guys weren't our regular certified crackheads. They were well-trained operators."

Carter could only imagine what Hunt must have felt when the motorcade SUVs started to blow up.

"What do you want me to do? I have a few leave days left if you need my help."

Hunt didn't reply right away. After a moment, Carter asked, "Are you there?"

"That's not all," Hunt said, his voice suddenly only a whisper. "They took Leila. My daughter's gone, Simon."

The words didn't make any sense to Carter. What the hell was Hunt talking about? Didn't his daughter live with her mother and her mother's NFL husband?

"What do you mean they took Leila, Pierce? Who's *they*?"

"The Black Tosca. She's behind all of this. Vicente's death, Leila's abduction. She orchestrated everything."

Carter stiffened. He hadn't expected this, and, for a moment, he was the one who went quiet. He didn't know Leila well. He had met her only a couple of times, but she seemed like a fantastic kid. Why would the Black Tosca kidnap Hunt's daughter?

"Pierce, buddy, I'm lost here. Why would the Black Tosca kidnap Leila? What is she to her?"

He heard Hunt clear his throat. "It was a mistake. She was traveling with Tony Garcia's daughter, Sophia, and—"

"Stop right there. What was Leila doing with Garcia's daughter?"

"Don't go there, Simon. I didn't know about it either, but it's beside the point."

Hunt sounded angry now, and Carter wondered what role Pierce's ex-wife had played.

"Okay," Carter conceded. "Not my business. When did this happen?"

For the next few minutes, Hunt told him everything he knew about the kidnapping and the Black Tosca's demand for Tony Garcia's head. Carter had known Hunt for a long time and was aware of some of the hardships his friend had endured, but it was the first time he felt Hunt wasn't 100 percent in control. There was a calculated edge to Hunt's voice that chilled him to the bone.

"I need you to keep feeding me all the intelligence we have on the Black Tosca and her organization," Hunt said. "I want to know everything there is to know about her. Who she knew growing up, who were her parents, does she have children, what—"

"I get the picture," Carter said. "Don't worry."

"Good," Hunt said. "Call me anytime at this number. You're the only one who has it."

Carter hesitated for a second, wondering if he should bring up the subject of Hunt's arrest warrant. He decided against it. The man had enough on his plate.

"Copy that. Give me an hour or so. I should have something for you."

CHAPTER THIRTY-SIX

Miami, Florida

Hunt placed his mobile phone on the coffee table next to Tony's laptop. Anna and Tony were both looking at him, their eyes desperate for answers he didn't have. Anna was seated ramrod straight in her chair. She was barely moving.

"Simon is a good man," Hunt told them. "He'll call back soon enough with additional info."

"So we're supposed to sit on our collective asses until *Simon* calls back? That's your plan, Superman?" Tony stood up, looking like he wanted to fight again.

Hunt hoped it wouldn't get to that, because the next time Garcia decided to spar, Hunt would put him down for the count.

"You'd better sit your ass back down and listen to what I have to say if you want to see your daughter again," Hunt said, looking him straight in the eyes and reining in his own frustration.

Hunt could tell that Tony was struggling to swallow his pride, but he managed to sit back down.

"Please, Pierce," Anna said, always trying to be the peacemaker, "tell us what you have in mind."

Hunt leaned toward Tony and said, "Are you ready to make a deal?"

Tony blinked, and a furrow appeared between his dark brows. He cocked his head and asked, "What kind of deal are we talking about?"

"I'll get Sophia and Leila back," Hunt said. "And once I do, I want you to start converting your illegal business interests into legitimate ones."

Tony's head snapped toward Anna. A look of complete surprise crossed his face. Anna let go a small, abrupt laugh but didn't respond otherwise. Even Tony seemed at a loss for words.

"We got a deal?" Hunt said.

Tony's face contorted in anger. "You're crazier than I thought," he said.

"I was under the impression you'd do anything for Sophia. I guess I was wrong."

"How dare you demand such things? Why does it even matter to you?"

Hunt's expression hardened. "Because your business is the reason our daughters were taken," he roared, "or are you too fucking blind to see that?"

A man like Tony didn't get to where he was by being stupid. He might have inherited the organization from his father when Vicente went to prison, but he was the one who had bullishly expanded it into many different and lucrative niches. Tony had invested heavily in real estate using money laundered through his numerous legitimate contracting corporations. He now owned several high-value lots and apartment buildings all around the east coast of Florida. In the process, Tony had made new enemies but also achieved a degree of diversification that provided the kind of synergy rarely seen in the drug-trafficking industry. A fifth of the family business income now came from genuine businesses. An organization like his would be a prime acquisition target for a powerful Mexican cartel like the one the Black Tosca controlled.

"Do you really think you can do better than the police can do?" Anna asked.

Hunt turned in his seat to face her. "Listen, Anna, the police are pretty good at what they do, and, to be honest, very few things grip an officer with more urgency than a missing child. There's something about this type of call that drives the officers to respond with everything they've got."

"But?"

"They excel at finding missing or runaway children," Hunt explained. "But Sophia and Leila, they were abducted by one of the most ferocious and powerful drug cartels in the world. The police are ill-equipped to deal with that, and with the red tape associated with a criminal investigation—"

"And you would know about these things, right, Terrance?" Tony asked, not hiding his sarcasm.

Hunt didn't take the bait. Instead, he looked at Anna for support. He didn't get any. It had been an exhausting day for everyone, and tensions ran high.

Hunt glared at Tony. "Yes, I know how to run a criminal investigation and how hard it is to successfully prosecute someone like you. I tried, and I failed, remember? We both know you were as guilty as your father. But here you are, reigning over his organization."

"What's your point, Pierce?" Anna demanded.

Hunt had long ago made up his mind about what he was willing to do to get Leila back. So when he replied to Anna, his voice was chillingly even. "I have no intention of following the rules. There's nothing I won't do, nothing I won't say, to get the girls back. I'll hurt as many people as I need to."

Flashbacks from his actions in Gaza flooded his thoughts. They came as short but violent bursts that shocked his brain with images so vivid that it was hard to dissociate them from reality.

A man is tied to a chair. Hamas terrorist scum. He's pleading—pleading for his life. A dark, reeking stain has already spread across his dirty combat trousers. His right kneecap has been shattered, and a finger is missing from his left hand.

Hunt pressed his hand against his forehead in an attempt to dislodge the brutal images.

"Pierce? Are you okay?"

Slowly, he managed to claw out of the images in his head. Once they were gone, he focused on Anna and said, "I've been through a situation like this before. Let's just say that in the Rangers, I acquired a particular set of skills. This skill set could come in quite handy in the next day or so."

"Where will you start?" Anna asked. "And what about the warrant against you?"

He looked at her, then at Tony. "Just give me everything you have on the Black Tosca's operations in Florida, and I truly mean everything. Together with whatever Carter sends me, I'll figure out something."

CHAPTER THIRTY-SEVEN

South Beach, Florida

Hunt glanced at Anna from time to time as he weaved through the South Beach traffic. She was looking straight in front of her, her head resting against the plush leather padding of the headrest. She wore a thousand-yard stare, the same one he had seen on the faces of soldiers right after they had lost a friend in combat. She hadn't exchanged one word with him since they had left Tony's compound, and Hunt was sure this was because he had told her and Tony—in no uncertain terms—that he didn't want Anna to accompany him. Tony had then volunteered, but Hunt had flat-out refused. Anna he could control. Maybe. But Tony—he was Sophia's father. There was no way he would keep his cool if they came close to finding the girls. The odds of Tony killing someone before Hunt could extract every bit of intel out of him were too great. Besides, the Black Tosca might well have Tony under surveillance.

Mercifully, the intelligence Simon Carter had sent his way was of great assistance in helping Hunt find a place to start in locating the girls. Cross-referencing it with the intelligence the Garcia family had gathered on the Black Tosca since her rise to power had been easier than he had originally assumed. The late Vicente had identified the Black Tosca as a potential threat early on and had kept close tabs on her, which surprised Hunt.

When he asked Anna how Vicente had recognized the menace Valentina Mieles could become years before she would appear on the DEA's radar, Anna had no idea why this would be so. Tony also denied knowing the reason behind his father's suspicion, but he wouldn't look Hunt in the eyes. Hunt had the feeling Tony knew why his father was interested in the Black Tosca but had deliberately decided not to share that reason, and it irritated the crap out of him.

What he did know, though, was that two years ago, Édgar Pomar, a cousin of one of the two dead assaulters Carter had identified through fingerprints, had been a person of interest in a DEA money-laundering investigation. No charges were ever brought against Pomar, but the DEA had spent a week following him around, trying to figure out his role in the scheme. Due to limited resources, they'd had to drop their surveillance, but not before two addresses were linked to Pomar's name. One was a two-bedroom condo in South Beach; the other was a luxurious oceanfront home in Hallandale Beach. The condo and the house were both rented through BlueShade Rental, an LLC owned by Graham Young, a Harvard Law School graduate and one of the most renowned criminal defense attorneys in the state of Florida.

Hunt wondered if Young was the real reason why the DEA had backed off of the investigation at that point. Young was well known for successfully defending controversial clients in court. His success rate was extraordinary. Though it was said he didn't have any political ambitions—something Hunt doubted very much, since most high-profile scumbags seemed to have some—Young's regular and generous contributions to the two main political parties made him almost untouchable.

This was all fine with Hunt, but if Young had anything to do with Leila's kidnapping, there would be no hand-wringing, no second-guessing about what Hunt would do to him. Untouchable or not, Hunt would break the man.

Since the condo was located on Ocean Drive, a major thoroughfare in Miami Beach consisting of ten city blocks of neon-infested, art deco overindulgence, Hunt decided to start with that property. Because Young's other property was tucked in a wealthy enclave of Hallandale Beach, he would have to be more cautious about his approach. Here on Ocean Drive, there was no such issue. It was almost midnight, and the streets were still filled with tourists and locals alike. Every hotel and restaurant was brightly lit, and the bars were packed so tightly that people were lining up on the sidewalks for the privilege of buying overpriced cocktails. The upbeat sounds of a rumba and the scent of delicious food made it to the interior of the red Grand Cherokee SRT. The Jeep wasn't the only thing he had borrowed from Tony. Three additional burner phones had found their way into his backpack. Just in case Tasis had "played" with the pistol he'd kept in the boat's cabin, Hunt checked to make sure the firing pin was still there and went through each of his three magazines to confirm all his rounds were still properly loaded. Tasis grinned the whole time, but Hunt didn't put it past him to try to fuck him up like that.

Hunt drove past the Colony Hotel, a 1935 art deco boutique hotel recognized around the world as the undeniable symbol of South Beach, and kept going for another quarter of a mile until he reached the address he was looking for. Parking in South Beach was slightly less difficult than getting a reservation at the Prime One Twelve, a bustling steak house not too far away, which meant it was almost impossible.

Hunt turned left and went west a couple of blocks until they stopped at a red light. A young man came to their window and waved a board that said, *Hungry. Not dangerous.*

Hunt slid down the window and gave the man a handful of one-dollar bills.

"Get something to eat."

"With what?" the man said. "What do you want me to do with five dollars?"

Most times Hunt gave money to homeless folks, they were grateful. This one was clearly on drugs—his pupils were as big as saucers. The sight saddened Hunt. He could easily replace the man's face with his brother's; he knew, just like he'd known with Jake, that the man would likely use the money for drugs, not food, but it was impossible not to try to help in some way.

He raised the window and mouthed *sorry* to the man just as Anna hit the automatic door-lock button. The click of the lock mechanism seemed to enrage the man. His expression changed into one of uncontrollable anger.

Hunt looked at the traffic light. Still red. He sighed.

"You know the doors were already locked, right?" he said to Anna.

"Sorry," Anna said sheepishly. "It's an old habit."

With a horrid roar, the man smashed the wooden end of his board into the driver's side front window. The window cracked but didn't break. The light turned green. Hunt slowly accelerated away just as the man lunged again; the SRT's side mirror clipped his shoulder. Hunt looked behind him and saw the man give him the finger.

The exhaust sound of the SRT V8 echoed over the nearby buildings as the car picked up speed. Hunt made a left on a street parallel to Ocean Drive.

"Tony lied to you," Anna said bluntly.

"About what?" he asked, even though he was pretty sure what her answer would be.

"Why my dad had a file on Valentina Mieles."

Hunt just grunted a noncommittal *hmm-hmm*.

A car pulled out of a parallel parking spot half a block away, and Hunt hurried to take its place.

"Don't you want to know why?"

He turned off the engine and looked at Anna. Shadows shifted in her eyes. Whatever she was keeping bottled up inside her, it was about to come out.

———

Anna was just a little girl when it happened. She didn't understand what her father did for a living. She knew people were scared of him, though, and that he commanded respect, because nobody bothered her at school. She had good grades, and the teachers never yelled at her. Her brother, Tony, was the most popular kid in the entire school. Everybody wanted to be friends with them for a chance to get invited to the next birthday party at the Garcias' mansion. Birthdays and Christmases were a big deal when she was growing up.

More often than not, her family vacationed at their large Colorado estate, less than a fifteen-minute drive from the Vail Ski Resort. Anna and Tony spent most of the days with their ski coaches while Vicente and their mother, Graciela, stayed behind doing whatever adults did.

One cold February weekend, her father had invited four friends from Mexico to spend a long weekend with them. The four men were well dressed and looked important. There was also a teenager with them. Anna still recalled how beautiful she was. An argument had flared up during dinner, and voices were raised. At some point, her father had sent her and Tony to their rooms with one of his bodyguards. Even from their rooms they could hear the yelling from the grand dining room. She remembered Tony holding her in his arms and how afraid she was. Then she heard the first shot. Three more followed in quick succession. She was screaming by then, terrified.

The bodyguard opened the door and told them to stay there, before running down the stairs with a gun in hand.

After he left, Tony had looked at her and said, "Daddy is in trouble. He needs me."

"Don't go, Tony," she pleaded. But he was already gone.

———

"So what happened next?" Hunt asked.

Anna was crying now. "I didn't know. He just . . . Tony just told me before we left."

Hunt searched for a box of tissues but didn't find one. "Tell me, Anna."

"Vicente, he . . . he forced the girl to set fire to her dad with her own hands," she finally said before bursting into tears.

Hunt was appalled. Of all the worst ways to die, this was the cruelest. He couldn't even begin to understand the damaging psychological effect this must have had on the young woman. No wonder the Black Tosca was a twisted witch.

Things were starting to fall into place in Hunt's mind. He was now convinced that even if Tony were to commit suicide, the Black Tosca would murder Leila and Sophia. It wasn't the Garcias' criminal organization she was after—though that was a nice bonus. She wanted revenge.

His throat had turned dry; finding the girls soon felt more urgent than ever. He grabbed his backpack from the rear seat and pulled out his 9 mm Glock. He screwed a silencer onto the end of the barrel and chambered a round. The bottom of his backpack had a sizable pocket, and Hunt used it to slide the pistol in, silencer first, before he unlocked the SUV's doors.

"Get in the driver's seat, Anna," he said, climbing out of the SRT.

At this point, Anna was going through the motions like a preprogrammed zombie. She exited the SUV and walked around to join Hunt next to the driver's door. Her eyes were puffy from all the crying. Small lines of tension creased her forehead.

"We'll get through this," Hunt said, even though he was barely holding himself together.

He put the Jeep's keys in her hand. "I'll let you know where to pick me up."

He was already across the street when she called his name.

He turned to glance her way.

"I'm glad you couldn't save my father," she said. "I'm happy the son of a bitch is dead."

CHAPTER THIRTY-EIGHT

South Beach, Florida

Hunt approached the condominium building. It was four stories high, and the developer's website indicated there were only four condos, all of them sprawling across two floors. The building had a minimalist look that Hunt didn't like. He noted two security cameras aimed to cover the area around the front door. From the real estate files he had downloaded at Tony's house, he'd studied the layout of the building carefully. The unit he was interested in occupied the third and fourth floors on the north side of the building. This was both a blessing and a curse. The unit would be more difficult to access since it was on the third floor, but the upside was that more people left their doors unlocked on higher floors than on the first or second floors.

Especially drug dealers looking for a quick exit.

There was no point waiting outside and trying to slip in behind someone. With only four condos, the owners or tenants knew each other and wouldn't hold the door open for someone they didn't know. So Hunt continued to explore the exterior of the building while making sure to keep his face away from the cameras. Since the front of the building was sleek and contemporary with lots of glass and steel, and the pedestrian traffic showed no sign of abating despite the late hour, climbing the facade on the east side or the wall on the northern side of the building was out of the question. The back of the building was a different matter. It was accessible through a small path between the building and the restaurant next door. The path led back toward an alleyway with no sidewalk. It was darker in the alley than on Ocean Drive, and the smell was different too, thanks to the open lids of the two dumpsters.

Hunt didn't care about the reek coming out of the dumpsters; he had found a drainpipe. He scanned his surroundings. He was alone. He grabbed hold of the drainpipe and pulled himself up like a spider. By the time he reached the third floor, his arms and lungs were burning, and his neck was slick with sweat. Hunt cursed under his breath. There were no entry points on the third floor, only a large window ten feet to his left. He had to keep going. His arms started to shake, but he continued, grimacing through the pain, until he reached the fourth floor. Three feet to his left was a small balcony overlooking the alleyway. A ledge—maybe three inches in width—ran from the drainpipe to the balcony. Hunt had his left foot on the ledge when he heard the back door of the restaurant open. He looked down and to his right and saw that a cook had lit up a cigarette. That couldn't have happened at a worse time. Any sudden movement he made could attract the cook's attention and prompt him to call the cops. Who wouldn't?

The fingers of his left hand struggled to maintain their hold on a small protruding brick while his left foot kept sliding off the narrow ledge. His right wrist and shoulders were cramping, his back was tensing up, and his shoulder blades were getting tighter by the second. The cook only had to look up to see Hunt hanging between the balcony and the drainpipe.

Hunt was stuck. He couldn't move left, and he couldn't move right. And he couldn't hold on much longer.

Édgar Pomar couldn't sleep. There was too much on his mind. Nothing that couldn't be handled, but he was a perfectionist. You had to be when you worked for the Black Tosca. The slightest slip could cost you your life and those of your loved ones. It made him anxious and in need of a cigarette. He thought about lighting up in bed, but his bitchy wife could come back at any time, and there was no chance of a late-night blow job if she caught him smoking inside. He opened his nightstand drawer and pushed aside the SIG Sauer to grab the pack of Marlboros and the lighter underneath. He stopped in the bathroom to relieve himself, thought about washing his hands but decided against it, and made his way to the second floor. Thank God for that small balcony. His wife hated it. "It fucking smells like shit in the alley," she kept complaining. But he didn't mind. It allowed him to smoke without having to go all the way down to the sidewalk. He slid the glass door open and stepped outside.

Damn! The missus was right. It did smell like shit. Maybe he didn't need that cigarette after all. He was about to shut the door when he saw movement to his left. His heart leaped in his throat, and he involuntarily took a step back before he dashed back inside to get his SIG.

———

Someone yelled from within the restaurant. The cook cursed out loud and replied with something Hunt couldn't make out. The cook tossed his cigarette in the alleyway and ground it under his heel before heading back inside the kitchen.

The sound of the balcony door sliding open next to Hunt momentarily caused his heart to pound even more violently than it already was. He'd be exposed to anyone stepping onto the balcony, and in this position, he was defenseless. He couldn't remember the last time he had been so vulnerable. He had less than a second to take action and only one move he could make.

Boosted by a surge of adrenaline and sheer will, Hunt ignored the pain coming from his legs and shoulders and leaped toward the balcony. The tips of his fingers grasped the railing, and he hurled himself up and over just in time to see a man run back inside the condominium. Hunt ran after him while alarm bells blared in his head. His entry should have been covert. How the hell had he ended up running after someone through an apartment he hadn't cleared? How many bad guys were inside? Were there even *any* bad guys inside? The man he was chasing had all the rights in the world to run away from him. Scratch that. The man he was chasing had all the rights in the world to fucking shoot him. What if he was simply trying to protect his family?

Damn it!

Under any other circumstances, Hunt would have retreated. But to find Leila, Hunt was ready to break all rules of morality.

Ahead of Hunt, the man started going down the stairs three at a time to reach the floor below, but he lost his footing and almost tumbled down the last five steps. He somehow managed to remain on his feet and careened right at the bottom of the stairs. Hunt lost sight of him and thought about going for his gun, but it would waste precious seconds, so he decided to accelerate instead. He jagged right the moment he reached the third floor, just in time to see the man run into a bedroom.

———

Pomar wasn't even halfway down the stairs when he heard the other man's footsteps hit the top step. He tried to glance back but nearly lost his balance. He jumped the last four steps, then sprinted to the bedroom. He reached his nightstand, opened the drawer, and grabbed his pistol. He didn't even have time to take it out of the drawer before the man jumped over the bed and tackled him at full speed. Both men crashed against the nightstand—with Pomar's hand still inside.

Its drawer closed, snapping Pomar's wrist. Pomar tried to yell, but his attacker threw him on the floor hard enough to knock the air out of his lungs. Before Pomar could recuperate, the man had a knee on his back and one of his hands cupped around his mouth. The tip of a knife was pressed to the back of his neck.

"Where are the girls?" the man barked at him.

With the man's hand solidly clasped against his mouth, Pomar could only make a few sounds. The man eased his hold to let him speak.

Mistake. The moment he did, Pomar sank his teeth into the man's hand; but, before he could rip a finger off, something hit him hard on the head. His forehead pitched forward and bounced twice against the hardwood floor, just like a basketball.

———

The man's teeth had barely touched his skin when Hunt elbowed the back of his head, knocking him out. Hunt went back to the nightstand and took the SIG Sauer from the drawer. Hunt withdrew his own pistol from his backpack and proceeded to clear the condo.

Better late than never, he thought. If there had been more than one bad guy, Hunt bet the man he had put to sleep would have called for help. The fact that he didn't indicated he was probably alone. Hunt nevertheless stayed vigilant and moved from room to room with speed, sweeping his gun left to right and back again. The condo was surprisingly clean and orderly. In less than two minutes, Hunt was confident they were the only two living things in the condo. He went back to the bedroom. The man was still on the floor, but he had regained consciousness. He was on his back, moaning in pain. Hunt grabbed him by the hair and dragged him outside the bedroom to a modern-looking dining chair. He lifted the man into the chair. From his backpack, Hunt pulled out a roll of duct tape. He secured the man's hands behind his back and his ankles to the legs of the chair. He then tore off two more

169

pieces and pressed the first one against the man's left eyebrow. He used the last piece to tape the man's mouth shut. Hunt slapped him to help him come around. The man looked at him and blinked his eyes as he tried to figure out how he had ended up tied to a chair. His forehead was swollen, and his eyes were unfocused. Hunt slapped him again, and it seemed to do the trick.

"I'll remove the tape covering your mouth now," Hunt said, pressing the tip of his silencer against the man's left knee. "Answer my questions and live, or don't and suffer. Then die. It's as simple as that. No bullshit. What do you say?"

The man's eyes were full of venom, but he nodded.

Hunt jerked on the tape. The man didn't even flinch, which told Hunt he was dangerous. "What's your name?"

The man seemed to hesitate, so Hunt banged the silencer on his knee.

"My name's Édgar Pomar."

That was good news. Pomar, as the cousin of one of the men killed during the ambush, was a direct link to the Black Tosca.

"Where are the girls?"

Something flickered in Pomar's eyes. Recognition, maybe? "Girls? What girls?"

"Where's the Black Tosca?"

For the briefest moment, there was another spark in Pomar's eyes. Fear? "Who? I never—"

In one quick movement, Hunt taped Pomar's mouth shut. Hunt's DEA training had included detecting micro expressions. Micro expressions were subtle and involuntary facial expressions that exposed a person's true emotions. Reading micro expressions was key to detecting deception, an important skill for an undercover operator.

Or when you were interrogating an uncooperative subject who might know where your kidnapped daughter was hidden.

Without any warning, Hunt shot Pomar in his right kneecap. Pomar tried to scream, but the duct tape muffled the sound. Tears ran down his cheeks. The kneecap was a nasty place to take a bullet. Not that Hunt knew from personal experience, but he had seen what it did to the Hamas leader he had "debriefed" in Gaza.

Hunt pressed the tip of the silencer against Pomar's other kneecap. Pomar shook his head vigorously. His terrified eyes gazed back at Hunt. His lips were trembling. Exactly what Hunt hoped he'd see. He needed Pomar to be more afraid of him than of the Black Tosca. He tore the duct tape from Pomar's mouth.

"Where's the Black Tosca?"

"She's not here, man. She's . . . she's in Mexico. I swear it!"

"Where in Mexico?"

Pomar shook his head. "C'mon, man!"

If Pomar was looking for compassion, he was looking at the wrong man. Hunt had none to give. He cut a new piece of duct tape from the roll and placed it on Pomar's mouth. The man didn't even resist this time around; he just sobbed. Hunt placed the barrel of his gun under Pomar's chin and lifted his head. Pomar was sweating now. His face and neck were covered with perspiration. His breathing had kicked up into high gear in anticipation of Hunt's next shot. But instead of shooting him again, Hunt pulled back, then went to the living room and picked up the clothes iron he'd seen earlier when he cleared the house. He made a show of plugging the iron into an electrical outlet next to Pomar. Hunt hated himself for what he was doing. He had sworn he'd never cross that line ever again, would never torture another man—and he was about to. It made him sick to his stomach, but for his daughter, he'd go to hell and back.

"I hate you for putting me in this position, Édgar," Hunt said honestly. "I don't want to do this to you. But one of the girls the Black Tosca kidnapped is my daughter."

Pomar thrashed against his restraints. The pain in his knee was unbearable. And now an iron? This man was crazy. He watched him lift the iron and press the red steam button. A cloud of steam blew out with a swoosh.

Fuck!

"Last chance," the man warned him.

Pomar nodded vigorously. The duct tape came off.

"Okay, man. She's in San Miguel de Allende," he confessed. "But it's not like you'll be able to get to her, you know? She's well protected."

"Where are the girls?" the man asked again.

"They aren't here, man—"

The iron flashed out so fast Pomar didn't even see it coming. The hot iron landed on his already swollen forehead and stayed there for what seemed like an eternity but was, in fact, less than three seconds. His already dazed mind had difficulty processing what he was seeing. From where he sat, it looked like the iron had some wallpaper stuck to the bottom.

Then the pain arrived in a surge of pure agony, and he understood it wasn't wallpaper but his skin glued to the iron. He screamed. A high-pitched, visceral scream that came from a place within him he didn't even know existed. But his cry was cut short when his interrogator moved behind him with the speed and agility of a panther and locked the crook of his arm around his throat. Pomar felt the blood pound in his temples as the man tightened his arm around Pomar's windpipe. His vision swam, and he could feel his face turning purple.

"Another stupid answer like that one and you lose the other knee," the man whispered in his ear. "Do you understand?"

Pomar bobbed his head up and down. He didn't want to die, didn't want to lose the other knee. He certainly couldn't picture himself spending the rest of his life in a wheelchair.

The man relaxed his grip. "Talk to me."

Hunt's patience was wearing thin. The only actionable intel he'd gotten so far was that the Black Tosca was in San Miguel de Allende. The DEA knew about her mansion but had never been able to send an undercover agent or even an informant inside. Only her close circle could come near the house. The next time Pomar opened his mouth, it had better be good. For his sake.

"There's another house. In Hallandale Beach," Pomar said.

The other property rented out in Pomar's name. *At least he's telling the truth.* "Go on."

"There's a team there."

"A team?"

"I don't know who they are, but they're heavy hitters. Hector Mieles might be on-site."

Hunt assumed these men were either part of the assault team that had ambushed Vicente Garcia's motorcade or part of the snatch team that had grabbed his daughter.

"How many of them?"

Pomar's shoulders sagged, and Hunt swore under his breath. Pomar didn't know the answer, so he asked, "Why do you think the girls are there? And think before you try to feed me some bullshit."

"Because it has holding rooms," Pomar explained. "It's either that or they're already on their way to Mexico to be sold or—"

Pomar didn't finish his sentence. He didn't need to. Hunt knew exactly what Pomar was thinking. Pretty teenage girls like Leila and Sophia were often beaten, raped, and—once their spirits were broken—forced into prostitution or slavery.

Just like the girls in Chicago, Hunt thought, remembering the twelve dead young women in the warehouse. To ensure Leila didn't meet the same fate, he'd break the promise he'd made after Gaza a thousand times.

Pomar suddenly started to shake violently. Hunt, alarmed, released Pomar's throat and tilted his head back. Pomar's eyes were empty pools, and his mouth hung open.

Not good.

———

It was becoming harder and harder to think through the throbbing in his shattered knee and the all-consuming agony coming from his forehead. Pomar felt his body starting to jiggle uncontrollably. The pain was unbearable now, and his mind started to drift. His body was shutting down, and his eyes were heavy with resignation. He hadn't done much good in this world. Beyond his extreme physical pain dwelled the gnawing feeling of utter failure. He should have joined the army instead of the cartel. The pay sucked, but at least he could have been proud of his accomplishments. He had so many regrets, but at least he had told the man everything he knew, which, he had to admit, wasn't much. For reasons he didn't understand, since it defied any kind of logic, he didn't hate the man for what he had done to him. As Pomar slipped into unconsciousness, the last thing he saw was the man's face and the glint of a knife.

———

There was nothing to gain from staying in the condominium any longer. Pomar hadn't been part of the team that kidnapped Leila—that much was clear—but it didn't mean he didn't deserve what Hunt had done to him. Hunt cut the duct tape around Pomar's wrists with his knife. Since Pomar was a cartel member, Hunt wasn't worried about him calling the police.

Hunt was halfway up the stairs when he stopped dead in his tracks and listened. He thought he had heard something coming from the third floor. He took a deep breath and held it in. He waited. There it was again. A soft scratching sound faintly touched his ears, followed by an even quieter click. It took Hunt a moment to place the sound. Was someone picking the lock? Hunt unzipped the bottom pocket of his backpack and pulled out his pistol. His heart thudded in his chest as he weighed his options. His exit strategy was to continue to the fourth floor and to go out the balcony and down the drainpipe. An alternative was to go back to the third floor and see who was trying to gain access to the condominium.

Hunt brought his gun up, and, praying for no squeaky steps, went down the stairs. He took position behind a doorframe so he could cover the front door. The door cracked opened. The hall light cast half a human shadow through the opening. Someone was waiting just outside the condo, listening. A moment later, the muzzle of a pistol appeared, and then a figure slipped inside the condo. The figure silently closed the door. There was just enough light for Hunt to recognize the intruder.

Anna Garcia.

"Anna, it's Pierce," Hunt said from behind the doorframe. "What are you—"

"Damn it, Pierce! You've been gone for more than fifteen minutes. What do you want me to do? For how long did you expect me to wait in the car? I came here to help you."

He switched the light on. Anna held a hand up to her face to shield her eyes from the sudden glare. Hunt was both pissed and impressed at the same time. The fact that Anna had the guts to gain access to the building, pick the lock, and come in with her gun drawn showed him she wanted to find the girls as much as he did.

"There were two cameras covering the front entrance of the building," Hunt said.

"No worries. I took care of them."

"You took care of them? How?" he asked, making his way to Pomar's bedroom.

"Through their Wi-Fi network," Anna explained, holstering her pistol.

Hunt squinted at her. "You know how to hack?"

"Don't look so surprised. You don't have to be trained in information technology to know how to break into a simple system."

Hunt shook his head. Given how much of himself he'd concealed from her, he supposed it was only fair that she had some secrets too. "Anyhow, this Pomar guy didn't know much. He said that Hector Mieles might be in Miami. More specifically, in Hallandale Beach."

"At the other Black Tosca safe house?"

"Yes."

"Hector is a cold-blooded killer."

That wasn't something Hunt needed to hear.

"He's a tall son of a bitch too. Rumors have him at seven feet tall. And big. He's former Mexican military," she added.

Seven feet tall. Hunt wondered if Hector wasn't the guy with whom he had exchanged gunshots the day before. A man with the lethal focus he'd witnessed wouldn't hesitate to kill two teenagers.

"I'm going to Hallandale Beach," Hunt said.

"I'm going with you."

Hunt elected not to argue.

"What are you gonna do with him?" she asked, pointing to Pomar, who had just started moving again.

"Nothing."

"You should kill him."

Hunt shook his head. "Not necessary. I don't expect we'll see him again. If he's smart, he'll disappear."

"I admire your moral code," she said sarcastically.

He raised an eyebrow. First, hacking. Now, bloodlust. What else was he going to discover about her? "You're very much your father's daughter, aren't you?"

A flash of anger appeared on Anna's face, and then it was gone.

"As you wish," she said. "But don't say I didn't warn you."

CHAPTER THIRTY-NINE

South Beach, Florida

Egan was on his way to Tony Garcia's house when Hector called.

"We have a visual on Pierce Hunt," Hector said. "He's in one of our safe houses. He's interrogating one of our men."

Hector sounded irritated, his shrill voice even shriller than usual.

"Which one?"

"Édgar Pomar."

"No. I meant which safe house?"

"The one in South Beach."

How had Hunt found the safe house? If he knew about that one, then he knew about the Hallandale Beach one too. And even if he didn't, Pomar would have told him. Hunt had a way of making people talk.

"Someone else joined in on the party," Hector added. "I'm watching it live."

"Somebody you know?"

"It's Anna Garcia, I think. Vicente's daughter."

Egan knew who Anna Garcia was. He didn't need Hector to lecture him on the who's who of the Miami drug trade. So Hunt and the Garcia family had joined forces. That was to be expected. No wonder Hector was concerned.

"Was Pomar privy to yesterday's operation?" Egan asked.

"He wasn't."

"Hunt's like a damn bulldog. You don't want him on your tail."

"I told you where he was," Hector said. "Go do your job."

"Where will you be?"

"Not your concern." Hector hung up.

Egan made a U-turn at the next streetlight. He drove south past Haulover Park, Bal Harbour, and North Beach without seeing them. His mind was on Hunt and how to take down the one man he owed his life to.

———

Egan parked his Ford Explorer four blocks from the safe house. Under his beige summer sport jacket was a SIG Sauer P229 in a leather shoulder holster. The serial number had been removed. He carried two extra magazines in the holster's pockets. The silencer was in his inside jacket pocket.

He dialed Hector's number to ask if Hunt was still inside the safe house, but the Black Tosca's cousin didn't pick up. Egan was surprised at how busy the streets were with cars and pedestrians at this hour. Vehicles were parked on both sides of the street, people strolling along the large sidewalks, talking, pushing strollers—which made no sense to Egan—and drinking as though they were in Las Vegas. To a tourist or an outsider—hell, to most people—it all seemed so welcoming and safe.

Egan had always thrived best in the underworld. No matter how hard he tried to fit into a normal life, he couldn't. Not after Gaza. In a way, the Black Tosca had offered him the best of both worlds. He operated with a foot on the fringes of society while living his day-to-day existence with someone like Katherine. *A good compromise*, he thought. *With just enough violence to keep me sane and happy.*

The staccato cough of a big engine startled him, and he glanced to the rear while his hand reached for his SIG Sauer. A Grand Cherokee raced around the street corner behind him, its tires screeching. The side windows were tinted black, but the windshield wasn't. As the Cherokee roared past him, enough light filtered through for him to make out a man in the passenger's seat. For one fleeting second their eyes met, and a look of recognition flashed across the man's face.

Pierce Hunt.

CHAPTER FORTY

South Beach, Florida

Anna exited the building first. Hunt had asked her to get the Cherokee while he took care of Pomar. She was glad Hunt hadn't killed him. She had been testing him when she'd suggested it, and he had passed with flying colors. He was nothing like her father, which was a good thing—nothing, even, like the man she'd assumed Terrance Davis was.

Anna was still struggling with her father's death. It had been much easier when she didn't know about the atrocity her father had committed. It had been somewhat comforting to pin his death entirely on Hunt's shoulders. But now that the Black Tosca was involved, it complicated things. She just couldn't push the thoughts away. What had her father done? Forcing a young girl to set fire to her own dad? It was a side of him she didn't know, didn't understand. How could someone in his right mind commit such a brutal, hideous act? In a strange way, she understood why the Black Tosca wanted revenge. How could she not?

But live streaming the murder of Sophia? That sickened her. She could comprehend the need to murder Vicente; the prick deserved it. But setting fire to two teenage girls?

Anna wept at the thought of what could happen to Sophia and her friend. She wept at the unfairness of it all. Then she became furious, enraged at the raw truth of her father's past actions. He, too, was responsible for Sophia's disappearance.

The bastard.

She must have taken a wrong turn because she found herself on a very dark, badly paved street she didn't recognize at all. Where was the Jeep again? She walked on, increasing her pace. She sensed movement behind her.

Before she could react or scream, an arm wrapped around her neck, and a hand covered her mouth. Anna tried to kick at her assailant's shins, but she was being dragged backward too fast. She tried to bite the hand but couldn't even open her mouth. Suddenly she felt herself flying through the air. She slammed into a brick wall and fell on the ground.

"What are you doing here, pretty lady?"

Anna lifted her head. A tall and beefy twentysomething kid with a boyish grin, wild eyes, and long, stringy hair that needed a good shampooing was looking down at her. He swept his hair back and said, licking his lips, "What am I gonna do with you?"

She reached for her gun, but he raced forward and tried to kick her in the face. She blocked the blow with her forearm, but the pain radiated through her shoulders. She managed to get up, but his fist smashed into the side of her head. Her vision blurred. Then his hands found their way around her throat, and he pushed her against the brick wall, grinding his lower body against her.

She tried to break free by bringing her arms up in between his forearms, but he was too strong. *Fuck!* She only needed to create enough distance between her back and the brick wall to get to her gun. His fingers were digging into her neck, cutting off her oxygen. She kicked at his knees, but there wasn't much strength in it. She clawed at his hands, but it only made him angry. He was saying something to her, but his words barely registered. She brought up her right knee as hard as she could. It landed directly between his legs. For a moment, the man stopped moving, and she took the opportunity to knee him again. This time she did it hard enough to rattle his yellow teeth. He involuntarily bent forward, and she seized his head by his long hair and pushed it down to meet her other knee coming up.

His head snapped back with a crunch. A broken nose? A vertebra? She didn't care. The man fell. She stumbled backward a step, panting. Oxygen was finally returning to her brain. She took a deep, shaky breath and thought about putting a bullet in the sexual predator's head. Instead, she kicked his head as if she were punting a football. The man rolled sideways, moaning. He coughed, and blood erupted from his mouth and nose. He rose to his knees.

Two muffled shots startled her. The man's body twitched as the bullets exploded in his back. Anna's arm was raised; her hand was holding her silenced pistol. She didn't remember grabbing the gun. She felt a stab of horror at what she'd done, but it lasted only a moment. What if the "pretty lady" he'd accosted had been a young woman like Sophia, unable to defend herself? She couldn't feel sorry that that young woman would now be safe because he was dead.

But what was she going to do with the body? *Tony.* Her brother would know what to do.

She called his number. *Where am I?* She looked around. The alleyway was quiet. All the windows facing it were closed, and no one seemed to be looking out. Good thing her pistol was suppressed. She used the location application on her phone to find out exactly where she was.

"Are you all right?" Tony asked as soon as he picked up.

"I'm fine," she replied. *I really am,* she told herself.

"Where are you?"

"I'll send you a screenshot of my location, Tony. Could you send . . . hmmm . . . could you send guys over?"

"Something happened? You found Sophia?"

"No, Tony," she said. "No, I didn't find Sophia. It's just that . . . I . . . someone's dead, and I need—"

"Don't say anything else," Tony cut in. "Not a word. You're injured?"

"I'm fine."

"Hunt?"

"He's fine too."

"I'll have men over very soon. Stay put."

"I can't. Pierce needs me."

It took her brother a few seconds to reply. "I'll take care of everything. Just be careful, okay?"

———

Hunt was getting nervous. What the hell was Anna doing? The SRT wasn't parked that far away from the condominium building. She'd been gone for over fifteen minutes. Something was wrong. *Shit.*

He was actually dialing her number on his burner phone when it started vibrating. Hunt tensed as he answered. "Yes?"

"I'm two minutes out," Anna said and then hung up.

Hunt exited Pomar's unit and used the stairs instead of the elevator to reach the ground floor. He had only one foot out the door when he came face to face with the homeless man who had tried to bust the window of the SRT.

Murphy's Law. Whatever can go wrong, will. Fucking always!

This time, though, the man wasn't alone. Two uniformed police officers were behind him.

"It's him! He's the guy who ran me over," the man said, pointing a finger at Hunt.

Hunt pretended he hadn't heard him and kept walking.

"Hey, you fuck!" the man yelled at him, frustrated.

Continuing to ignore him now would raise suspicion. Hunt glanced his way and said, "Excuse me? Do we know each other?"

"You ran me over with your Cherokee? I saw you! You were driving it."

One of the officers gently pushed the man away and stood in front of Hunt. The cop almost looked like he was sorry to disturb him.

"I'm sorry, sir," the cop said, rolling his eyes, "but this man claims someone ran him over with a Jeep Cherokee. Do you own a Cherokee?"

Under any other circumstances, Hunt would have described the encounter that happened, trusting that the evidence—the man's lack of injuries, traffic light cams—would show he hadn't run the man over. But there was no time to get embroiled in an investigation. Leila needed him. "I do not," Hunt said.

"Fucking liar!" the man yelled. The taller of the two officers warned him to shut up.

The other cop asked Hunt if he lived in the area.

"I'm visiting a friend," Hunt said. "I live north of here."

"Just so we can show our sarge we made an effort, could I see a piece of identification?"

Hunt sighed. What was he supposed to do? If they ran his name through the system, they'd see the warrant for his arrest. And even if they didn't run it, they might recognize his name. He was in a jam. To make matters worse, he heard the now familiar deep roar of the SRT. And he wasn't the only one to recognize the sound. The homeless man did too. The man's eyes flamed with triumph.

"Here! That's the Cherokee I talked about. See? See? I wasn't fucking lying."

Intrigued, the officers turned to watch the SRT race toward their location. Alarmed, one of them whipped back toward Hunt, but he was too late. Hunt was already moving.

———

Anna looked in her rearview mirror, anxious that someone had called the police and that she was about to be pulled over and put in handcuffs. Were there any witnesses or security cameras that had recorded her deed? There was no way to know. She simply hoped her brother would take care of it like he'd promised.

She questioned the wisdom of telling Hunt what she'd done. His knowing about it wouldn't help in any way.

Oh my God! How did this happen? She had executed a man. *No, not an execution. Self-defense.* She made a right turn on Ocean Drive and accelerated south, pushing the negative thoughts away. At some point, she'd have to deal with what she had done, but now wasn't the right time. Too many people were counting on her.

She was less than three hundred feet from the condominium building when she noticed a commotion in front of it. She sucked in a breath. *What now?*

———

In a flash, Hunt took in the tactical situation. *Two police officers, one civilian, and less than five seconds to neutralize them.*

Hunt delivered a well-placed right hook to the shorter officer's chin. It was all very unfair. The officer was caught by surprise, and even though his neck was as thick as one of his legs and his jaw could have been built from granite, his knees buckled under him. Hunt took a side step toward the second officer, who, to his credit, had managed to pull his service pistol out of its holster. But Hunt was just too fast. His speed, his precision—all of it drilled into him through years of training—came naturally. The officer had no chance. Hunt slapped both hands over his weapon, effectively trapping the officer's hand against the frame of his pistol. He rotated the gun away from him and then directed it upward while twisting it against the rotation of the officer's wrist. The officer screamed in frustration and horror as Hunt disarmed him in less than half a second. Hunt delivered a powerful, open-palm strike to the officer's chest, forcing him to take a few steps back.

The officer was in a bad spot, and he knew it. Hunt released the magazine and let it fall on the sidewalk. He stripped the slide and barrel from the gun and tossed it back to the officer.

All the while the homeless man just stood there, eyes wide and mouth agape.

"Sorry about your partner, brother," Hunt said to the officer as Anna came to a stop next to the curb. "I didn't hit him too hard," Hunt added, climbing into the SRT.

Anna accelerated away.

———

"What took you so long?" Hunt asked Anna. In the side mirror, Hunt saw the officer he had knocked out get to his knees.

"Just be happy I didn't leave your ass on the street."

He looked at her. "Thanks," he said. "And I mean it."

She nodded but remained silent. There was a deep purple mark on her right cheek. "What the hell happened to you?" Hunt asked.

Anna sniffed and looked away.

There were red finger marks on her neck, as if someone had grabbed her and tried to strangle her.

"No, seriously, Anna, what happened? Were you mugged?"

"Later, okay? Let's get out of here."

Hunt didn't push it. He was about to tell her they needed a new vehicle when someone walking on the sidewalk caught his eyes. Hunt did a double take. For a split second their eyes met, and there was a jolt of recognition.

Cole Egan?

Could it really be him? What was he doing here? A coincidence?

"What is it?" Anna asked.

"I'm not sure," he said, his mind racing. "I'm not sure."

CHAPTER FORTY-ONE

South Beach, Florida

Egan kept walking. He didn't turn to watch where the Jeep was going. He had memorized the license plate and could get all the information he needed from it. With lights flashing and sirens blaring, two police cars sped past him and stopped in front of the condominium building. Car doors flung open, and the officers jumped out. It was futile to get any closer to the safe house. It was compromised.

Had Hunt left Pomar alive? If he had to bet on it, he'd say Pomar was dead. But with Hunt, you never knew. He was a man capable of great sympathy but also of extreme violence. If Pomar was alive, he wouldn't talk to the police. He might have spilled his guts to Hunt, but the police would have to follow the rules. Egan retraced his steps back to his car and thought about his next move. Hunt was probably on his way to the second safe house. That was the only thing of value that Pomar could have shared with him.

Egan dialed Hector's number.

"Hunt and Anna Garcia are on their way to you," Egan said.

"What happened on your end?"

"Let's just say that the South Beach safe house is no longer safe."

"I'll send a crew to torch it."

"I wouldn't do that if I were you," Egan cautioned. "There are at least half a dozen police officers on the scene."

"I see. What about our man?"

"I don't know."

"Then please tell me what you do know," Hector said, obviously irritated.

For $400,000, Egan would give Hector a little wiggle room, but he didn't appreciate Hector's tone.

"No doubt Hunt squeezed out of your man everything he knew about you and your team. All your safe houses are effectively compromised. And they're driving a late-model red Cherokee SRT."

"I'll tell my men to get ready."

Had Hector left a small contingent behind? That would be a grave mistake. "Tell your men to leave now," Egan said. "I just told you Hunt's on his way."

"They'll handle him," Hector said.

Hadn't he made it crystal clear that Hunt was dangerous? *Hunt single-handedly slaughtered half a dozen men to find me*, Egan thought. *He won't hesitate to kill twice that number to find his daughter.*

"For Christ's sake, Hector, pull them out."

Egan didn't really care what happened to the Black Tosca's men, but he didn't want to be the only one left standing at the end. The crazy bitch would blame him.

"I see no reason to. Pomar was alone. They aren't. They'll take him down."

"I'll tell you this one more time, Hector," Egan said. "Hunt is the last man you want to cross. He'll fucking kill anyone who is even remotely connected to the kidnapping of his daughter. Get out while you can. You understand, Hector? Hello? Hector?"

Hector had hung up on him.

Fuck!

Egan started the car and thought about his options. It was his job to take care of Hunt. He was under no illusions about what would happen to him—and his family—if he failed.

CHAPTER FORTY-TWO

Hallandale Beach, Florida

Hunt would give a year's salary to have Simon Carter and the rest of his former RRT teammates with him right now. He needed guys he could count on to have his back. Arrest warrant or not, his men—his friends—would drop everything to come to his assistance. He'd do the same for them. But with the exception of Simon Carter, he hadn't called upon them. Not yet anyway. There was no time. Every minute away from Leila was a minute she was spending with Hector Mieles and the rest of the Black Tosca's crew.

And they were animals.

Over sixty thousand people had been killed since 2006 in relation to drug-trafficking organizations. Not all of them could be attributed to the Black Tosca's network, but she was a big part of the problem. The Justice Department had estimated that the sale of heroin, marijuana, and cocaine added over $3 billion annually into the Black Tosca's coffers. Illegal drugs, though, were only one of the products her cartel offered. Her revenue streams had become increasingly diversified over the past couple years and now included human trafficking and the shipment of illegal immigrants and sex workers. She had ordered the construction of an extensive network of skillfully constructed tunnels under the United States–Mexico border. Some experts Hunt knew thought she was getting ready to sell her services to terrorists. They would pay her dearly for the right to use her network to transport weapons and sleeper cells into the United States. And that scared the shit out of Hunt.

There wasn't much traffic this time of night, and Hunt could see the headlights of oncoming cars from afar. That went for anyone trying to follow them too. Cole Egan's face resurfaced in his mind. Was it purely a coincidence that Egan was a couple blocks away from Pomar's condominium? He hadn't seen the man for years, and now, on this night, here he was. Hunt's gut told him that Egan's sudden reappearance wasn't a fluke. It was more than that. It meant trouble. The only link connecting Egan to this whole mess was McMaster. Was his new boss dirty? The thought had crossed his mind earlier, but he took advantage of the quiet drive to give it more consideration. McMaster was the one who had introduced him to Chief Inspector Zorita, the man who had tried to kill Vicente Garcia.

Good Christ!

Why hadn't he seen this before? McMaster was on the Black Tosca's payroll, and he had hired Egan to do his dirty work. With Cole Egan in the picture, the operation had just gotten a whole lot more dangerous. Had McMaster issued the warrant too? Had he lied to Hunt that the FBI was behind it? Warning Hunt about the warrant might have been a ruse to lure him in or to guarantee his trust. Did this mean that the only people he could trust were Anna and Tony Garcia? The very same people he had once betrayed? How screwed up was that? But that wasn't entirely true, was it? He wasn't alone. He could trust Simon Carter and the rest of his former teammates. Of that he was sure.

"We're one mile out," he said, looking at Anna. At her request, he had moved into the driver's seat the moment they were out of Miami.

Anna hadn't been the same since they had left Pomar's condominium. He could tell something bothered her, but she had yet to share it with him. What was he going to do with her? She had spent the past five minutes typing furiously on her laptop. A video started playing.

"What are you watching?"

"Did you know the house we're about to hit was for sale three years ago?"

"Why would I know that?"

"They were asking eleven million dollars for it."

"Not the type of listing I usually look at. A bit outside of my budget."

"The real estate broker who listed the house uploaded a superb video."

That sparked Hunt's interest. "It's still up?"

"It is. We're a quarter mile away. It will be on your right."

Hunt let up on the gas pedal a couple hundred feet away from the house and let the Jeep coast by. The Black Tosca's Hallandale Beach safe house was a huge estate. It wasn't part of a gated community, and it didn't need to be. It was located directly on the A1A next to similar estates. High brick walls surrounded it on three sides. The only access from the road was through a fifteen-foot iron fence secured by an electronic latch. A tank could bust through it, but not a Grand Cherokee.

"Looks like a fortress," Anna said.

"Yeah."

"How are we gonna go in?"

"The beach is an option," Hunt replied.

"But they'll be expecting that, won't they?"

"Not only that, but they probably have motion detectors all around the back of the house, and every door and window will be wired."

"So?"

"I'll be fine," Hunt said, making a right at the next intersection. "I'll park the SUV and watch the video you found. That should give me a better idea about what to expect inside the house. Don't worry. I'll find a way. Trust me."

"I don't think you meant that."

"What?"

"Trusting you."

"I simply meant I know what I'm doing, Anna. Nothing else."

"I'll ask Tony to send some men to help out. And just so you know, I'm not staying in the car."

Hunt thought better than to pick another fight with her. Two miles past the safe house, he made a right turn into an almost empty parking lot. He took a space between two vehicles next to a Taco Bell.

"We need new transportation. There aren't many SRTs on the streets, and the police probably have a BOLO out on it. A BOLO is—"

"I know what it means," Anna snapped back. "Be on the lookout."

"Okay, I'm sorry. Relax a bit, will you? We're on the same team."

He regretted his choice of words the moment they came out of his mouth.

"Are we? Because last time you said that, you fucked us all."

She had a point. There wasn't much he could say to soothe her, so he remained silent.

"I sent Tony an email," she told him after a moment. "He'll be here shortly with another SUV."

"He knows where we are?"

"He's been tracking us the whole time."

"How?"

"Through me, of course."

It made sense that Tony didn't trust him to keep his little sister safe. They both knew Anna's safety wasn't Hunt's priority.

Still, Hunt wasn't happy about this new development.

"I specifically told the both of you I didn't want him around."

"And you're a fool if you thought you could keep him at bay. His daughter might be in there too. Don't forget that."

Hunt sighed. The sort of help he needed was trained operators, not gunslingers. "How long before he gets here?"

Anna looked at her phone. "Five minutes."

"Show me the video."

"Stop right there!" Anna said.

Hunt paused the video.

"Back up a few seconds."

Hunt did. "What did you see?"

She reached over him and clicked on the play button. "Look at the door handle."

The video focused on the main entrance. A large, modern wooden front door with no window occupied the whole frame. The door was beautiful and looked expensive.

"There's no lock," Hunt said. "Only a keypad."

"Correct," Anna said. "It's a Schlage lock."

"And that's good news? The door looks heavy as hell. We can't pick that kind of lock."

"Maybe you can't pick it, but I can hack it."

"You're serious?"

Anna flashed him a mischievous grin, but there was no warmth to it, only contempt. "You're not the only one who can keep secrets."

———

She watched the green words of code flicker across the screen of her laptop, her fingers burning up the keyboard. She brought up a hidden sign-on screen and entered a code, and just like that, she was in the security mainframe.

"I never asked you where you learned to do that."

"And you're asking me now?"

"I am."

"None of your damn business," she replied bluntly.

———

Anna remembered the first time she had cracked into a computer. She was fifteen and still in high school. She did it to change her best friend's math test result. A handsome young man—Agustín was his name—who used to work for her father had patiently shown her how to do it. For close to two years, every afternoon after school, she spent half an hour or so with Agustín and watched him work. He was incredible. Within minutes, Agustín was able to hack into someone's bank account and transfer money out of it. After moving the money around the world, it ended up in one of Vicente Garcia's Bahamian bank accounts. For his services, Agustín—at least this is what he had told her—was getting 20 percent of whatever he sent to her father.

Then, one day, she came back from school, and Agustín wasn't at his desk. He wasn't there the next day either. When she inquired about his whereabouts, her father told her Agustín wasn't working for him anymore.

"Why?" she asked him.

"He stole from me."

Her father's reply—the way he said it—had chilled her to the bone, but she'd summoned the courage to say, "I thought you liked him. Didn't he make you lots of money?"

Vicente banged his fist on his desk, making Anna jump. "I said, he stole from me," Vicente roared. "If someone steals from me, there are consequences."

Anna, too terrified to ask what the consequences were, had run back to her room. For a while, she didn't dare touch another computer. But when the time came to go to college, she couldn't help herself. She hacked into the mainframes of most of the colleges she applied to just to see how she ranked among her peers. There was no need to change the rankings. She was high enough to pick where she wanted to go. She ended up graduating with a master's degree in computer science from the Florida Institute of Technology and working for her father doing pretty much the same thing Agustín had done. But better. She beefed up her father's network security while keeping an eye on their competitors' vulnerabilities and exploiting them whenever she could. After a few years, though, she needed a new challenge and had gone to work for a couple of start-up companies. That was what she'd been doing when she met Terrance Davis. To be completely honest, she was as angry with herself for being so naive as she was at Hunt for his treachery.

———

But that was a topic for later. Now wasn't the time to let her personal feelings or animosity toward Hunt encroach on what they needed to do. For now, Hunt was her best shot at getting Sophia back. Anna simply couldn't imagine a world without her. She had loved Sophia from the very moment she was born. She had loved her niece every single hour of every day as she watched her grow into a beautiful young woman, and as much as she distrusted Hunt, she knew he felt the same way toward Leila. They had no choice but to work together.

Breaking through a Wi-Fi network, however strong the password, was child's play for someone like her. She easily wiped clean all the previous passwords and reset them to the factory setting before replacing them with her own. The Schlage lock was linked to a network that gave her access to all the systems linked to that network. In this case it meant that from the relative safety of the Jeep, she could control all the interior and exterior lights, the blinds, the house's three air-conditioning units, the security cameras, and the alarm system. She could even open the front gate.

"I got us our way in," she said.

CHAPTER FORTY-THREE

Hallandale Beach, Florida

Emilio looked at his watch. Hector had left for the Hypoluxo safe house ten minutes ago. He had taken with him the rest of his team and the two girls, leaving Emilio and two other local shooters behind. The inside of the house was in total blackness. He had ordered all the interior lights to be turned off. The outside lights were turned off too, so they'd be able to pinpoint exactly where the intruders came from. *If anyone's really coming*, thought Emilio. Hector had said a man—the father of one of the girls—and a woman were on their way.

"He's dangerous, Emilio, so be ready," Hector had said.

Emilio was used to dealing with dangerous men. This one wouldn't be any different. His orders were clear: Kill the man and the woman. Bring their bodies inside, and torch the house.

Easy enough.

Emilio had positioned the two shooters on the ground floor, both covering the rear of the house since it led directly to the beach, the most probable approach. High brick walls topped with glittering shards of broken glass protected the three other sides of the house. Six inches above the broken glass, strands of razor wire ran the length of each wall. It was a nasty but effective way to deter petty thieves—or a DEA agent. Even if the man successfully scaled one of the three walls, there was a multitude of motion detector lights positioned outside the house. Getting close to the house undetected would be impossible.

Then the doorbell rang. *What the fuck?*

CHAPTER FORTY-FOUR

Hallandale Beach, Florida

Hunt spotted a dark late-model Range Rover turning into the parking lot.

"Is that him?" he asked.

"Yes."

A moment later, Tony and Tasis climbed out of the car. Anna unlocked the doors of the Jeep, and both men joined them inside.

"Get your stuff, and move it to the Range Rover. Mauricio will dispose of the Jeep," Tony said without preamble.

"But Tony, I thought you wanted me to help with—" started Tasis, but Tony cut him off.

"Mauricio, take the Jeep, do what you got to do, and then go back to the compound. Make sure the guys fixed Anna's issue. I don't want the body to pop up, so burn it if you can. I'll call you if I need your assistance. Understood?"

Anna's issue? Burn it if you can? What the hell is Tony talking about?

Hunt looked at Anna. She was massaging her neck. She locked eyes with him and shook her head. "Not now. Please."

"You didn't tell him?" Tony asked.

"Tell me what?" Hunt asked.

It was Tony's turn to look at his sister, a scowl of annoyance on his face. "Tell him."

Hunt didn't like to be kept in the dark, but what he liked even less was Anna being bullied into revealing something she was clearly not ready to divulge.

"She said later, Tony. Let it go."

Anna thanked Hunt with a small nod.

Tony's body tensed, but he let it go. "Whatever," he said, and then turned toward Tasis. "You can go, Mauricio."

Hunt could see Tasis wasn't thrilled about leaving his boss with Hunt.

"Give me the damn keys, Hunt," Tasis said.

Hunt grabbed his backpack and the rest of his gear and handed the Jeep's keys to Tasis.

"Okay, let's go," Tony said.

Tony got behind the Range Rover's wheel while Hunt took the passenger seat. Anna settled in the back seat with her computer and mobile phone. A moment later, the Jeep exited the parking lot and accelerated away. Hunt was glad to see it go. It had become a liability.

Tony shifted in his seat and handed Hunt and Anna a small digital radio and an earpiece each. "So what's the plan?"

————

"If Anna can open the front gate, shouldn't we go in this way?" Tony asked after Hunt shared his plan.

"Absolutely not," Hunt said. "They'd see us coming."

"And there would be no way for me to hide the fact that the gate is being opened remotely," Anna added.

"It would tip our hand, Tony," Hunt explained. "Better to approach stealthily by the beach, get in position, and then let Anna work her magic."

Tony thought it over for a minute and then said, "Are you sure they'll come out of the house?"

"Not at all."

"If they don't, we're fucked."

That was stating the obvious. The objective was to get covertly in position with Tony at the front door and Hunt waiting by the large patio door at the back of the house. Once they were in place, Anna would remotely activate one of the motion sensors in the backyard to draw at least one man out to the back. Because Hunt wanted to get in the house by two different entry points—from the door leading to the rear terrace and the front door—they needed someone to unlock the patio door, as Anna had determined there were no electronic locks she could hack at the back of the house. The moment Hunt confirmed he had gained access, Tony would enter from the front door, the point of entry where Hunt expected the least resistance.

That was the plan, anyway.

———

Hunt took a gamble. A calculated one, but a gamble nonetheless. Anna told him there were motion detectors but couldn't say what kind they were. Motion sensors usually fell into two categories. There were those that worked by infrared—heat sensors—and those that worked by ultrasound. The infrared motion detectors detected infrared energy—heat—given off by animals or humans. When there was an upsurge in infrared energy, the alarm sounded. They worked well outside in cold-climate countries, or inside any residence, but they weren't the best in Florida. With nighttime temperatures often reaching the midnineties, the sensors weren't effective at distinguishing a human from the ambient air. With that in mind, Hunt bet that the outside motion detectors were ultrasonic devices. If he was wrong, he'd know soon enough, and their plan would go bust.

After parking the Range Rover on a side street, they found a public pathway to the beach about a dozen or so mansions north of the Black Tosca's safe house.

"How will you know if it works?" Tony asked.

"If no light comes on, it means it's working," Hunt said. A bead of sweat rolled down his back. It was a warm and muggy night. There was no breeze, which was unusual. Crouched on the beach with his back toward the ocean, Hunt scrutinized the house with his ATN night-vision monocular. Was Leila there, only two hundred feet away? He was sure that, right behind him, Tony was wondering the exact same thing about his daughter. Hunt didn't like what he was seeing with his monocular. The house was in total darkness. Not a single light was on.

It could be a trap. He said so to Tony.

"What choice do we have?"

"The trick is to go slowly at first," Hunt said.

"Okay."

"If a light comes on," Hunt said, "run back toward the beach and get back to Anna."

"You know I won't do that, so stop bullshitting me."

"If this is indeed a trap, they'll have automatic weapons," Hunt warned him. "We have pistols."

"Aren't you supposed to be some kind of super-hotshot DEA agent?"

"A bullet in the head is a bullet in the head. It doesn't discriminate. It doesn't matter how well trained you are. If they have superior fire-power and we're outnumbered, our only chance is our stealth and the violence of our action when the shooting starts. Let's try to keep the element of surprise for as long we can."

Without another word, he crawled toward the house. He held his pistol in his right hand while the left held a small radio scanner. Fifty feet and five minutes later, he stopped his painstakingly slow crawl and turned on the device. They had reached the edge of the property. Hunt doubted they were close enough for the scanner to detect the motion sensors—which were generally reliable to about thirty feet—but there was no room for error, so Hunt checked anyway.

Nothing. He continued forward, stopping every five feet to check the detector, half expecting the motion-sensor-activated floodlights to beam on them. On the fourth stop—they were now well inside the property line—the scanner vibrated twice, announcing that it had found the wavelength of the sound waves the motion sensors were using. It was too dark for Hunt to see where the sensors were located, but if he had to guess, he'd say they were positioned on the numerous palm trees lined up about fifty feet from the rear of the house. Hunt matched the scanner's frequency to the one emitted by the sensor. By squawking in the same frequency, the scanner masked any other returning waves, making Hunt and Tony invisible to the motion sensor. Hunt repeated the process three more times. He glanced back at Tony. The moonlight was just bright enough to illuminate his face. He was staring right back at Hunt, his face blank—no trace of a smile, but no anger or animosity either.

"Let's do this," he mouthed.

Hunt wiped his forehead with his arm. He never minded the heat, but tonight the humidity was killing him. His shirt was stuck to his back, and sweat trickled into his eyes. He looked ahead. Another fifty feet and they would reach the terrace. They wouldn't be able to keep going in a straight line, though; there was a massive pool in their path, so they hooked to the right. As much as Hunt forced himself to focus, he couldn't help thinking about Leila. The closer they got to the house, the more he felt she wasn't there. The house was too dark, too quiet.

He couldn't let his pessimism get the best of him.

One step at a time, Pierce, Hunt told himself. *Take it one step at a time. It's the only way to move forward. She's counting on you.*

"Stop!"

Hunt turned his head to his left. Tony had caught up to him.

"What is it?"

"There's a pathway to our right. Looks like it tracks the side of the house."

Hunt had missed it. *That's what happens when you aren't attentive to your surroundings. You're lucky someone wasn't waiting for you with a rifle. You'd be dead.* They were so close to the house that Hunt was confident there were no more motion detectors between him and where he wanted to go. He gave the detector to Tony and whispered, "Take this, and slowly make your way to the front door."

"I'll let you know when I'm there," Tony told him.

Tony had already moved toward the path when Hunt reached out and grabbed his ankle. Tony glanced back.

"Make sure you know who you're shooting at before pulling the trigger."

"Let me worry about this," Tony whispered back, kicking Hunt's hand away with his opposite foot.

Once Tony was out of sight, Hunt continued inching his way toward the house while making sure to stay out of direct view from the patio door. If someone were to take a peek from one of the second floor windows, he'd be done for.

Tony's voice came squawking in his earpiece. "I'm a few feet away from the front door. Are you ready?"

Tony had gone his separate way less than three minutes ago. *Didn't I tell him to go slow?* He loathed working with civilians. They had no tactical awareness. Tony was tough and a bright guy. Hunt wasn't surprised that the Garcia family had thrived under his leadership. But in their current situation, Tony was out of his depth. He should have listened to Hunt.

"Stand by," Tony told him.

"I'm good to go when you're both ready," Anna informed them.

"Copy that, Anna," Hunt replied. "Wait for my command."

It took him another two minutes to reach his spot. Hidden behind the built-in kitchen, Hunt had a perfect view of the patio door fifteen feet away. He was about to use the bottom of his shirt to wipe the sweat from his face but remembered it was full of sand. He used his hand instead and rubbed it dry against his jeans.

"Anna, this is Pierce."

"Yes?"

"On my command, open the front gate, then wait twenty seconds and ring the doorbell."

"What about the floodlight?"

"I'll let you know when to turn it on."

"Okay."

Hunt took a moment to gather his thoughts and picture what was about to happen. They were as ready as they were going to be. Hunt had conducted raids similar to this one more times than he could count, and he usually had a pretty good idea of how things would go. Not this time. Having Leila in play changed things. There was no point denying it.

"Anna from Pierce, open the front gate."

Three seconds later, Anna replied, "Front gate opening now."

Hunt counted to ten and closed one of his eyes in anticipation of what was about to happen. There was a chance he'd need his night vision. He heard through the wall the ring and chimes of the front doorbell. When Hunt reached the count of sixty, he asked Anna to turn on the floodlight. A moment later, half the backyard was bathed in light as two powerful floodlights were turned on. Crouched in the shadows of the built-in kitchen, Hunt aimed his silenced Glock at the sliding door and waited.

———

"Stand by," Emilio said, loud enough so the two shooters positioned at the back of the house heard him. "I'll check who's there."

Emilio pulled out his phone and tapped on the application that allowed him to see who was at the door. It didn't work.

Strange, but not unusual. The timing, though, couldn't be worse. He carefully made his way to the office—which had a window with a direct view of the front of the house—and looked outside with his gun drawn and at his side. The front gate was open. Emilio relaxed. Hector had probably forgotten something and sent one of his men to retrieve it. That meant it was Hector's man waiting for Emilio to open the door for him. He holstered his pistol and headed to the foyer. He was ten feet away from the door when one of his men shouted a warning.

"Two floodlights just switched on! North side of the lot!"

"Go check it out," Emilio ordered. "It's probably one of Hector's men, so hold your fire."

Probably one of Hector's men. That wasn't good enough. "Hey," Emilio said to the other shooter, "cover him. Just in case."

The humming sound of the keyless door-lock mechanism behind him grabbed his attention. Who had activated it? Only he and Hector had the eight-digit code to the keyless lock. If Hector was at the front door, he wouldn't have bothered ringing the doorbell. He would have simply called in advance to warn them of his arrival and come in.

Joder! Emilio's hand had just reached his holster when the front door burst open.

———

Hunt heard at least two different people yelling inside the house. If whoever was in charge was going to fall for it, they'd do it now. His pulse quickened.

C'mon, assholes. Come outside. Hunt welcomed the sound of the sliding door latch as if it were the Messiah's second coming. Someone had unlocked it. A moment later, the door slid open.

"Anna from Pierce," he said into the mic. "Hit the inside lights!"

Hunt held his breath and readjusted his pistol grip as a rifle barrel appeared in the gap between the doorframe and the sliding door. A tall man stepped out, and the ashen glow of the moonlight allowed Hunt to take a good look at him. He had wide shoulders and a big, beefy neck with arms to match. His hair was cropped short, and the man wore a two-day-old beard. The man squinted, trying to adjust his eyes and waiting for his night vision to return. Then the interior lights came on. Hunt had a clear shot but decided to wait an extra second to see if another man stepped out.

"I'm going in through the front door," Hunt heard Tony say over the radio.

Before Hunt could reply, a shot rang out. Then another.

Tony!

The gunman spun around, bringing his weapon up.

Hunt broke cover and stood upright from behind the built-in kitchen with his pistol grasped in both hands and its muzzle pointed at the gunman's head twenty feet away. The black suppressor of Hunt's pistol coughed twice. The first round hit the man in the jaw, destroying the lower half of his face. The second round entered his neck below his right ear. By the time the gunman's body collapsed on the terrace, Hunt was already halfway to the sliding door. He had no intention of spending any more time in the open than absolutely necessary. Being in the open had always given Hunt a sense of vulnerability. He squeezed into the opening and charged into the house, checking his right and then sweeping to his left. He saw another gunman running toward the front of the house. He had an MP5 in a sling around his neck and a pistol in his hand.

Hunt shot him in the back. The gunman, carried by his forward momentum, crashed headfirst into a wall. Hunt scanned for more threats. When his eyes returned to the gunman he had just shot, he was raising his pistol toward Hunt. Hunt rolled to his right as a bullet whizzed to his left. He reengaged the gunman with three quick rounds to the upper body. The man dropped his gun, and his body went limp. Hunt continued toward the front of the house.

More gunshots came from the foyer, and the sound of two men fighting forced Hunt to move faster.

Then he heard Tony scream in pain. The kind of guttural and uncontrollable scream that came from the depths of a man afraid to die.

———

The man came in so fast that Emilio's first shot went wide. By the time he realigned his pistol, the man was almost on him. A muzzle flashed in front of him, and Emilio felt a bullet graze his cheek. Emilio fired again, and he heard the man grunt as the bullet ricocheted off his gun and nicked his hand before embedding itself in the drywall. The man yelled in pain but nevertheless managed to tackle Emilio just below the belt. Emilio's pistol flew out of his hand, and both men crashed to the floor, locked in a deadly embrace. Emilio grabbed the man's hair and pulled back to create some distance. The moment the man's face was a few inches away from his, Emilio head butted him on the nose with a sickening crunch. The man cried out, blood gushing out of his nose and splashing across Emilio's face. Emilio pushed the larger man off him and jumped to his feet.

A shot rang out behind him, and for a second, Emilio lost his focus. He glanced back to see if he was in immediate danger. It was all the other man needed to make a move. This time, he swung a knife.

Where did the knife come from?

Emilio's pistol was behind him, and he had no idea where the man's gun was. The knife came in fast, directly at his stomach. Emilio parried with his arm, knocking the man's knife arm to the right. But the knife swung again, and this time it sliced his right forearm open. Emilio, enraged, swung wildly and got lucky. His fist connected with the man's already broken nose, forcing him back a few steps. Although Emilio was in an unbelievable amount of pain, his mind was still in the fight, and he dived for his gun. He slid on the sleek marble and reached his pistol on his stomach. He crashed against the wall with a loud thud, still holding his pistol loosely in his left hand. He rolled to his side just in time to see the man lunge at him with his knife, his eyes wild with rage.

Emilio had time to fire only once before the man's blade plunged into his chest.

———

Hunt gasped at the scene in front of him. Tony, huddled against the wall, was clutching his stomach, blood pouring from between his fingers, his eyes open wide in disbelief. Next to him was a man in even worse shape. A knife was embedded to the hilt in his chest.

"Anna from Pierce—"

"What's going on?"

"Tony's been shot," Hunt said, rushing to Tony's side.

"Get the girls, Pierce. I'll be fine."

The boldness in Tony's voice surprised Hunt.

"Go," Tony insisted. "Please."

Hunt ignored him and said to Anna, "Come to the safe house. Drive through the front gate and come right in."

Tony grabbed his arm, and shook his head. "No—"

"He's in the main entrance. Take him to a hospital."

"On my way," Anna replied, her voice breaking. "I'm only two minutes away."

"I have my own doctor—"

"This is serious, Tony," Hunt insisted, trying to place Tony in a more comfortable position. "You need surgery."

"What are you doing?" Tony asked. His voice had lost its strength now, and his eyes were closed.

Hunt inserted a fresh magazine in his Glock and pocketed the other one. "I'm gonna find our daughters, Tony. Or I'll die trying. I promise."

Tony slowly opened his eyes. They were glazed and distant. He nodded slowly. A tear trickled down his cheek. "I want to see her again," he said. "She's my everything, Pierce. You understand?"

Yeah, I understand.

"Anna will take care of you. Hang tight," Hunt said.

Without another look at Tony, Hunt stepped out of the foyer, half expecting to get shot. If there were more shooters in the house, they would have flocked to the ground floor and surrounded them by now. Instead, the house was dead quiet. With any luck, nobody had heard the gunshots, or if they did, they thought they were fireworks—a daily late-night beach occurrence nowadays. His gun up and in front of him, Hunt started searching the rest of the house. He began with the second floor, where he found six large bedrooms and as many bathrooms. But there were no signs of Leila and Sophia ever having been there. He checked every room and closet, hoping to find a clue that would at least confirm whether the girls had been in the house. By the time he returned to the ground floor, Tony was gone.

"Anna from Pierce," he called over their communication system.

"What?"

"Are you on your way to the hospital?"

"Did you find Sophia?"

"No trace of the girls yet, but I'm not done."

"Shit!"

My thoughts exactly.

"I'll be at the hospital in less than five minutes," she added as he was about to ask her that very question.

"I want you to leave him at the emergency room, Anna. Then you head straight back to his house and ask Mauricio to take care of the Range Rover."

She didn't reply.

"Anna, did you hear what I just said?"

"Yes! Yes! Yes!"

Hunt could only imagine how she felt. During the past twenty-four hours, she had lost her father, a powerful Mexican drug cartel had kidnapped her niece, and now her brother had been shot and was fighting for his life. That wasn't counting the fact she'd been forced to work with Hunt, the man who had wrecked her life.

"How's he doing?" he asked, entering the living room.

"I'm not a doctor, Pierce!"

"You're doing a hell of a job, Anna. Just focus on one thing at a time. And right now, it's getting Tony to a hospital."

"What about you?"

"Thank you for everything you've done tonight. But I'll do the rest on my own," he told her. "Goodbye, Anna. And I'm truly sorry. You're a good and kind woman."

He took the earpiece out of his ear and put it in his pocket. He also turned off the radio. He continued his search of the ground floor. He checked the pantry and the appliances and looked under the sofas and armchairs for anything the girls might have left behind.

Nothing.

There was only one place left to look. The basement.

CHAPTER FORTY-FIVE

South of Hypoluxo, Florida

Hector wasn't worried, but he wondered why Emilio hadn't called him yet. The application on his phone that monitored the Hallandale Beach safe house wasn't working. He loved new technologies, but he was frustrated when they didn't work as advertised.

Leila and Sophia—blindfolded, gagged, and with their hands tied behind their backs—were in the back of the Ford Transit. He touched his ear. To help with the extreme bruising and tenderness, he'd swallowed four two-hundred-milligram tablets of Advil. Still, his entire head rumbled with the worst headache he'd ever had. He would have ripped the girl's throat out right on the spot if it wasn't for his cousin, who'd insisted on keeping the little pest alive for a few more hours. Despite the constant pain, Hector laughed at his own stupidity. Never before in his life, whether in the military or at the service of his cousin, had he underestimated an adversary. And here he was, in total agony, because he had misjudged an *unarmed* fifteen-year-old teenager. *Serves me right.*

Hector reached up and flipped open the mirror on the sun visor and angled it so that he could look at the bandage wrapped around his head. Blood had already begun to darken the white bandage. A little blood loss wouldn't kill him, but damned if it didn't hurt like hell. He checked his watch and decided to call Emilio for a situation report.

Why isn't he answering his phone? Emilio always picked up, usually on the first ring. Hector checked that he'd dialed the right number. He had. He punched the number a second time. Nothing.

He tried the mobile application again, but he was still unable to connect with the safe house's Wi-Fi. Hector murmured a curse and dialed another number. This time his call was picked up right away.

CHAPTER FORTY-SIX

Hallandale Beach, Florida

The nondescript gray van was parked on a quiet side street with a direct view of the front gate of the Black Tosca's Hallandale Beach safe house. Inside the van, Egan pressed his sniper rifle to his shoulder. He peered through the scope, his finger on the frame, not yet caressing the trigger. He'd stolen the van from a twenty-four-hour grocery store in Aventura. He'd then stopped at a Walgreens in Fort Lauderdale and pinched a license plate from an identical van.

His phone, placed on the van's floor next to his SIG Sauer P229, chirped twice.

"Where are you?" Hector growled.

"Across the street from your Hallandale Beach safe house."

When Hector replied, his voice was clear and calm, but there was an added urgency to it. "Emilio isn't picking up. Have you been inside the house?"

Egan centered his scope's crosshairs on a large window on the second floor of the house. "No, I haven't."

"I'm getting tired of having to squeeze every simple answer out of you, Mr. Granger. Fucking exhausted, in fact!"

"Are you done with your tantrum?" Egan asked, keeping his voice even.

Here you are, Egan thought, adjusting his aim. The lights were on, but most of the curtains and drapes were closed. Egan switched to infrared, and through a heavy curtain he saw someone, but only for a fraction of a second.

"You asked me if I've been inside the house. I said no. What else do you want to know?"

"You're a fucking pain in the ass," Hector said, the heat of his anger sizzling through every word. "Did you see anything unusual? Did anyone else enter the house?"

"I told you to pull your guys out, didn't I?" Egan replied matter-of-factly. "I warned you, Hector, but you hung up on me instead."

If there was one thing he knew and respected about Hector, it was his commitment to his men. If Hector was as good of a leader as Egan believed him to be, he was sure Hector was feeling pretty miserable right now. Egan's objective wasn't to torture Hector about the probable death of the team he had left behind to ambush Hunt; his goal was to make him realize that when it came to Pierce Hunt, he'd better listen to what Egan had to say.

Egan heard Hector take deep breaths, hold them for a second or two, and then let them out slowly, just as though he was laboring to control something gargantuan. *His anger.*

"You were right," Hector finally admitted. "I made an error."

"Don't feel too bad about yourself, Hector," Egan said. "You know what they say, right?"

"What are you talking about?"

"A mistake admitted is a mistake half-forgiven."

"Are you done?"

Whoever was moving from room to room on the second floor of the safe house knew not to hang around a window for too long. "There's movement inside the house."

"Hunt?"

"Most likely. Anna Garcia picked up her brother a couple minutes ago. Poor Tony looked like he was in bad shape."

"You saw them, and you didn't engage?" Hector sounded annoyed again.

"They aren't under contract, Hector."

Hector cursed in Spanish, and Egan could almost imagine the big man shaking his head.

"Anything else?" Egan asked.

"Call me when it's done."

———

Hector hung up. He was furious. *What a fucking twat!* But he knew his anger was directed mostly at himself. Mr. Granger had been right. Hunt was indeed a dangerous man. Too bad he hadn't been able to put him down at the ambush site. If Hunt had killed Emilio and the two other shooters, he couldn't ignore the possibility that the Hypoluxo safe house was compromised too.

The Black Tosca had always allowed him maximum flexibility regarding how he accomplished his missions over the years. What he had in mind this time around, though, would require her approval. The only question was if he should call her now or once he had set the wheels in motion.

"Sir," his driver said, pointing outside.

Hector looked up from his phone and spotted a number of police cars parked on the highway's shoulder about a quarter mile ahead of them.

A knot formed in his stomach. Could the police be looking for them? Doubtful. Still, Hector had a hard time believing how fast this mission was turning into a clusterfuck. He didn't need any more problems. He had enough shit to deal with.

"Make sure you aren't speeding," Hector said to his driver. "And relax."

The driver nodded, but his fingers tightened on the wheel. The presence of the police cruisers clearly bothered him.

His two men in the back shifted in their seats. A quick look confirmed they were getting ready to face the new threat if it materialized. A moment later, they drove past three marked Florida Highway Patrol cruisers. Six officers, coffee cups in hand, were standing in front of their vehicles, laughing.

Keep laughing and having fun, guys, and you'll go home at the end of your shift, Hector thought.

But he knew that wasn't to be when, one minute later and only five minutes away from Palm Beach County Park Airport, he saw a riot of flashing red emergency lights in his mirror.

CHAPTER FORTY-SEVEN

South of Hypoluxo, Florida

Corporal Ryan Steck from the Florida Highway Patrol was looking forward to the end of his shift. His wife, Mary, had given birth to their fourth child forty-eight hours ago. In two days, he'd be on paternity leave for a full month. Mary was a fantastic mother, but he knew she was looking forward to getting some help. She kept an immaculate house and was also a great cook, but with a newborn and three children all under the age of five, it was about to get very, very busy.

It was three in the morning. His shift would be over in four hours. It had been a slow night. A few routine traffic stops, a drunk driver, but nothing too serious. For Corporal Steck, staying awake at this hour was the hardest part of the shift. He had stopped at the Dunkin' Donuts to pick up six large coffees and six donuts—three vanilla-frosted and three coconuts—for his crew. He hoped the coffee and sugar would keep them alert until the end of their shift.

He asked his crew to meet him on the highway at a specific mileage sign a few miles south of Hypoluxo. By the time the rest of his team arrived at the meeting point, his partner, Trooper Erica Eiderzen, had gulped half her coffee and eaten all of her donut.

"I don't understand, Erica, I really don't."

"What?" she asked, licking her fingers.

"Your fitness level is light-years ahead of mine. How many donuts do you eat a day again?"

"I don't count," she replied, drinking the last of her coffee. "Three or four, maybe? It really depends who's buying."

Erica was a tall, hardy woman with a handsome but serious face. She wasn't talkative by nature, but Steck liked her very much. They'd been partners for three years, and she was the godmother of his third child.

"I wish I had your metabolism," he said, opening the door of his police cruiser.

She shrugged. "How many hours do you spend working out, Ryan?"

He didn't work out anymore. He'd love to, but with three kids—now four!—there weren't enough hours in the day. And he felt it too; his stomach wasn't as hard as it used to be.

"I walk my dog twice a day," he said. "Does that count?"

Steck loved his crew. They were hardworking guys and girls—and they trusted each other. He was sad to see one of them go. Tonight was Trooper Linda Farrell's last night shift. Two weeks from now, she was to report to the FBI Academy to begin training. Steck was convinced Farrell would become a great FBI special agent. She had the strength, tenacity, wits, and guts to reach the higher echelons of the federal police force. Steck had always known the highway patrol was only a stepping-stone for her, but he didn't mind. He'd shared with her everything he knew about the job. She had repaid him in kind with hard work, loyalty, and dependability.

"I'll miss you guys," Farrell said, accepting a coconut donut from Steck. "What I'm not gonna miss are these romantic highway impromptus."

Steck was big on dissuasion. He was a firm believer that motorists would change their driving habits if they saw enough FHP cruisers on the highways. Statistics supported his claim, so he continued to hold team meetings off the highway's shoulder.

They exchanged a few jokes and anecdotes before Steck asked them if anything had spiked their attention since the beginning of their shift.

"The report about the red Jeep SRT was kind of out of the ordinary," Farrell said.

Steck had thought so too but hadn't dug any deeper. "Why's that?"

"It said a man knocked out two patrol officers before climbing into a red SRT."

"And?"

"Well, I took the liberty to investigate a bit further," Farrell said.

"What did you learn?"

"The patrol officers said that the man who had assaulted them had also savagely beaten up the occupant of one of the units."

"Drug deal gone bad?"

"Not sure yet, but Édgar Pomar, the man they found unconscious, had a bullet in his right knee, among other things. And what's even more interesting is that a company named BlueShade Rental, an LLC owned by Graham Young, owns the unit in which they found Pomar."

"The name Graham Young rings a bell," Steck said, staring down the highway with a thoughtful expression. "Isn't he an attorney?"

Farrell acquiesced with a smile. She took a sip of her coffee and then said, "The *Miami Herald* once named him one of the top ten most influential criminal defense attorneys in the city."

"How do you know all this?" Erica Eiderzen asked.

"I called the department and asked about the case. There's a BOLO out on the SRT. I wanted to know why. Officer safety and all that, you know?"

Steck was impressed. Linda Farrell was a good cop. She had made the right decision to join the FBI.

"But you know what truly grabbed my attention?" Farrell asked no one in particular.

Knowing his protégée wasn't one to waste anyone's time, Steck was curious. "Tell me."

"Young's LLC owns eight vehicles and two properties."

"Probably to host and drive his wealthy clients around," Eiderzen offered.

"Yeah, maybe."

"You think there's more to it than that, Linda?" Steck asked.

"I'm just saying, it's kind of weird that an attorney owns two residences—in which he doesn't even live—and eight vehicles."

"What types of vehicles are associated with the properties?"

"Two minivans, two sports cars, two Mercedes SUVs, and two Ford panel vans."

"Nothing illegal about any of this," Eiderzen said.

"I know," Farrell admitted. "I just find it strange. Why would he need panel vans? It's not like he's an electrician or something."

"You believe it's a front for an illicit business?" Steck asked.

"Édgar Pomar has a rap sheet that includes drugs, car theft, and weapons charges."

"He could be one of Graham Young's clients," Steck suggested.

"I'm sure he is," Farrell replied. "I just wish we could investigate this further."

"Not our jurisdiction," Eiderzen said.

"That's not true, and you know it, Erica," Steck intervened. "We—"

His partner raised her hands in mock surrender. "I know, Ryan, I was just kidding. What I meant to say was that investigating these cases isn't our primary mandate. We're short-staffed enough as it is."

Eiderzen was right, of course. Even though the troopers of the Florida Highway Patrol were state law enforcement officers and had the power to enforce state laws and make arrests, their main obligation was to ensure the safety of the highways and roads of the state.

"I understand this, Erica," Farrell replied, "but that shouldn't prevent us from keeping an eye out for the vehicles connected to Graham Young's two residences, right?"

Eiderzen snorted. "No, I guess not."

Steck wondered why Eiderzen was so pushy and was a bit surprised that she was giving Farrell such a hard time on this issue. As the second-most senior trooper of the team, she should be encouraging initiative among the junior members, not dismissing it as she just did. *Maybe she's a bit jealous?*

"Anyway," Farrell said, unfazed by Eiderzen's criticism, "I emailed you a list of the license plates of the eight vehicles owned by BlueShade Rental."

"The FBI will be lucky to have her, won't they?" Steck grabbed Farrell by the shoulders and pulled her close. "Good job."

Eiderzen rolled her eyes but smiled nonetheless. She asked Farrell, "Isn't this your last shift?"

Farrell tapped the glass of her watch with her finger. "Yes, but there's a few hours left."

"All right, everyone, saddle up," Steck announced. "Let's finish this shift on a high note, and don't forget to check the list Linda sent us."

Just as they were about to break, a Ford panel van drove past them. It was in the middle lane, and Steck estimated it was driving at the speed limit. Steck tried to catch the license plate but only got a partial from the last three characters. D79.

He sat behind the wheel of his police cruiser and turned on the cruiser's computer. Eiderzen took her seat and said, "You'd think Linda would have called in sick or at least taken the day off, this being her last shift."

"Not her style," Steck said. He compared the license plate from the Ford panel van he had just seen to the two license plates Farrell had forwarded to them via email.

I'll be damned.

"One of them is a match," Steck said, looking at his partner.

"What are you talking about?"

"The list Linda sent us," Steck explained. "One of the Fords' plates matches the panel van that drove by us a minute ago. Weren't you paying attention?"

Steck made a quick executive decision and decided to pull over the van. He'd find a legal reason to do so later. He put the gearshift into drive and pressed the gas pedal to the floor. Dust and small rocks shot out from under the rear tires and peppered the concrete buffering wall separating the two sides of the highway.

"What are you doing?" Eiderzen asked, clipping her seat belt in place.

"We're gonna check it out."

Eiderzen grabbed the microphone from the dashboard clip and said, "Trooper Farrell from Trooper Eiderzen."

"Go ahead for Farrell."

"A Ford panel van with a partially matching license plate drove past us a minute ago. Corporal Steck will intercept and pull it over. You want to back us up?"

"You serious?"

"The last three digits matched one of the plates," Eiderzen replied.

Steck smiled. Police work often involved pure sweat—talking to people on the street, canvassing an area to find a weapon, finding witnesses willing to share their stories. Out of the hundreds—and sometime thousands—of pieces of information a team brought in over the course of an investigation, it wasn't unusual to get only one or two solid leads. Equally important, though, was that success in police work largely depended on luck and on a cop's instinct to follow his or her gut. Farrell had done so with this case, and as long as it didn't take him or his team too far from their primary mandate, Steck was ready to probe deeper into BlueShade Rental.

Steck looked in his rearview mirror. The rest of his team was right behind him. They were now traveling at close to ninety miles an hour. At that speed, it didn't take long to catch up to the Ford panel van. When they were about seventy-five feet behind the van, Steck's foot came off the gas pedal.

"Can you confirm the license plate?" he asked Erica.

"Yep," she said. "That's one of them."

"Okay. Let the others know. We'll pull it over."

It didn't matter how many years of service he had behind him. Every time Steck initiated a traffic stop, a rush of adrenaline surged through him. All traffic stops are potentially dangerous. Every year, officers of the Florida Highway Patrol were injured or killed during what Steck was sure the injured or dead officers thought was a routine traffic stop. There was nothing routine with traffic stops. Ever. About one out of ten physical attacks against police officers occurred while engaged in a traffic stop.

As he activated the emergency equipment of his police cruiser, Corporal Ryan Steck turned over in his mind everything he could think of that could go wrong.

Never could he have foreseen what was waiting for him and his team.

CHAPTER FORTY-EIGHT

Hallandale Beach, Florida

Hunt began his controlled descent down the stairs leading to the basement. He kept his back pressed against the wall and his gun in front of him but close to his body. When he reached the final step, a chill coursed through him.

Leila. She was here. I can feel it.

He listened closely for any sound. Once he was satisfied that the only noise was his own breathing, Hunt moved rapidly, room by room, searching for any signs of his daughter. The first room consisted of a double bed, which had been slept in, a dresser with a large mirror, and a night table with a lamp. A sink and a toilet were tucked next to each other in one corner. A video camera hung from the ceiling in a back corner. A lump formed in his throat.

Was it here that they kept her?

He tossed the mattress aside and opened all the drawers but didn't find anything connecting the room to his daughter. The next room was a perfect replica of the previous one. With one major difference.

The blood.

Something terrible had happened in this room. *To Leila?* He blinked a few times and shook the dark thoughts away. If whatever had happened here had taken place more than an hour or two ago, the blood would be dry and brown. Instead, it was dark red and fresh.

And frightening.

Hunt let loose a slew of curse words. He was too late. They'd whisked Leila and Sophia away. Were they already in Mexico? Pomar had told him that was a possibility. There was one more room to check. As his eyes swept across the bedroom one last time, Hunt caught something on the floor, glistening in the murky darkness. He moved closer, shining the beam of his flashlight around.

There. *What the hell was that?*

Upon closer examination, Hunt realized it was an ear, or at least a chunk of one. It was still wet with blood. His heart sank, and his knees wobbled. In his mind's eye, he saw Leila's life from when she was a baby to a young woman. He loved her so much. His eyes began to tear up.

Christ, a fucking ear! How much more can I take?

He picked up the piece of flesh, almost dropping it twice it was so slick with blood, and rinsed it at the sink. As the blood washed down the drain, swirling in the white porcelain sink, a tremendous sense of relief surged through him. His legs no longer able to hold him, he sank to his knees and wept.

The ear wasn't hers. The skin was too dark. His daughter—he was sure it was her—had put up a good fight. She hadn't surrendered to her captors. He was proud of her. A smile creased his eyes and replaced the tears.

She hadn't given up on him. *Hang on, Leila. I'll find you.*

A soft creaking behind him made Hunt lunge to his right. He rolled once and came up on his knees, his pistol pointed at the door. Too late. A shadow on his left turned on a flashlight, temporarily blinding Hunt with its powerful beam. Hunt reacted immediately. Instead of staying put, dropping his gun, and hoping not to get shot, Hunt ducked below the beam of light and rolled forward before lunging low and hard at the shadow. With immense force, Hunt's right shoulder rammed into the shadow's midsection. Hunt dropped his gun in the process, but the shadow—Hunt could now see it was a man—was taken completely by surprise and expelled air in a loud groan. But the fight wasn't over yet. The man wrapped his right arm around Hunt's neck and began to squeeze with an almost superhuman strength. Hunt tried to pull down on the man's arm with both his hands, but the man was just too strong. His arm didn't budge an inch. Both Hunt's carotids were being constricted.

Someone yelled. Hunt didn't know if it came from him or the man he was fighting with. What he knew for sure, though, was that he was about to pass out. He was quickly running out of options and oxygen. He wanted to open his mouth and swallow great gulps of air, but it was physically impossible to do so. The man was just too strong. His head felt as if it was being squashed and was about to implode. The man was tightening his viselike grip, trying to choke the life out of Hunt. Hunt brought up his clenched right fist between the man's legs with all the force he could muster. The man's knees buckled, but he somehow managed to hold on to his choke. But Hunt had destabilized him and bought himself a precious second. Hunt pushed against the man's thigh and turned his head to the side. He encircled the man's right knee with his arms, and, using the last of his strength, he lifted the man in the air and threw him to the ground. Hunt went with him. They hit the ground hard, with Hunt on top. With a whiplash effect, the man's head slammed on the floor with a resounding thud. The flashlight rolled out of his hand, its beam revealing Hunt's pistol. Before his opponent could gather his wits, Hunt jumped to his feet but struggled to keep himself upright. He staggered backward a few steps before recovering his pistol. The flashlight, which had finally come to a stop, illuminated the man's face.

Hunt gasped, and his eyes shot wide open.

Cole Egan.

———

Cole Egan's ears were ringing. When his head had hit the floor, there had been a series of blinding flashing lights and a loud thud unlike anything he had heard before. The back of his head, slick with blood, was throbbing. When he opened his eyes, Pierce Hunt was standing in front of him, a gun pointed at his chest.

"Hey, Pierce," Egan said, massaging his temples in tiny circles with his fingertips.

He tried to sit up, but Hunt planted his foot on his chest. With anyone else but Hunt, he'd try something to get out of this annoying situation. With Hunt, though, he'd end up with a double tap in the chest. Plus, he wasn't here to kill his former colleague and friend; he was here to warn him and offer his help.

"What the fuck are you doing here, Cole?" Hunt said, his voice wavering. "Don't tell me you're involved with this shit. I'll drill one in your forehead."

Egan could see Hunt was struggling to understand what had just happened. Egan knew he was just one piece of a large puzzle. With luck, Hunt would give him a minute or two to explain before shooting him in the head.

"Look around you, Pierce. Do you see a weapon? I came in with a flashlight, for God's sake."

"Keep talking."

"Your daughter was here," Egan said. "Can I get up?"

Instead of removing his foot, Hunt dug it even deeper into Egan's chest. Egan winced in pain.

"C'mon, Pierce, if I wanted you dead, I would have brought more than a goddamned flashlight."

"Leila was here?"

"And so was Garcia's daughter."

"Whose side are you on, Cole?"

"Do you really have to ask?"

"Answer the fucking question," Hunt growled. "You're not the same man I once saved."

There was no denying it. He wasn't sure how much—if anything—Hunt knew about Mr. Granger, but Gaza had changed him. For the last decade, Egan's loyalty had been to whomever paid him the most, and the Black Tosca had been quite generous. But how could he live with himself if he turned against the man who had sacrificed so much of his soul to save him? Gaza had tainted Egan; Hunt, on the contrary, seemed to be the exact same.

"True," Egan admitted, looking Hunt straight in the eyes. "But I'm on your side."

Hunt seemed to hesitate, and Egan feared he was about to punch out and meet his creator.

"The Black Tosca hired me to kill you. By reneging on that contract—"

"You piece of shit," Hunt said, shaking his head in disbelief.

"Weren't you listening? I'm not following it through. Believe it or not—"

"You'd better hope I'm a believer, Cole. If not . . ." Hunt didn't finish his thought. He didn't need to. "My daughter's been taken, and I'm in no mood to play games, even with you."

"My wife's pregnant, Pierce," Egan said defensively. "I had to at least pretend to take the contract. That's the only thing I'm guilty of."

In Egan's mind, there was nothing to gain by admitting he'd actually intended to kill Hunt. His only play now was to team up with Hunt and go after the Black Tosca. Only with the Black Tosca dead could he assure the safety of Katherine and the baby.

"What changed your mind?" Hunt asked.

"Nothing changed my mind," Egan replied immediately, not falling for Hunt's trap. "I'd never do that. Never. You hear me?"

"Oh, I hear you, but the question is whether I believe you."

"What do I have—"

"Was Daniel McMaster in with you on this?" Hunt cut in.

"What? No." Egan's head was spinning. What did McMaster have to do with any of this? Hunt wasn't making sense. "McMaster is my father-in-law, Pierce. That's it. He doesn't know anything. He's the reason why I'm with Katherine. I've being spying on him for years."

A look of disbelief appeared on Hunt's face.

Egan took a couple of deep breaths, which wasn't easy, as Hunt had all his weight on his chest, and said, "If you think I'm against you, or lying to you, pull the damn trigger and be done with it. But if you believe me, help me up, and let's get your daughter back."

Hunt's stare didn't vacillate. Egan's words hadn't gotten through his friend's defenses. In fact, Egan saw Hunt's finger slowly getting tighter around the trigger.

"I want to be a father, Pierce," Egan pleaded.

———

Hunt relaxed his finger. He believed Egan. It all made sense now. McMaster had unwittingly found himself trapped in the Black Tosca's web. He was a victim too.

"Can you really help me?" Hunt asked Egan, lowering his weapon.

"Yes, but I need to call McMaster first. I need him to relocate Katherine. If the Black Tosca learns I've double-crossed her, she'll kill Katherine."

"McMaster won't be happy, but he'll do it," Hunt said.

"Once he learns who I really am, he'll ask Katherine never to see me again."

"What have you got yourself into?"

Egan averted his eyes. Hunt could tell the question made Egan uncomfortable. Whatever shit Egan had gotten himself into, he was in neck-deep. *Too deep, maybe? Am I being played?*

Egan had told the truth about not being armed. He was a skilled operator—one of the best Hunt had worked with—and Hunt had only heard him at the last moment. If Egan had come in with a weapon in hand, there was a good chance Hunt would have a hole or two in him.

"I fucked up, Pierce. I really did," Egan said with a sigh. "The only thing that counts now is protecting Katherine. The only way to do that is to take down the Black Tosca. I'm tired of being her puppet. So please, let me help you. Maybe it will be my redemption. Sort of, anyway."

Hunt holstered his gun and extended his hand. Egan, still on the ground, took it. "Really?" Egan asked.

"Yeah, really."

CHAPTER FORTY-NINE

South of Hypoluxo, Florida

Hector hung up. He had just spoken to the chief pilot. His instructions had been short and to the point. The plane needed to be ready to depart in twenty minutes with a flight plan to Nassau, Bahamas.

"What should I do?" his driver asked.

The three police cruisers were right on the van's tail, their emergency lights blitzing in a synchronized pattern of red and blue. Hector had no choice but to order his driver to stop. Now wasn't the time to be angry or to start questioning how they had ended up being pulled over. Now was the time to react and to adapt to the current situation.

"Change of plan, gentlemen," Hector said, loud enough for all his men to hear. "Once we're done here, we'll head directly to the airport. We'll figure out what to do once we're in the air. Understood?"

His men nodded. They were ready for action. They were outnumbered six to four, but there was no way the police officers were prepared for the tremendous amount of firepower his men were about to lay down upon them. And even if the officers were prepared, his men were much better trained than the highway cops.

"Pull the van over at the next off-ramp," Hector said to the driver. "Let's go to work."

———

The Ford panel van's driver tapped the brakes numerous times to indicate he was about to pull over—at least, that was Steck's interpretation. The driver then activated his right turn signal. Steck followed the van as it pulled onto the shoulder of the off-ramp. The panel van stopped four hundred feet later at the end of the ramp. Steck stopped his cruiser about three or four car lengths behind it. Trooper Eiderzen turned on the cruiser's powerful spotlight and shined it on the van.

"You see anything?" Steck asked.

The panel van's windows were heavily tinted, and there were no windows in the back. It was hard to tell how many occupants were inside the vehicle save for the driver and at least one passenger. The driver's door opened, and a man climbed out. He wore a pair of black jeans and a dark-colored T-shirt and appeared to be holding a cigarette in his right hand. The man waved at the police car before shielding his eyes. With the beam of the spotlight shining in his eyes, there was no way he could see Steck or the rest of his team. A small burning circle of tobacco glowed orange as the driver drew on his cigarette. Steck looked away from the driver, his eyes searching for anything suspicious. The shocks on the van were somewhat compressed, but that didn't mean anything. Maybe they were carrying a heavy load? But Steck had to put everything in perspective. There were almost no vehicles on the road. It was late at night—or very early in the morning. The panel van was owned by a holding company belonging to a notorious attorney. One of the properties within the same holding company had been the scene of a crime that same night. These were all things that Steck kept in mind as he disembarked from his vehicle.

"Call it in," he instructed Eiderzen, placing his hand over his holster. "And please, Erica, keep the spotlight's beam on the van."

Eiderzen nodded.

Steck keyed his radio and said to his team, "Linda, get behind me. Jack and Ricardo, take the passenger side, and watch out for oncoming traffic."

He got a series of acknowledgments. He then added, "Erica will operate the spotlight, and Carrie will stay in reserve and keep an eye on the back of the panel van."

Steck started his approach. His gut told him he was missing something. The panel van's driver turned his head toward the van and said something. Steck didn't hear what it was, and it made him nervous. He had an unsettled feeling in his chest. Steck's right hand casually released the strap on his holster.

———

Hector thought his driver was playing his role perfectly. It was even money the cops would ask him to get back in the van, but they ended up allowing him to stay outside.

"They're all there," his man told him hastily. "Two approaching on my side, two more on your side, one manning the spotlight, and the last officer is staying back. Light body armor and pistols only."

Hector nodded his thanks and said to his team, "Wait till they get to the back of the van, then be precise, fast, and deadly. I want us on our way in thirty seconds."

Five seconds later, Hector gave the order to execute.

———

Even with the mighty beam of the spotlight, Steck had difficulty seeing inside the van. And he didn't like it. The back of his neck tingled. He knew the feeling well. He'd had it many times since joining the Florida Highway Patrol, and he had learned to listen to his sixth sense. Steck was still two steps away from the vehicle when he stopped. Farrell, who'd been following a little too closely, bumped into him. For a fraction of a second, the angle was just right, and Steck saw there were at least two more occupants in the panel van.

And they were on the move.

"What's going on?" Farrell asked, immediately alert.

Before Steck could reply, the side doors opened. Steck instinctively pulled out his firearm and ducked. The driver reached for something behind his back. Steck had a clear shot, but he hesitated, afraid this was all a mistake and that he was reading too much into the situation. Farrell didn't hesitate, though. She sidestepped him to the left and fired at the driver while yelling, "Police!"

The driver, hit twice above his left nipple, crumpled to the ground. Then everything happened at once. A man dressed in black combat gear and armed with what looked like an MP5 exited the van in front of Steck and opened fire on full automatic. The first bullet ripped Steck's pistol from his hand, and then several caught him on his left side and lower abdomen. It felt like a series of sharp, stinging punches. Steck heard Farrell scream as bullets slammed into her, making her dance. More bullets slapped through the windshield of his police cruiser, right where Eiderzen was seated. Steck fell to one knee and managed to retrieve his pistol. He tried to return fire, but his hands were shaking so much he couldn't pull the trigger. Steck looked down and noticed blood oozing out of his shirt and pants.

Christ! What have I done? I led my team right into a slaughter.

When he looked up again, the man in black had his eyes fixed on him. *Is he smiling?* Then the man fired.

———

Hector advanced, swinging his MP5 left and right and looking for additional threats he might have missed. Nothing. His side of the van was clear. The spotlight had been shattered and so had the front windshield of the first police car.

A few cars sped by, but none stopped.

"Back in the van!" Hector yelled.

"Man down!" one of his men yelled back.

Fuck! He hurried to the other side of the van, where his driver lay on his back next to the front left tire. Hector knelt next to him. He cursed all the gods he knew. The driver's heart, at least for the few beats it had left, was pumping blood through two holes, circular and neat, where the bullets had struck him. Hector took his man's hand in his own. He wished he could do something for him, but the man was too far gone. Hector knew he wouldn't want pity, so he simply said, "You did well, my friend."

A moment later, the driver's eyes rolled back in their sockets, and Hector heard the death rattle as his man breathed out for the last time.

CHAPTER FIFTY

Hallandale Beach, Florida

While Egan called Daniel McMaster to explain the situation and to beg for his help in temporarily relocating Katherine, Hunt searched the room at the end of the hallway. It was the only room left in the basement he hadn't gone through. What he found took his breath away.

Dear God, they recorded everything.

On a large curved desk, two computer screens linked to the video cameras inside the bedrooms displayed live feeds of the surveillance footage. Opposite the screens was a twin bed, unmade, with clothes strewn all over it. None of the clothes belonged to Leila, which was a relief. Hunt sat behind the desk and pulled the keyboard tray toward him. On it was a wireless keyboard and a wireless mouse. Maybe he could see what had happened in the bedrooms. It took a minute to figure out how the system worked, but it was pretty simple. With a click of the mouse, he rewound the digital recording until he saw Leila.

Hunt couldn't catch a breath, his throat locking the moment he caught sight of his Leila. His heart pounded in his chest. Even though Egan had told him so, it was a relief to confirm he was only an hour or so behind the animals who had stolen his daughter from him.

Hunt remained motionless as he watched Leila fight one of her captors, a tall and muscular man four times her size. His face grew hot as he witnessed Leila being flung across the bedroom. Hunt almost threw the computer screen against the opposite wall when he recognized the brute. *Hector Mieles.*

How could a man do that to a fifteen-year-old girl? Tightness swelled in his chest. *I'm gonna fucking kill you.* Hunt couldn't take his eyes off the screen. Unconsciously, he clenched and unclenched his fists as Hector Mieles approached his daughter, who seemed to have lost consciousness after rolling on her side a few times. Hunt stared at Mieles, a man he could and should have killed the day before, with the hypnotic fascination of a predator looking at its prey.

Suddenly Mieles jerked back, and Leila spat the piece of flesh Hunt had discovered in the bedroom. Despite everything he'd just seen, a grin pulled at his mouth.

Leila was alive and still in the fight.

———

Egan was thankful Daniel McMaster hadn't asked too many questions. He knew there would be hell to pay in the future, but at least Katherine and his unborn baby would be safe. As a DEA special agent in charge, McMaster had a lot of resources at his disposal. One of those resources was the ability to hide high-value assets or witnesses. There was no doubt in Egan's mind that McMaster would use his power to ensure the safety of his daughter and future grandchild. Egan wished he could have explained everything to Katherine prior to requesting her father's assistance, but there was no time—and, to be honest, he wasn't exactly sure how he would explain the situation. It wasn't the easiest thing to admit to your wife that you were a hired gun for a drug cartel. This was especially true when your wife's dad had made a career out of arresting cartel members.

Egan made his way back to the basement. He found Hunt in the room at the end of the small hallway, staring at two computer screens. When Hunt glanced back, there was a murderous rage in his eyes.

"They drugged the girls," Hunt told him. "Do you know where they went?"

"The Black Tosca owns another safe house in Hypoluxo. Hector planned on taking Leila and . . . what's the name of the other girl again?"

"Sophia. She's Tony Garcia's daughter."

"Tony Garcia?" Egan asked. *What was Pierce's daughter doing with the daughter of the head of one of the largest crime families in Florida?*

"That's what I said, Cole. It's a long story, one I won't share with you either, so please continue."

"Hector's original plan, before you rampaged into Pomar's condominium, was to keep the girls here. When he realized you were coming after him, he left a crew behind to ambush you."

"You included?"

Egan shook his head. "No, I was hired to track you down and kill you," he said simply.

Hunt's eyes penetrated deep into his, but when Hunt said nothing, Egan added, "You gave me a second chance, Pierce. When those assholes took me in Gaza, I never thought I'd see the light of day again. I fully expected to be tortured for weeks on end. I later learned that the brass ordered you not to come after me. But you did. I hope you'll give me the chance to repay you."

And maybe, just maybe, redeem myself for all the stupid shit I've done since then.

"Okay."

"Okay? Okay what?"

"Tell me where the girls are. You don't think they brought them to the Hypoluxo safe house?"

"I was supposed to call Hector the moment I put you down. Obviously, I didn't, so it makes no tactical sense for him to go to Hypoluxo. He'll have to assume that I'm either dead—"

"Or that you've been turned," Hunt interjected.

"Yeah, that too."

Egan hoped his father-in-law would move in quick to protect Katherine. Because if Hunt was right and the Black Tosca had even a soupçon of suspicion that Egan had betrayed her, she'd move mountains to destroy him and everyone he held dear.

"So where's Hector headed if he ain't going to Hypoluxo?"

"To Mexico. He's taking them to San Miguel de Allende."

CHAPTER FIFTY-ONE

Palm Beach County Park Airport, Florida

Hector briefly considered hijacking a vehicle, but they were so close to the airport that it wasn't worth the risk. He sat behind the wheel, started the engine, and redlined the Ford through the red light at the end of the off-ramp. He sped onto the on-ramp across the intersection. Less than three minutes had elapsed since they had been pulled over by the cops.

In the back, one of the girls woke up and started to moan. It started with little sobs every few seconds but quickly grew in intensity. It almost sounded like an injured animal. Had one of them been wounded? Had a stray bullet hit one of the girls? He hoped not. The Black Tosca wanted two healthy and *uninjured* children.

Within minutes, if it was not already done, all local, state, and federal law enforcement agencies would learn about the slaughter of the six highway patrol officers. Then all bets would be off. A massive search operation would be launched, and the police would seal off all the major roads leading to the bus stations, cruise ship terminals, and international airports. He doubted Palm Beach County Park Airport would get the same treatment, but he didn't care to wait and find out. The sooner they were in the air, the better.

"Check on the girls," Hector said, keeping his eyes on the highway. Now wasn't the time to get distracted. "See what the commotion is about."

———

Leila woke up with a start. She opened her eyes, but her vision remained a dark blur. A face slowly coalesced next to her.

Sophia?

She tried to speak but couldn't open her mouth. She couldn't move any part of her body. Her feet and hands were bound with zip ties, and duct tape covered her mouth. She had never felt so claustrophobic before. She struggled to break free, the zip ties digging into her flesh. She moaned in pain. Leila's heart battered her rib cage. At least there was no black bag over her head to keep her from seeing where she was. *A van?* Sophia was next to her. She could see her friend's face clearly now. She was gagged and tied the same way Leila was.

The fact that they were alive meant that their captor had something in mind for her and Sophia. That in itself wasn't good news. Was it in retribution for what she had done to his ear? Maybe, but she couldn't let fear cause her to lose her capacity to think clearly. As long as they were alive, there was hope of a rescue. Her gaze settled on Sophia as she wished her friend would open her eyes. But she didn't. Leila listened carefully. She heard men talking in Spanish—weird, she hadn't noticed them before—but she didn't hear any breathing coming from her friend. Sophia's chest wasn't moving either. Fear clouded Leila's eyes.

Oh my God, she's not breathing. Sophia's not breathing!

Leila tried to yell, but the duct tape on her mouth muffled her voice. She kept trying, but it did no good. She was powerless and angry. She lifted her bound feet and kicked at the side wall of the van. She only managed one soft thump before a man grabbed her elbow from behind. He yanked it back so hard he almost dislocated her shoulder. Then he grabbed her with both hands and pulled her up to a seated position. With one hand, the man reached for one of the edges of the duct tape over her mouth.

"This will be painful," the man said in accented English.

He ripped the duct tape off in one swift motion. Her whole body shuddered. She screamed. In response, he slapped her across the face. Tears ran down her cheeks. She could feel the imprint of his hand on her skin.

"Sophia's not breathing!" Leila screamed between two sobs. "Do something!"

A look of abject fear crossed the man's features. He climbed over the rear bench seat and pushed Leila over. He removed the duct tape over Sophia's mouth. The man's back was toward her, and Leila wished she had use of her hands. She'd try to get the gun free from the holster on his hip or, at the very least, dig her fingers deep into his eyes.

She could spout all the wishful thinking she wanted; she couldn't do anything for Sophia. Her mind slowed to a sluggish crawl, only able to focus on one thing.

Don't die, Sophia. Don't die. Please don't die.

———

"Sophia's alive, Hector," his man said a minute later. "But she's having spasms. Her breathing is depressed. The drug you used must have slowed her heartbeat. She'll be fine."

Hector breathed a shallow sigh of relief.

"Retape Leila's mouth, and keep the girls quiet until we get to the airport."

They were a few miles away from the airport. He called the chief pilot again.

"Is the plane ready?"

"It will be in five to ten minutes. We just started the engines."

Hector grunted. "I want to take off the moment we get there, and I want you and your copilot to stay in the cockpit. I don't need a welcome committee."

"Yessir. May I ask where we're headed?"

"Nassau." The pilot needed to know which flight plan to file. "Can I drive directly onto the runway?"

It was an unusual question, but the pilot didn't seem to care. "Usually no, but if you're in a rush, I can ask the private aviation clerk to keep it open for you. Would that work?"

"Perfectly."

"Very well. We'll be ready for you."

As Hector took the exit off Highway 95, three Florida Highway Patrol cruisers flew by in the opposite direction with sirens blaring and flashing lights whirling. An ambulance followed shortly after. Then another. It would take the authorities a few minutes to get organized, but there was no time to lose. At the end of the off-ramp, Hector made a left turn onto Lantana Road. He traveled westward for a mile and then was forced to come to an abrupt stop when a pair of Palm Beach County fire rescue trucks—sirens screaming—raced out of their bay and cut him off. Less than a quarter mile later, Hector made a right onto the access road leading to the airport. He slowed down to get his bearings. In front of him was the gate leading to the tarmac. It was opened, and Hector was able to drive the Ford close enough to the King Air 350 passenger door that they would have only a few steps to take before reaching the stairway and disappearing inside the aircraft.

His men climbed out of the panel van, fanned out around the plane, and took up firing positions. Hector opened the rear doors of the van, cut the zip ties around the two girls' ankles, and, none too gently, dragged Leila out. He lifted her as though she were a doll and tossed her over his right shoulder. He climbed the small steps and dropped her roughly in the first available seat. He touched his damaged ear again, and his hand came back with a little blood on his fingertips.

"Don't move," he barked at her. She looked petrified. Good.

He repeated the process with the other girl but seated her in the third row, making sure she was facing the rear of the plane. Hector was about to order his men to board the plane when the cockpit door opened. A man dressed in a pilot's uniform—the first officer, not the captain, since he was wearing only three stripes—stood motionless, a stunned look on his face. The pilot's eyes darted back and forth between Leila, who still had her wrists tied behind her back and duct tape over her mouth, and Hector.

"Weren't you asked to stay in the cockpit?" Hector asked, reaching the pilot in two strides.

Hector's right hand shot out like a bolt of lightning. He buried his fist in the man's solar plexus with such force that, had he hit the man over the heart, it might have stopped it cold. The man curled up, but Hector didn't allow him to go down. Instead, Hector spun him around, grabbed his left arm, and twisted it behind his back while locking his own arm around the man's throat.

The captain, with whom Hector had had numerous chats over the phone, twisted his head to see what was going on. The look on his face wasn't what Hector expected. The whole incident with his associate seemed to have amused him.

The man's actually smiling, Hector thought.

"What's so funny?" he asked the pilot.

The man's smile disappeared, and he said, "I told him to stay in the cockpit, but when he saw your men and the guns, he panicked."

"You didn't?"

"You're paying me well not to."

"Can you fly this plane by yourself?"

There wasn't even a hint of hesitation. "Absolutely. And I can keep my mouth shut too."

Now it was Hector's turn to smile. "Good," he said.

The conversation's implications weren't lost on the first officer. His face was turning dark red as he tried to break free from Hector's grasp. Hector let go of the man's arm and pulled his knife out of its sheath. He stabbed the man twice in the chest before embedding the knife deep into his neck. Hector angled his body and threw the first officer out of the plane's door.

He looked at the captain. "All set?"

CHAPTER FIFTY-TWO

Stafford, Virginia

Simon Carter got the phone call in the middle of his workout routine. He was an early riser and preferred hitting the gym when there was nobody else around. His call display told him it was an unknown number. He picked up anyway. He knew it was Pierce Hunt.

"Any news?" he asked his friend.

"Kind of. I have a favor to ask."

"You got it, Pierce."

"You don't even know what I'm about to ask you. It could be dangerous."

Carter chuckled. "I'm sure it is. That's why you're calling me, right?"

"And illegal too," Hunt added.

Hunt was toying with him, so he said, "But is it honorable, and will it serve justice?"

"I need your help getting my daughter back."

"I already knew that. I'm in."

"But this time it isn't only to check stuff in the DEA database, Simon. I need a shooter."

If Pierce Hunt needed a shooter, that meant he had a target. "How many of us do you need? You know the guys will do anything for you, right?"

"I do, and I appreciate that. But this operation will be black. No footprint whatsoever."

"So only you and me?" Carter asked.

"And an old friend of mine from the Seventy-Fifth."

"You trust him, Pierce?"

"Not as much as I trust you, brother. That's why I need you."

"Tell me what you need, and consider it done."

CHAPTER FIFTY-THREE

Coral Gables, Florida

"Will Tony be okay?" Hunt asked Anna.

"Don't know," she replied, her eyes moist with tears. "He's still in surgery." Hunt watched her take a long sip of vodka straight from the bottle.

It had been six hours since Tony Garcia had been shot. The police were asking a lot of questions, and Hunt wouldn't be surprised if, supposing Tony pulled through, they brought him in for questioning. Since the news that six Florida Highway Patrol officers had been butchered on an off-ramp of Highway 95 had hit the major outlets, every law enforcement officer in the region was looking for the perpetrators. Everybody was on edge. The slain officers were fathers, mothers, sisters, and brothers. They were pillars of their communities who had paid the ultimate price. Their brother cops wouldn't hesitate to break a few bones to get to those who had killed so many of their own. They didn't know the culprits were long gone, out of their reach.

But not from my reach, Hunt thought.

I'm gonna mess that fucking bitch up, he added, thinking about the Black Tosca. With only twelve hours left to the Black Tosca's original deadline for Tony to deliver his own severed head, Hunt was anxious to hear back from Simon Carter. He checked his watch for the fifth time in ten minutes. Since Carter's connecting flight from Houston to

Querétaro, Mexico, was on time—Hunt had checked via the United Airlines application—he would land in about two hours. Upon landing, he would be met by DEA special agents, men who didn't mind risking their careers to help Hunt. They wouldn't participate in the actual takedown, but they would take care of all the logistics. They would provide Hunt and his team the necessary weapons and transportation options. They all knew Hunt could never repay them. What they also knew, though, was that if the roles were reversed, Hunt would be there for them.

Simon Carter was Hunt's reconnaissance element. There was no point in Hunt and Egan traveling all the way to Mexico only to find out that Leila and Sophia weren't there. Carter's mission was twofold. First, he was to confirm Leila and Sophia's position or, at the very least, verify that Hector was there. Second, he needed to scout a location from where they could establish their base of operations.

In the meantime, Hunt wanted updates from Daniel McMaster regarding the bystander he had accidentally shot during yesterday's ambush—the cause of the warrant for his arrest.

"You have a phone I can use?" he asked Anna.

She got up from the sofa and disappeared from the living room. Tasis, though, was still there, standing in a corner and looking pissed off as usual.

Egan leaned toward Hunt. "Thanks for keeping my involvement with you-know-who between us," he said, his voice low.

The truce Hunt had forged with the Garcia crime family was fragile. If Tasis, Anna, or any members of their family learned that Egan was a contractor for the Black Tosca, he'd never live to see another day. Thoughts of the Black Tosca reminded Hunt that if he couldn't find his daughter within the next—he checked his watch again—eleven hours and thirty-two minutes, Leila would be burned alive, her execution live streamed.

This is your fault, Vicente Garcia, you piece of shit. What were you thinking, burning a man in front of his young daughter? Now it's your own granddaughter and my Leila who'll pay the price for your stupidity.

"Hey, Pierce, you okay?"

Hunt looked up. Anna was inserting a SIM card into a prepaid cell phone. She handed him the phone. He mumbled his thanks and walked out to the terrace to place his call.

McMaster didn't pick up, so Hunt left a quick voice mail letting him know he'd call again in exactly five minutes. When he turned around, Tasis was there, his jaw locked so tight that Hunt could see a muscle twitching.

"What do you want?" Hunt asked him.

"What can I do to help?"

Hunt cocked his head. *This is unexpected.* "I thought you wanted to kill me?"

"A part of me still does. Your betrayal is my failure, I told you."

"But?"

"Anna said you tried to save Tony's life, so I'll ask again: Can I help?"

There was no way Hunt would let Tasis travel with him and Egan to Mexico to meet with Carter. As loyal and ruthless as Tasis was, he wasn't a trained operator. He had no idea how to work within a team or employ the unconventional tactics used during a hostage rescue operation. Still, he could be useful here in Florida. But first, Hunt had a question for him.

"What was Tony talking about earlier? Anna's issue. What is it?"

Tasis looked at the floor. "It's not my place—"

"Don't fuck with me, Mauricio."

Tasis crossed his arms with a heavy sigh. "She killed a man," he said, then quickly added, "but it was legitimate self-defense."

Hunt ought to have been surprised, but he wasn't. He couldn't say why, but deep down he had known, or at least suspected. Something in her demeanor, maybe?

"In Miami," Hunt said, remembering how shaken she'd been when she had picked him up in the Cherokee.

"That's right. A man attacked her. She killed him."

Hunt felt terrible for Anna. Killing someone—self-defense or not—placed a black mark on one's soul. He didn't know when it would come, but down the road she'd need someone to talk to. He would be there for her.

"You know where my daughter lives?" Hunt asked, changing the subject.

"Chris Moon's residence, yes?"

"If our op in Mexico fails, they'll come for my ex-wife. She's Moon's wife now, but she's Leila's mother, and I still care for her."

"I don't think you'll fail, Mr. Hunt, but if you do, I'll make sure she's safe."

Hunt kept his mouth shut but offered a slight nod.

Tasis turned around and headed back inside the house. It was time to call McMaster again. This time the DEA man answered right away.

"Is that you, Pierce?"

"I'm calling to check on the bystander I shot. Last time we talked, he was in surgery. Tell me he's okay."

"He's okay. Last I heard, they were about to release him. He'll be fine, but that doesn't mean he won't sue. And there's the warrant."

The innocent victim he'd hit with a bullet was safe, and that was all Hunt cared about. He'd deal with the potential lawsuit and warrant later. McMaster wasn't about to rat him out to the local cops. He knew what was at stake.

"Thanks for letting me know, sir."

McMaster changed the subject, and his voice grew cold—almost stern. "Is Cole with you?"

"He's close by, yes."

"What's his role in this, Pierce?"

"I think it would be better if you—"

"He's my daughter's husband, damn it! He's with the CIA, isn't he?"

The CIA? Cole? That was ridiculous. The CIA wouldn't touch Cole Egan with a ten-foot pole. Hunt was about to ask McMaster what kind of weed he smoked but thought better of it. Maybe it wasn't such a bad idea to play the CIA card. Those guys were involved in a lot of shit overseas. If Egan wanted to keep his family—and stay out of jail—hinting that he was CIA wasn't a bad idea, at least for the short term. He'd have a chat with Egan about it.

"As I suggested earlier, I really think you guys should have a serious man-to-man talk, you know?" Hunt replied, staying vague.

"I fucking knew it!" McMaster exclaimed. "I knew it. A goddamn spook! Did you know, Hunt, that he called me in the middle of the night to ask me to either relocate my daughter or, at the very least, to send a security team to her house?"

Of course I know. I was with him.

"I had no idea, sir."

"Why can't the CIA protect their own? You'd think they'd have special teams for that, wouldn't you?"

"I don't know their procedures."

"Where are you headed next?"

"Not sure yet," Hunt said, still keeping things vague.

"Well, let me know if you need anything," McMaster replied, his tone indicating he understood Hunt's reticence about sharing more information. "And, Pierce, please tell Cole I'll make sure Katherine's safe."

CHAPTER FIFTY-FOUR

San Miguel de Allende, Mexico

The Black Tosca's close circle of advisors was once again reunited in her lavish dining room. The only senior member missing was her cousin Hector, so there were four instead of the usual five. The men seated around the dining room table were getting jumpy. It wasn't a secret that Hector's operation on American soil hadn't been the complete success they were hoping for. The Black Tosca wanted to reassure them, to let them know that everything was under control. There was no reason to expect any blowback from the local authorities—most of them were in the cartel's pocket—or the Mexican government. As for the United States government, it would never dare an incursion deep into Mexico, especially an urban area like San Miguel de Allende.

"Why didn't Hector eliminate the girls in Miami? Is there really a need to go through all of this here?"

As a businesswoman, Valentina Mieles understood her advisor's concerns. The man—a fifty-year-old accountant—was a math genius and an essential element of her organization. But he wasn't a risk-taker. This was something she had long ago accepted, but what she couldn't tolerate was his tone. Defiant. Insubordinate. She'd give him one chance to retract.

"What are you afraid of? Tell me. I'm curious."

All eyes turned toward his end of the table. They all knew she didn't care for subordinates questioning her judgment, and even less so in front of the group. He swallowed hard before he looked at her again, his face flushed. He had definitely caught her drift.

"With all due respect, Valentina, and I apologize if I sounded impertinent—believe me, it wasn't my intention—what I wanted to say was that this end of the operation won't generate any revenue for you and that, perhaps, this could have been dealt with differently."

He was right, of course. It would have indeed been preferable if the whole operation could have been carried out in the United States, but a series of unfortunate events had forced Hector's hand. She'd never heard of Pierce Hunt before, and, to be honest, she was surprised that one man could have caused Hector to change his plans. Even Mr. Granger had failed to check in with a progress report, something that had never happened before. Mr. Granger was a valuable asset; his access to Daniel McMaster was priceless. This access would become extremely helpful to her organization once Tony Garcia and his top lieutenants had been taken care of.

Mr. Granger better be alive, she thought. Nicolás was good, but he wasn't Cole Egan.

Nevertheless, she wanted to see this through. For once, she wasn't propelled by greed but by vengeance. Her taste for revenge wouldn't be satiated until she heard the screams of agony from Tony Garcia's daughter. Only then would her mind allow her to think of something else. She let the silence stretch out a few more seconds, taking pleasure in seeing her accountant sweat bullets. She considered different possibilities and options. That was why she was so good and the one standing at the head of the table. Her ability to seize an opportunity in a chaotic situation and to adapt quicker than anyone else to a changing environment was her key to remaining in power.

She narrowed her eyes on the accountant, but she spoke to everyone.

"I understand your concerns, gentlemen, but you know as well as I do that to succeed in our business, we need to constantly revise our business plan. Taking over the Garcia family's distribution network will allow us to move a lot more product, and the cost associated with its distribution will drop significantly. I've been communicating very closely with our major trading partners, and I've assured them that we'll be operational within the next thirty days."

"What if Tony Garcia doesn't surrender?" one of her deputies asked. "His men are very loyal to him."

"I'm well aware of their loyalty to him," she hissed, but she continued more calmly, "Tony Garcia's world is crumbling around him. Within the last thirty-six hours, we killed his father and kidnapped his daughter. He also managed to get shot by one of our men on the ground."

The Black Tosca gazed at the four stunned, silent faces around the table. They were all looking at her, wide-eyed, waiting for her to continue.

"He's straddling the threshold between life and death, I'm told."

A few smiles appeared on the men's faces. One of them said, "So even if he doesn't chop his head off, we'll get him in prison."

The Black Tosca nodded. "Inside the system, he won't have the kind of protection he's accustomed to on the outside. He'll be an easy mark."

"So why's Hector bringing the girls here? I was under the impression that the kidnapping was to bring Tony Garcia to his knees."

"Let's just say that there's another, more personal reason too," she said, almost shaking in anticipation.

"Will they be here soon?" the accountant asked, cleaning his glasses with a tissue.

"Oh, they're already here."

CHAPTER FIFTY-FIVE

San Miguel de Allende, Mexico

The last leg of his flight had been uneventful, just like the first one. Upon landing, he cleared Mexican customs under the fictitious name of Terry Lewis—an alias the DEA had prepared for him in case he ever needed to be deployed to Mexico quickly. He exited the terminal and looked for someone holding a sign with his fake name on it. Two dozen taxi drivers were standing around with names on signs. He spotted a tall, dark man with a mustache and slender build holding a sign with the right name on it. The man fit the description Hunt had given him. Carter hoisted his only bag more securely on his shoulder and walked toward the man. They made eye contact, and Carter followed the man at a distance. The man walked silently but briskly through the terminal to the arrivals curb. He hopped into the passenger seat of a waiting late-model Toyota Land Cruiser. Carter climbed into the back seat, and the SUV rolled forward. The driver was an attractive Latina woman with long, dark brown hair that fell to her shoulders.

"Welcome to Mexico, Simon," she said, her big green eyes looking at him in the rearview mirror. "I'm Abigail. This is my husband, Dante."

"You guys are really married, or it's a cover?" Never before had he met a pair of DEA special agents who were married and posted together outside the United States.

"Let's just say that we work and sleep together."

Carter chuckled. "Got it."

"There's a cooler behind your seat with a couple of sandwiches and a bottle of water," Dante told him.

"Thanks," Carter said, opening the cooler. "I appreciate you picking me up."

"Our pleasure. Hunt told us what this is about. We'll do our best to help."

"How do you know Pierce?" Carter asked, grabbing a sandwich and the water bottle.

"I flew helicopters in Iraq," Dante said. "We crossed paths a few times."

"If he's asking you to risk your career for him, I'm sure it was more than a few times."

"No, not really. But I guess it's what he did on one of those times that matters, isn't it?"

"Pierce saved Dante's life," Abigail said. "That's why we're both willing to risk anything for him."

Carter didn't want to push for more information since it wasn't his business, but Dante was quite forthcoming.

"My Black Hawk was shot down over Latifiya," Dante explained. "It's a small town south of Baghdad. It's dominated by native Sunni Arabs and was one of the hottest spots for our troops between 2003 and 2007. The Iraqi army couldn't get a grip on the insurgents, so Hunt and a bunch of Rangers were sent in to help them. I was bringing in fresh troops to the zone when my chopper was hit broadside. I did a controlled crash landing—"

"I didn't know such a thing existed," Carter said, biting into the ham-and-swiss sandwich.

"What?"

"A controlled crash landing."

"You wanna know the story or not?" Dante asked, but he was smiling.

"I'm sorry. Please continue," Carter said, twisting the cap off his water bottle.

"Hunt saw the chopper go down and, with six other Rangers, left his covered position and charged five hundred feet across open ground to provide suppressive fire."

That sounds like Pierce, Carter thought. *Crazy motherfucker.*

"I'm glad you made it," Carter said. "Pierce is a good man."

"The best. I'm in his debt, and this little op of ours, it won't even cover the interest."

"I hear you," Carter replied.

"It sucks what happened to his daughter. That's not right, man. Will they really set his daughter on fire? On live video?"

"Not if I can help it."

They drove the next fifteen minutes in silence, staring out their respective windows and considering what could happen to Leila if they failed.

"So what's the plan?"

"Since this morning, Abigail and I are officially on leave. We don't have to report our whereabouts for the next thirty-six hours."

"One way or the other, this will all be over in less than twelve," Carter told them.

"We got a two-bedroom apartment in Centro," Abigail said. "We created an Airbnb account using one of our aliases. We booked it for a week."

"Centro is the old town?"

"Yes, and a UNESCO World Heritage site. Narrow streets lined with homes in different shades of yellow, red, orange, and brown terracotta. All very pretty, but that isn't why we put you there."

"Because of the expats?"

"You got it," Dante said. "About ten percent of the seventy thousand residents are expats. You'll blend right in."

"What about the list of items Pierce sent you?"

"That was a bit trickier, I'm afraid," Dante admitted. "Since Pierce wanted to keep this black, we couldn't access the armory. Nevertheless, in addition to our own personal firearms, we were able to secure three Glock 22s, and three silenced MP5s with enough ammunition to kill half the population of San Miguel."

"Body armor?"

"Yes, we got that too. Light body armor only, though. But we got the Ops-Core FAST helmets and NODs you asked for. We had to buy the Nikon, the binoculars, and all the other electronic items Pierce wanted."

"Transportation?" Carter asked, taking notes.

"We rented a compact SUV through Hertz and used the same IDs we used to reserve the apartment on Airbnb. The Land Cruiser is ours to use too."

"Do you have any info regarding the Black Tosca's mansion?"

Abigail shook her head but kept her mouth shut. Dante ran his fingers through his hair.

"What is it?"

"We don't know much," Dante confessed. "A couple of agents tried to fly a drone over the mansion a few months ago, but it got shut down."

"How the hell do you shut down a small drone?" Carter asked.

"There are devices that detect drones using radio frequency methodology. It's effective up to about twenty-five hundred feet. And it's quite difficult to circumvent. The most expensive systems—which I'm sure the Black Tosca has—automatically detect and disable incoming drones."

"So where does that leave us?" Carter asked.

"We have a few shots that were taken by a satellite a few years back, but they won't be of much value. Having said that, the Mexico City office arrested a midlevel member of the Black Tosca's cartel three weeks ago."

"I doubt he said anything of importance. These guys prefer to do time rather than talk to us."

"You never worked in Mexico, did you?" Abigail asked.

Carter narrowed his eyes, wondering what she meant.

Dante jumped in and said, "We do things differently here, Simon. Our methods are, let's say, a little more invasive than they'd be back in the States. You know what I mean?"

Carter knew what *invasive* meant. Whatever intelligence the DEA got from the cartel member, they wouldn't be able to use it in a court of law.

"Okay, so he talked to you. Anything I should know?"

Dante handed Carter a file containing the satellite pictures and drawings of the perimeter surrounding the residence.

"He said that the grounds of the residence were patrolled twenty-four hours a day by half a dozen heavily armed guards, and that wasn't counting the two at the guardhouse outside the main gate."

Six guards. That wasn't a good start. That was a lot of enemy personnel.

Dante continued, "He also said that security cameras were set up strategically around the property with infrared motion detectors."

Shit! What did you expect, Simon? You knew Valentina Mieles would be a hard target to get to. That didn't change the fact that it would be almost impossible to breach the perimeter during broad daylight.

"Tell him about Nicolás," Abigail said.

"Who's Nicolás?"

"Nicolás is her lead bodyguard."

That was good to know. "What's his background?"

"Since we don't have a last name for him, we're not sure."

"But you did find something?"

"It's only a guess—"

"Ah, c'mon, Dante, it's more than a guess. He fits the physical description that was given to us."

"Anyway," Dante continued, ignoring his wife, "I wouldn't put too much thought into this if I were you, but there's a Nicolás Gomez born in 1981 who was dishonorably discharged from the *Fuerzas Especiales* for leaking intelligence to a known drug cartel associate."

"The Mexican navy special forces?"

"Yes. Supposedly they're a tier-one unit, but I doubt they really are."

"Still, he's someone we'll need to be careful about."

Carter ran his hands over his face. His three-day beard was beginning to itch. "How many road access points are there?"

"That's the good news," Abigail said, stopping the Land Cruiser to let an old woman cross the street with her dog. "There's only one."

Carter was still studying the satellite pictures when they reached the Airbnb rental twenty minutes later. The rental was a small but charming three-story house.

"We'll drop you off here," Abigail said. "You'll find everything you need on the kitchen table. It's apartment number one, and the code to unlock the door is four-nine-two-three-four."

"You're not coming in?"

"We each have our own place," Dante said, tossing a mobile phone to Carter, "so if one of us gets caught, the whole thing won't collapse."

"Check your gear, take what you need, and we'll link up in thirty minutes," Abigail said, unlocking the doors. "Dante's number is the first contact. I'm the second, and the Guadalajara DEA office is the third one."

Carter climbed out of the Land Cruiser and watched the SUV as it smoothly accelerated away before coming to a stop at an intersection packed with shoppers, commuters, and tourists. Carter stretched and arched his back a few times to loosen up before he made his way to the rental unit. He punched in the five-digit code Abigail had given him, and the door unlocked. He opened it and slid inside.

The place wasn't big, but it was clean. Carter used the toilet, washed his hands in the sink, and brushed his teeth before he headed to the tiny dining room, where he found a set of car keys and a handwritten note telling him where the vehicle was. He carried the keys with him to the bedroom. On the bed were three medium-size Pelican cases and two duffel bags.

Carter spent the next twenty minutes checking the equipment, loading the weapons, and making sure the NODs had new batteries. Exactly thirty minutes after he was dropped off, Carter called Dante.

"Everything was to your satisfaction?" Dante asked.

Carter, a perfectionist, and exceptionally so when it came to marksmanship, wished he could have test-fired the Glocks and the MP5s, but he had no choice in the matter. "Everything's fine."

"How do you want to play it?"

"Our only objective is to confirm that Leila and Sophia are here."

"What about Hector Mieles?"

"I think it's fair to assume that if Hector's here, the girls are here too, agreed?"

"Makes sense."

"So I'll head in the direction of the Black Tosca's residence and drive around once. I'll call you back once I'm done, and, depending on my findings, I'll let you know what we'll do."

———

Carter brought the powerful binoculars to his eyes and focused on the Black Tosca's residence half a mile away. The house—one of the biggest Carter had ever seen—was a custom-built fortress. It had the style of a Spanish colonial home and was perched high on a hilltop with spectacular views of the Sierra Madre mountains and the rolling countryside.

Carter wondered if the citizens of San Miguel de Allende knew—or cared—about the high number of criminal organizations whose bosses had elected to reside in the city *Condé Nast Traveler* magazine had named the best in the world. Carter had to admit that the small city exuded so much charm, history, and beauty that even though he was tracking the man who'd kidnapped Hunt's daughter, he couldn't help feeling he had been transported to another dimension. Towering churches, sunset-colored houses, and charming cobblestone streets added an indescribable something Carter would be hard pressed to explain to the guys back in Stafford. But he wasn't here to relax, explore, or see the sights. His initial reconnaissance showed him a couple of good spots from where he had good views of the front gate and the east side of the third floor of the house. The tall walls surrounding the property and its sheer elevation from the street hindered Carter's ability to see anything below the third floor.

He had been in his position for a little more than two hours when a pair of white Range Rovers came out the front gate at the end of the long asphalt driveway leading up to the Black Tosca's residence. The side windows of both Range Rovers were heavily tinted, and the sunlight glinted off the windshield, but Carter, his eyes glued to his binoculars, was able to confirm that there were at least two occupants per vehicle. He quickly exchanged the binoculars for his Nikon P900 camera. Both Range Rovers made a right turn and accelerated toward his location. Carter brought the camera to his eye and snapped eight pictures. The vehicles were still a quarter of a mile away when Carter crouched behind the steering wheel and got as low as he could, his right hand drifting toward the passenger seat where his Glock 22 was hidden under a local guidebook. Not that the Glock would make much difference in a shoot-out with Hector's men. In about fifteen seconds, he'd know if he'd been seen. He started to count in his head. At the count of seventeen, the Range Rovers drove slowly past his position. If they were going to hit him, it was going to happen right about now. Carter's grip tensed around the Glock. He held his breath and strained his ears for a full minute and listened for signs of trouble. Nothing.

He risked a look in his side mirror. The Range Rovers were stopped at a red light five or six hundred feet behind his SUV.

That was close, Carter thought. He chuckled to himself, mostly from relief.

Carter looked at the Nikon's display to analyze the pictures. The first five showed the first Range Rover and its occupants: two Latino males whose faces Carter didn't recognize. The last three photos, though, made his heart jolt. With a lump in his throat, Carter dialed the number Hunt had given him.

"It's me," Carter said once he had his friend on the line.

"What did you learn?"

"Hector Mieles is in San Miguel, Pierce. Get your ass over here."

CHAPTER FIFTY-SIX

Miami, Florida

It took Hunt less than fifteen minutes to get to Jasmine's house from Tony Garcia's house. He rang the doorbell twice. Jasmine opened the door wearing only a light-blue terry cloth robe with a matching towel on her head. She looked tired, worn out. The lines on her face were too pronounced for someone her age. Her eyes, which had been so vibrant in the past, were now dull. He wondered if his eyes looked the same way. Clearly, Leila's kidnapping had hit his ex-wife very hard. Jasmine probably thought he was bearing bad news because her legs buckled, and before Hunt could catch her, she collapsed to her knees. Hunt knelt next to her.

"I think Leila's still alive," he said into her ear. "But I need Chris's help."

She shook her head in what Hunt could only assume was disbelief.

"Oh my God," she managed to say. "I . . . I thought you were here because—"

"Not at all, but I need to hurry up. Can we talk inside?"

Jasmine nodded, and Hunt helped her up.

Chris was jogging down the hallway. "You okay, Jasmine?"

Jasmine removed the towel she had on her head and used it to wipe her tears away. "Pierce thinks Leila's alive."

Hunt saw a look of genuine relief wash over Moon's face. The quarterback actually closed his eyes and crossed himself.

"Where is she?" he asked.

"In Mexico."

"Mexico? What's she doing in Mexico? How did she get there? How—" Jasmine unleashed, but Hunt interrupted her.

"Valid questions, all of them. And I promise I'll explain everything, but not now. Okay?"

"Is there anything I can do?" Moon asked. "I told you before, Pierce, I know I'm not her dad, but I love her very much."

Hunt placed a hand on Moon's shoulder and squeezed gently. "I know, and that's why I'm here."

"Shoot. What do you need?"

"I need you to charter a jet for me."

Moon didn't even blink at the request. "When do you want to fly, and where do you want to go?"

"I'm needed in San Miguel de Allende," Hunt said. "It's a small town—"

"I know exactly where it is. Jasmine and I spent a long weekend there last year."

"You think Leila's in San Miguel?" Jasmine asked.

"I do," he replied. "And I need to go now."

Moon was typing furiously on his smartphone. He said, "We can leave from Miami International in fifty minutes or from Fort Lauderdale in ninety. What do you prefer?"

"The sooner the better, Chris, but what did you mean by 'we'?"

"I'm coming with you. And since I'm paying, my request isn't negotiable."

"Count me in too," Jasmine said.

"No!" Hunt and Moon shouted at the same time. "Listen, Jasmine," Hunt said, taking one of her hands in both of his. "If anything happens to me downrange, I want our daughter to have a mother. I know it sounds clichéd, but it's too dangerous. Trust me on this."

Jasmine sighed but nodded reluctantly. "Be careful. Both of you."

CHAPTER FIFTY-SEVEN

Del Bajío Airport, Guanajuato, Mexico

Hunt caught up on his sleep while Egan and Moon talked football. Anna spent the whole flight studying the intelligence Carter and the two other DEA special agents had sent their way prior to takeoff. Due to favorable winds and their request that the pilot push the throttles a touch more than usual, the flight to Del Bajío airport took just over three hours.

The plane landed smoothly on the runway, and the engines roared in reverse to slow it down. They taxied to the private aviation hangar, where Dante stood next to his Land Cruiser, talking to an immigration officer. Through his window, Hunt saw the men shake hands. A moment later, the immigration officer disappeared inside his four-door sedan and drove away.

Hunt unbuckled his seat belt and sat in the empty seat next to Moon.

"I'll call you every hour on the dot to let you know we're okay," Hunt told him. "If I miss a timing, I'll call ten minutes past the hour. If I miss that too, I'll call at the half hour. If you haven't heard from me or Cole by then, I want you and Anna to return to Miami and call this man."

Hunt gave him McMaster's business card. Moon frowned as he read the name. "Isn't he your father-in-law?" he asked, his eyes on Egan.

"Yep," Egan confirmed with a smile.

Hunt wondered how much of his personal life Egan had shared with Moon. Not that it was any of his business. Anna was seated behind him, and Hunt felt her gaze burning into his back. He stood up to face her.

"I know this isn't what you wanted, Anna, but I'd appreciate you staying in the plane."

"If it's what you need," she replied without much enthusiasm. Then she added, her voice a shade warmer than usual, "Be careful, okay?"

"Okay."

"I mean this."

"Okay," he repeated, unsure of her meaning. "I will."

"Go get our girls, Pierce," Anna said, touching him gently on the arm. "I'm counting on you."

He took a deep breath and remained silent. He had so much on his mind, but he had a hard time staying indifferent and calm when Anna's simple touch sent his heart into overdrive and his blood pounding in his ears. Hunt realized right there and then that he still wanted her. Would she want him, though? Would she take him back despite everything that had happened between them? Despite everything she'd endured because of him? Would she forget the emotional pain he'd caused her? The betrayal?

And don't forget, Pierce, you're a DEA agent, Hunt reminded himself. And wouldn't he be betraying his brother's memory by being with Anna? It was *her* kind of people who had killed Jake. But before he could dwell on that further, he needed to get his daughter and Sophia back. That was what he needed to focus on. Nothing else.

So shut this useless internal debate off, Hunt thought.

"I'll bring them back," he assured her. She gave him a quick hug and then took a step back.

Hunt told her, "Remember that if the shit hits the fan, you'll be our last line of defense. We're counting on you too."

Anna's job was to take care of the logistics in case they had to ditch the plane. Hunt had asked her to reserve rental cars and to find accommodation between San Miguel de Allende and Mexico City. She was also to book numerous flights from Mexico City to Miami and Fort Lauderdale.

"Ready?" Hunt asked Egan.

"I've been standing here for the last three minutes, haven't I?"

———

Dante met him outside the vehicle. Dante offered his hand, but Hunt embraced him instead.

"Thanks for everything, Dante."

"Don't thank me yet. We still have plenty to do."

Hunt nodded and introduced Egan to Dante. "Cole and I served together in the Seventy-Fifth," he said, then added for Egan's benefit, "Dante was a Black Hawk pilot in the army. A real pro."

Egan and Dante shook hands. "A real pleasure, Dante. I've always been jealous of anyone who can fly."

Dante laughed out loud. "Weird. I'm jealous of anyone who can shoot straight."

They all climbed into the Land Cruiser with Dante behind the wheel and Hunt in the passenger seat. In the back, Egan had already found the cooler with the Gatorade. He passed a bottle to Hunt, who drank half of it down before he took a breath.

"Thirsty?" Dante asked.

"Nervous."

For the next forty minutes, Dante went over the intelligence they had gathered so far and the equipment they had available. Finally, they brainstormed ideas about how to gain access to the Black Tosca's residence.

"We haven't come up with anything solid yet, Pierce," Dante confessed. "Her defense is airtight. With four shooters and Abigail in reserve, I wasn't able to figure out a way to get in, rescue your daughter and her friend, and make a clean exit."

"Can't you guys call the DEA offices in Guadalajara and Mexico City and ask for support?"

"Not happening," Dante said. "Too many hoops to jump through. Too many regulations."

"What if we forced her to come out instead?" Hunt offered.

"How?" Egan asked. "She has her own water supply, two or three power generators, and probably enough food and wine to last a year. I'm pretty sure she also has tunnels under her residence that lead to different houses in the neighborhood."

"Cole's right, Pierce. She'd never come out through the front gate."

"Then we'll have to figure out something else, and fast."

CHAPTER FIFTY-EIGHT

San Miguel de Allende, Mexico

They arrived at the Airbnb apartment rental five minutes later.

Dante showed him where the weapons were. Hunt selected one of the MP5s and a Glock 22 with a silencer. From a duffel bag, he picked two flashbangs, a hip holster for the Glock, and seven magazines of ammunition—five for the MP5 and two for the Glock. Dante handed him a bulletproof vest from another duffel bag. Hunt adjusted it so that it wouldn't interfere with the rest of his equipment.

He picked up the magazines and placed them into the magazine pouches on his stomach. To expedite any magazine changes, he inserted the magazines with the bullets down and facing to the right. He checked the MP5 to make sure the weapon was clear and did the same with the Glock. Hunt inserted a magazine into the pistol and pulled the slide back, allowing the first bullet to feed into the chamber. He then released the magazine, holstered his pistol, and inserted another round into the magazine to top it off. He pulled the Glock out from its holster once again and reinserted the full magazine before holstering the pistol. He followed pretty much the same routine with the MP5, his hands working fast and expertly.

To clear his head, Hunt took a deep breath and then slowly exhaled. He repeated the process three times.

Hunt was in his element. He was ready.

Then Carter called. Leila was on the move.

———

The time to move cautiously had passed. They needed to speed things up. Hunt's conversation with Carter had been short but to the point. Abigail, who had taken Carter's position close to the front gate, had spotted the same two white Range Rovers that Carter had seen earlier in the day. Using her own Nikon, she was able to get two good shots of the inside of the first SUV. She had sent the pictures to Carter, who had immediately confirmed that the girl seated in the second row of the SUV was Leila. No word on Sophia, though, so that complicated things. Hunt had hoped that the two girls would still be together. That would have allowed them to maximize their efficiency by not having to split up.

Hunt had just placed his hourly call to Moon when Carter phoned him.

"Where are you?" Carter asked.

"We're leaving Centro now. What's up?"

"Abigail and I followed the two Range Rovers to a neighborhood called Candelaria. You need me to spell it?"

"Negative, Simon. I know where it is," jumped in Dante, making a U-turn. "We're less than ten minutes away."

Carter gave them the address. "Hurry up. I have a feeling we might have a play here."

———

Carter and Abigail had no choice but to give the Range Rovers considerable leeway in order not to be spotted. The fact that Abigail and Carter each had their own vehicle was great, but they really needed six cars to

271

pull off this kind of surveillance operation. That wasn't going to happen, so they had to tread carefully.

The neighborhood of Candelaria consisted of very large and very private estates. There wasn't a lot of traffic, so Carter had to play it safe. The last thing he wanted was to spook Hector. Carter had allowed four cars to pull in front of him as a buffer between his vehicle and the last Range Rover. Abigail hung back two cars behind. Up ahead, the Range Rovers made a right turn into private property.

Carter called Abigail to let her know.

"I'm not turning into the driveway," Carter told her. "I'll try to get an address and see what we can find out."

As he drove by, Carter marked the address on his GPS. The house was a big bungalow—at least eight or nine thousand square feet by Carter's estimate—and the owner had set it back far enough from the road to not be disturbed by passing cars but close enough to flaunt his wealth. Keeping one hand on the steering wheel, Carter texted the address to Hunt.

His phone vibrated in his hand. It was Abigail.

"I'll pull over at the next intersection and run the address against our database," she said. "I'll let you know what I learn, if anything."

"I'll find a spot from where I can keep my eyes on target."

He made a left at the next intersection and twisted in his seat to see if he still had a visual on the house. He didn't. If he couldn't see the house, they couldn't see him either. He stopped on the narrow gravel shoulder and turned off the engine. He climbed out of his compact SUV and opened the trunk, from which he removed a DJI Matrice 100 quadcopter drone. Since the drone was made of waterproof aluminum and plastic, its weight—without the camera—was only slightly over six pounds, which made it incredibly light and easy to carry around. But what really sold this unit to Carter was that it could be controlled from a distance of one and a half miles without a problem. It was the same model he had used on many occasions with the RRT.

Within thirty seconds, the drone was in the air. Carter reacquainted himself with the controls by circling the drone a couple of times overhead. Two minutes later, the drone was hovering a quarter mile away from the Range Rovers at an altitude of one hundred feet. Carter zoomed in on the house just in time to see Leila being carried inside by Hector Mieles.

CHAPTER FIFTY-NINE

San Miguel de Allende, Mexico

Hector popped a couple of Dexedrine capsules in his mouth and washed them down with four huge gulps of water. As his adrenaline rush from all the events of the past thirty-six hours finally crashed, Hector realized he was seriously tired. He was running on empty. His age, even though he had just touched forty, and the years of abuse he had subjected his body to since his days in the army were taking their toll. He still had a few good years in front of him, but at some point he would have to stop.

But to do what? He had always been a soldier. He would die a soldier. He had known that all his adult life. At first he had thought it would be for his country, but when Valentina had called for him, he hadn't had the heart to turn her down. Not after what had happened to her father.

Sometimes he wondered if she'd be the Black Tosca if it weren't for his help. Not that he was jealous or wanted to take her place; on the contrary, he had absolutely no desire to become the face of the cartel.

"We're almost there, Hector," his driver told him.

"I know. It's not my first time here," Hector snapped back.

Óliver Sáez, the man they were about to meet, was one of the richest men in San Miguel de Allende. Through grit and shrewdness, the real estate agent turned real estate developer had become a man of wealth and influence. He was also an importer—and sometimes provider—of everything that was forbidden by Mexican law. One of these forbidden things was the trafficking of clean, white, underage virgin girls. During an international online auction, a pretty American like Leila could easily fetch a quarter of a million dollars.

Hector grunted at the thought. Sáez appalled him; the man embodied everything Hector hated. Sáez was a disloyal, dishonest, lying son of a bitch. Hector had even considered killing the man not so long ago. But today, he was glad Sáez was alive. In fact, without him, Hector was convinced that Valentina would burn Leila too.

Upon his arrival in San Miguel, his cousin had given him a thorough tongue-lashing. She was furious that he had taken the initiative to bring the girls to Mexico without consulting with her first.

"It was either that or killing them both in Florida. A single bullet to the head, not that crazy shit you have in mind," he had told her.

"You mean the crazy shit her grandfather did to me?"

"And I killed the son of a bitch for you, Valentina. I lost good men doing so, not counting Chief Inspector Zorita," he had reminded her.

"I've made my decision, Hector. You won't change my mind."

"It could bring us all down," Hector had pleaded with her. "Leila's father is a DEA special agent named Pierce Hunt. Do you really think the Americans won't hit us back if we live stream the death of his teenage daughter? And you want to burn her alive? Hunt's also a veteran, and the Americans worship their veterans. I'm telling you, Cousin, the pressure the public will put on their elected officials to do something will be such that they'll have no choice but to come after us."

"They'll never succeed. They've tried before. I'm still here. And that Pierce Hunt . . . I thought Mr. Granger was supposed to take care of him?"

"I haven't heard back from him. So perhaps Hunt's dead. Who knows? But we have to consider the possibility that it is Mr. Granger who's six feet under."

"That would be a shame."

"Listen to me, Valentina. The only reason we're still alive and able to operate our business is because the Americans are playing within the set of rules they imposed upon themselves. Kill that girl by burning her on the world stage for everyone to watch, and I can guarantee they'll scorch the rule book. Next thing you know, one of their Predators will fire a couple of Hellfire missiles and—"

"They don't have the guts!"

"Two years ago I would have agreed with you. But now? With this president? I think he's just looking for a reason to give the order to shoot."

In the end, he had won his point. The Black Tosca had agreed to sell Leila to Sáez for $100,000. It was much lower than she'd get for her on the open market, but at least she wouldn't have to incur the Americans' wrath.

Sáez lived in a large house in Candelaria, the most exclusive countryside development in San Miguel and only five minutes from the center of the city. Bordered by beautiful and mature trees, Sáez's house had splendid views of the Picacho Mountains. As Hector's driver turned into the long driveway leading to Sáez's estate, the sun began to set behind the large house.

In the rear of the SUV, Leila gave a small whimper. Hector turned in his seat and looked at her. She had promised to behave, so he had removed the zip ties around her ankles and cuffed her hands in front of her instead of behind her back. There was no duct tape on her mouth either.

She was crying, tears streaming down her face. He handed her a tissue, and she used it to wipe her tears and blow her nose.

I saved your life, Hector thought. *Now I'm wondering if I shouldn't just put a bullet in your head to save you from the misery that's about to come.*

———

"Where are you taking me?" Leila asked, hating the way her voice betrayed her fear.

Hector didn't respond. Usually arrogant and self-assured, he now looked confused, and she didn't know why. It made her anxious. As much as she abhorred him, something about Hector made her feel safe. How twisted was that? *He's the one who kidnapped me and almost knocked me out, but with him I feel safe?*

Through the front windshield of the Range Rover, she saw that the driveway split into a circular loop outside the steps of the large wooden front door. A panoply of luxury cars was parked around the loop.

"Where are we?" she asked Hector, but he once again failed to reply. Instead, he hopped out of the SUV and climbed the six steps leading to the front door. He rang the front bell, and a moment later, a man greeted him. He offered his hand to Hector, but Hector slapped it away. The man seemed offended, and he looked long and hard at Hector, who stood his ground. The whole situation was driving her crazy. She couldn't shake the tingling feeling that something very wrong was about to happen to her. Her body began to shiver—out of fear, surely. Just a few short days ago, she had been safe and happy and eating pizza with her dad. Now, here she was, trembling like a leaf, hungry, and scared out of her wits.

Hector walked back to the Range Rover and opened the door for her.

"Follow me," he said, his face completely devoid of any expression.

Leila lifted her chin slightly and said, her voice quavering, "No. I'm not going anywhere."

He seized her arm and started pulling her out of the Range Rover. She wrenched her arm out of his grasp and tried to grab on to the headrest in front of her to keep from being dragged out of the SUV, but Hector was too strong. Her hands slipped on the smooth leather, and he roughly tugged her out of the vehicle. The moment her feet hit the ground, she screamed and kicked out at him before she lunged, her tied hands in front of her, aiming for his already injured ear. He easily sidestepped to his right, and she landed face-first on the asphalt. He picked her up effortlessly and, without another word, tossed her over his shoulder.

It was pointless to resist, so she didn't. He set her onto her feet once inside the house. The man who'd wanted to shake Hector's hand was standing next to her, a big, ugly smile on his face.

"I'll take her from here, if you don't mind," the man said.

Hector took one long last look at her, and, for a fleeting moment, she thought he was about to take her back to the SUV, but he turned away. Tears welled up in her eyes again, and she wiped them angrily with her forearm.

"Welcome, Leila. Welcome," the man said. "I'm Óliver Sáez, and you're mine."

CHAPTER SIXTY

San Miguel de Allende, Mexico

Hunt had kept the line open with Carter so they could communicate in real time.

"Hector's coming out of the house, Pierce. Leila isn't with him. She's still in the house."

Forget this is Leila. This is just another rescue mission. What would you do if it were someone else's daughter?

Hunt made a snap decision. "We're going in."

"What about the Range Rovers?" Egan asked. "Do we let Hector go?"

"Do you think they're armored?" Hunt asked Carter.

"No doubt about it."

Hunt cursed. They weren't equipped to deal with armored SUVs. "We're letting them go," he said.

"Copy that," Carter replied.

Hunt continued with a bunch of instructions. "The moment they're off-site, we're moving in. Cole and Carter, you're on me. We'll move together."

"Copy," said Carter.

"I got it," Egan said.

"Dante will stay in or around the Land Cruiser. You'll have our six."

"Understood."

"And let Abigail know I want her to keep an eye on the end of the driveway. I want to know if someone's coming."

"Will do," Dante said as he turned into the driveway.

For a second, Hunt closed his eyes. He had worked with Egan in the past and with Carter more recently. They were both extremely capable operators, but the three of them weren't a team. They would have to be careful. Rushing around like a bunch of chickens with their heads cut off was a sure way to end up the same way. It would be his job to take the lead and to make sure they stayed focused on the objective. *Get Leila back.*

CHAPTER SIXTY-ONE

San Miguel de Allende, Mexico

Hector couldn't wait to get out of there. Óliver Sáez's house creeped him out, and he was furious at Valentina for ordering him to sell the teenager to this monster. Before the week was over, Leila would be abused, beaten, and most probably savagely raped.

But she would live, he reminded himself. *She. Would. Live.* But what kind of life would it be? *Fuck!*

He slammed his hand against the dashboard so hard that the glove compartment popped open.

"Everything okay, boss?" his driver asked him.

Hector flashed him a murderous look. The man's eyes returned to the road ahead, and he didn't speak another word.

Hector glanced at his watch and shivered. Sophia's execution was in two hours. He was glad Valentina hadn't asked him to partake in that foolishness. Nicolás, her beau, had volunteered. Hector didn't like Nicolás. He never had. Nicolás was a heartless son of a bitch. You couldn't have a heart if you were willing to set a fifteen-year-old on fire. Nobody deserved to die that way. It hurt him to see how his beloved cousin had turned into someone willing to inflict such pain on a child. But these thoughts were dangerous.

You're getting weak. Get a grip. Or she'll crush you.

But the facts didn't change. Valentina was slowly but surely turning into a real-life monster. It was true that as a child she had suffered a great deal, but, in Hector's mind, that was no reason to start killing children.

With a shock, Hector realized he had failed her. It was he who had promised to keep her safe—saving her sometimes from herself—and to keep her away from her self-destructive course.

He would try to reason with her one more time. He couldn't let her kill Sophia, because if he did, he'd be just as guilty.

And what about Leila? You're gonna leave her with Sáez?

His gut told him to ask his driver to turn the Range Rover around and to get rid of Sáez and the other pigs in his house. In the Black Tosca's book, though, that would be considered treason. Even for Hector Mieles. Was he actually considering going rogue? Hector, a man who had never hesitated to make a decision in the heat of battle, couldn't think straight. His mind was being pulled in two diametrically opposite directions. He was confused.

Hector looked outside the Range Rover window and saw a bunch of kids—some of them about the same age as Leila and Sophia—playing soccer on a makeshift field. He shook his head. *Confused?* Hector chewed on the word for a moment. He was a lot of things, but confused wasn't one of them. He knew what he had to do.

He ordered his driver to turn around.

CHAPTER SIXTY-TWO

San Miguel de Allende, Mexico

Leila's heart sank as she nervously looked around her. The house was stunning, but its occupants weren't. Behind Sáez stood three men in dark suits. They were looking her over as if she were a fresh piece of meat. They made her skin crawl.

Sáez said, "Don't be afraid of these fine gentlemen, my dear Leila. They represent foreign buyers who are looking for someone like you to add to their collection."

Their collection?

"But let's not get ahead of ourselves," Sáez continued. "Let's get you ready for the auction, shall we?"

Sáez clicked his fingers, and two men she hadn't realized were there grabbed her from behind. She kicked the man to her left on the shin with her heel, and he let out a low groan of pain. She screamed at the top of her lungs, a loud, piercing sound that reverberated throughout the first floor of the house. The man to her right clamped his hand over her mouth.

Mistake. He should have asked Hector what she did to people who pissed her off.

She bit down hard. She sank her teeth into the fleshy part of his hand, between the thumb and forefinger, with the clear objective of biting right through it. But before she could draw blood, Sáez punched her in the ribs, the blow sending her against the wall. Sáez wrapped his hands around her throat, choking her until she gagged. He pressed his body against hers and began to grind his midsection against her back. She felt his arousal. She wanted to vomit, but there was too much pressure on her throat. No air was coming through. She tried to fight back with every ounce of energy she had left, but he had her completely. She was at his mercy. She couldn't breathe, couldn't scream, and couldn't escape.

Her vision tunneled.

Then the front door burst open.

CHAPTER SIXTY-THREE

San Miguel de Allende, Mexico

The Land Cruiser screeched to a halt. Hunt was ready and out of the door even before the SUV came to a complete stop. He raced to the front door of the house, not bothering to slam his car door shut. He pressed his back against the wall as he waited for Egan and Carter to take their positions on either side of the front door. Hunt stretched his arm and checked if the door was locked. It was.

He heard a commotion from inside the house. Someone screamed.

Leila! His heart racing, he looked at Carter and mouthed, "Detcord."

Carter let his MP5 fall to the end of its sling and grabbed his back-pack. From it he pulled a coil of detonation cord. Even though it looked as harmless as a dock line, the tiny and flexible plastic tube Carter held in his hands was filled with PETN—pentaerythritol tetranitrate—a substance capable of exploding at a rate of approximately 6,500 meters per second. Carter cut off a ten-inch piece. He used duct tape to attach it to the handle and dead bolt. He then connected the blasting cap, the fuse, and the handheld detonator.

Carter signaled them to move back before he scurried away.

Hunt nodded.

The detcord blew with a cracking sound. Hunt was the first to move through the smoke. The front door was half off its hinges. Hunt kicked the door open and went in with Egan on his tail. Leila was twenty feet in front of him, pinned to the wall by a man Hunt quickly identified as Óliver Sáez from the photo Abigail had sent him. Hunt felt a presence to his right but focused on his target, knowing Egan would take care of the other threat. Hunt fired twice, striking Sáez in the upper neck and jaw, his throat spewing a mist of air and blood into his daughter's face. As Sáez fell, three men wearing dark suits appeared in Hunt's field of vision. If they were here, they were complicit. Two of the three men reached inside their jackets. Hunt fired four rounds in quick succession, hitting each man twice in the chest. He swung the MP5 sights around on the last man standing. Behind him, Hunt heard Egan's MP5 bark three times and the sounds of someone falling about and stumbling around furniture. The man in front of Hunt wore an expensive suit and looked like a rich Saudi prince. The man raised his hands in surrender. They hadn't been inside the house for more than five seconds.

Then Leila screamed, "Shoot him! Shoot him!" And Hunt did.

———

Carter was about to go in when two Range Rovers turned into the driveway. *Shit.* He peeked inside the house and saw that Hunt had already secured his daughter and was on his way out. Egan was right behind him, covering his retreat.

"We have company," Carter shouted.

CHAPTER SIXTY-FOUR

San Miguel de Allende, Mexico

Valentina Mieles looked at Sophia Garcia as she tried to break free from Nicolás's arms. She enjoyed watching Nicolás. It was arousing to watch him try to tie Sophia to the bed frame. She had set up a special room in her basement for tonight's event.

He flashed her a smile, and she noticed his eyes—cold as a snake's. She shivered. Sophia was twisting and screaming, unwilling to cooperate. She tried to hold her legs together, but Nicolás pried them apart. Sophia punched him on the chin. He slapped her hard across the face and used the opportunity to tie her legs to the bedposts.

"Careful, Nicolás," the Black Tosca warned. "We don't want to hurt her too much before the show, do we?"

Sophia must have regained her senses because she lunged at Nicolás from her seated position. The Black Tosca could only admire her tenacity. She was thrashing and struggling with all her might and giving Nicolás more trouble than he'd bargained for. Nicolás punched Sophia in the stomach, and even though she was fifteen feet away, the Black Tosca heard the air expel from her lungs. Nicolás grabbed her hands and tied them together before securing them to the bed frame.

"Well done, Nicolás. Come here," she said to him.

His bottom lip was bleeding. The little bitch had punched him harder than she had thought. She grazed her tongue over the inside of his bottom lip. She sucked away the blood, relishing its rich, metallic taste.

"There," she said. "Better."

"I can't wait," he said, clearly looking forward to what was coming next.

"Is everything ready?"

Nicolás nodded. "It is. We've already set up the online accounts. We'll route the video through so many different layers that it will be virtually impossible for anyone to find the original IP address."

"Good."

"There's already over five thousand viewers waiting for the event."

"How interesting."

"I wouldn't be surprised if we have over one hundred thousand viewers," Nicolás said. "People love this kind of stuff."

"Go get dressed for the occasion, Nicolás."

"Yes, ma'am."

Once Nicolás had walked out, she approached Sophia. The teenager was crying, either from anger, pain, or confusion—the Black Tosca didn't know.

"Where's Leila? What have you done to her?" Sophia asked between sobs.

The Black Tosca didn't reply right away, surprised by the question.

"So kind of you to worry about your friend, Sophia. You're so very cute."

"Where's my friend?"

"She exchanged her life for yours, my dear."

Ouch! From the look on her face, Sophia was buying it. There were only a few things in life the Black Tosca enjoyed more than torturing people. It was funny, really. Some people loved to take care of abused puppies; she, on the other hand, loved to manipulate others to the point of great emotional pain. Sophia had started crying again, which warmed the Black Tosca's heart.

"She's my best friend. She'd never do that," Sophia moaned. But she didn't sound convinced.

"Oh, but she did," the Black Tosca said. "She did."

Sophia's tears were running freely down her cheek now. "Why would she do that?"

"I offered the deal to her first. And she took it."

"What deal?"

"Oh my, Nicolás didn't tell you about tonight's event? I am so, so sorry. How rude of him."

Sophia was afraid now; the Black Tosca could see she was trembling.

"In a few minutes, we'll pour some gasoline onto your legs, arms, and torso, and then we'll set you on fire for the world to see. How does that sound?"

From Sophia's mouth came a weird, hideously inhuman shriek of pure emotional pain that caused every hair on the Black Tosca's body to rise up in pleasure.

CHAPTER SIXTY-FIVE

San Miguel de Allende, Mexico

Impossible, Hector thought, recognizing Pierce Hunt as he rushed out of the house and into a waiting Toyota Land Cruiser.

"Who are these people?" his driver asked.

Hector's eyes stopped on another man. *Mr. Granger, you fucking traitor.*

A man jumped out of the driver's seat of the Land Cruiser and opened fire. Several rounds ricocheted off the armored windshield, and Hector ignored the scratches as he scanned ahead, trying to figure out how many enemy combatants he and his three men were up against.

For a moment, Hector considered ordering his men out of the vehicles but thought better of it. He grabbed the radio and calmly asked his men to disengage.

"Sir?" his driver asked him.

"This ain't our business anymore. We sold the girl, remember? Turn around."

The driver continued straight down the driveway. "But this is Pierce Hunt, sir!"

"I ordered you to disengage," Hector screamed, as rounds continued to hit the Range Rover. "Do it now!" They were getting dangerously close. The Range Rovers were armored, but they weren't built like tanks. The driver jerked the wheel to the left, but it was too late. Hector ducked behind the dashboard just as the windshield disintegrated and bullets peppered his driver's chest.

Hector felt the Range Rover accelerate, and he braced for impact.

———

"Get down! Get down!" Hunt yelled as he pushed his daughter to the ground. He covered her body with his own as Egan and Carter joined their fire to Dante's.

Two seconds later, Carter screamed at him at the top of his lungs to move. He was waving Hunt off. Hunt didn't understand why Carter wanted him to move. He and Leila were in the safest place, right in front of the Land Cruiser and using its engine block as cover. Then, amid the chaos, Hunt understood. He heard an engine revving.

The Range Rovers.

Hunt forced his daughter up and saw one of the Range Rovers racing toward them. Leila was screaming, immobilized by fear. Summoning all his strength, Hunt pushed his daughter away just as the Range Rover crashed into the Land Cruiser.

Then something struck him hard in the back, throwing him from his feet and sending him sailing forward.

———

Carter started firing at the first Range Rover, concentrating his rounds just above the steering wheel, knowing the windshield would eventually crack. Half a second later, his magazine almost empty, he realized his rounds were getting through. The driver's body jerked as round after round hit him in the chest, neck, and face. But instead of slowing down, the Range Rover accelerated.

He looked to his left where Hunt and Leila were. They were directly in the path of the incoming SUV.

"Move, Pierce! Move!" he yelled at his friend. "Get up! Get up!"

For Carter, it seemed to take an eternity for Hunt to actually stand up and realize what was going on. Carter sprinted to them, knowing he wasn't going to make it in time, but he tried anyway. By the time Carter reached his friend, Hunt had already shoved his daughter out of the way. Carter crashed into Hunt, sending him flying off to the side, his momentum carrying him forward. The grinding metallic crunch of the collision between the Range Rover and the Land Cruiser came a millisecond before he felt a tremendous punch to his legs. The jolt of the impact launched him into the air like a crash test dummy. He landed on his back with a jarring thud that sent a tidal wave of pain up his spine. Then everything went black.

———

Egan couldn't believe what had just happened. Dante ran toward Hunt and Leila to render assistance, but Hunt waved him off. He was fine. Carter, though, wasn't moving. His eyes were closed, and his legs were twisted at odd angles. Egan tried to move in his direction, but the second Range Rover came to a stop. Two men jumped out. They opened fire, and Egan scurried for cover behind the crashed vehicles. The bullets followed him, sending shards of asphalt through the air. The fact that the two SUVs could explode at any time wasn't lost on him. He needed to get out of there. But where to? The two shooters had taken position behind their Range Rover. He tried to get a fix on them, but bullets whizzed past his head. Egan was growing more frustrated by the second. They were in a standoff.

———

Simon Carter had saved his life. It was that simple. Now Hunt's friend lay motionless, and Dante and Egan were pinned down. Leila looked startled but unhurt. Hunt crawled toward her.

"You okay?"

"Yeah, I think so."

"Stay down, Leila. Okay?"

She nodded. The tears he had seen earlier were gone, replaced by a glint of determination. "Can I help?" she asked.

Brave girl. "Just stay where you are."

"Dad?" she said, just loud enough for him to hear. He looked at her. "Thanks for coming. I knew you would."

Right now, there was nothing he wanted more than to hold his daughter in his arms. He kissed her on the forehead and then went to work.

CHAPTER SIXTY-SIX

San Miguel de Allende, Mexico

The smell of fuel woke Hector up. He flung his eyes open, and light flooded in. He remembered being violently thrown forward. And then nothing. He was bleeding and broken, and he cursed his driver for his stupidity. He looked around him. The Range Rover was upside down. All its windows had shattered on impact. He checked the driver, or what was left of him. There was nothing Hector could do for him.

Sporadic gunfire drew his attention.

MP5s. Not ours.

And AR-15s. My guys.

He looked around the interior of the smashed SUV for his own AR-15 but couldn't find it. He pulled his pistol out and crept toward the shattered window. He felt pieces of glass beneath his hands and muffled a curse as they dug deep into his skin. He fought the weakness that swam through his limbs. His strength was sapped, but he managed to pull himself out of the Range Rover. He lay on the ground a moment, catching his breath. He got to one knee to orient himself and felt a presence behind him.

He turned sharply, raising his pistol as he did so. But he was too late. Hunt had already fired twice. The two bullets slammed into Hector's abdomen. His pistol slipped through his fingers. He moved his hands to his abdomen, clutching his wounds. The first round had hit no vital organs, so if Hunt had only fired once, he would have had a chance.

But the second bullet had been awfully effective. It had mangled his intestines and kidneys. Never before in his life had he been in such agony. Hector yelped in pain as he forced himself into a sitting position. He supported himself with his left arm but kept his right hand pressed against the entry wounds. Bright red blood poured through his fingers. He chuckled but didn't know why. He looked at Hunt. The expression on Hunt's face was one of utter contempt. His eyes, cold and dark, showed no sympathy, no mercy whatsoever.

"I hope it hurts," Hunt told him.

Hector looked down. The front of his shirt was a deep crimson and so was the top of his pants.

"Sí, it does. Very much so."

"Where's Sophia Garcia?"

Hector wanted to answer. He wanted Hunt to stop Valentina, but he felt himself drifting away. He was losing too much blood too fast.

Pain brought him back. He opened his eyes. Hunt's face was inches away from his, and he was holding Hector's injured ear with his left hand. A searing ache filled Hector's senses as Hunt twisted. He screamed. Hunt let go of his ear.

"Where's Sophia Garcia?" he repeated.

"She's in San Miguel," he said weakly. Another wave of pain racked his entire body. He waited for it to subside and then said, "At the Black Tosca's house. And Hunt?"

Hunt's eyes had turned murderous. "Careful, Hector."

Suddenly, the pain was gone, leaving behind exhaustion and numbness. His left arm buckled, and Hector slowly slid to the ground, panting.

"I'm . . . I'm sorry. This . . . should have never happened."

"No, it shouldn't have," Hunt confirmed. The last thing Hector saw was a flash of light. He never felt the first bullet enter just below his nose, or the second one, which pierced his heart.

Hunt scanned his surroundings to make sure he wasn't being flanked. He caught a glimpse of Egan, who had taken position behind what was left of the Land Cruiser. Dante was in a prone position next to Leila. Hunt rushed to Egan's side just as bullets pinged off the metal behind him. Egan returned fire with his MP5.

"I'm down to one mag," Egan told him, firing a couple of shots. Then he added, "I had to keep their heads down while you were having your little chat with Hector."

Hunt gave Egan one of his magazines. "We need to haul ass, Cole. Abigail will pick us up, but we need to take these two bozos out."

"Agreed," Egan said. "But these guys aren't dumb. They know how to shoot, and the angle is all wrong from here. I can't hit anything."

"But you can keep their heads down, right?"

Egan frowned. "What are you thinking?"

"Change your mag."

Egan obeyed and inserted the magazine Hunt had given him into his MP5.

"On three, you pin them down with a full mag. Copy?"

Egan nodded, and Hunt counted, "One, two, three."

Egan inched out of cover and sent rounds toward the Range Rover at a rapid rate. Hunt waited until Egan had fired a dozen rounds before he sprinted the sixty feet of open ground separating him from the front door. He reached the front door just as Egan fired his last round. Hunt moved inside and to the west side of the house. He hunched over, keeping low to the floor to stay below the windows. There were no blinds on the windows, so Hunt was extra vigilant when he peeked outside, leaving only a tiny part of his head exposed.

From there, he had a nice angle on the two cartel members. Since Egan had returned to his normal rate of fire—one round every ten or fifteen seconds—the two men were taking more chances and were swapping turns at risking a lucky shot. Hunt didn't dare open the window to engage his targets, so he moved his MP5's firing selector from single shot to three-round bursts. He aligned his sights on where he thought the closest man would appear—at the front of the Range Rover, just over the engine block. Hunt estimated the distance at two hundred feet. Not impossible, but not an easy shot either, especially as he had to shoot through a window. Hunt would have only one chance to hit his target. If he missed, his target would know exactly where Hunt had fired from, and he would lose the element of surprise.

There! The man appeared, just right of where Hunt had bet he'd be. Hunt adjusted his aim and slowly pulled the trigger. His three-round burst shattered the window, showering the porch with broken glass. Hunt's target was hit, and he fell forward, out of cover. He tried to get up but only managed to get on one knee before falling again. Hunt was about to send him the gift of another three-round burst, but remembered what Egan had told him.

These guys aren't dumb. They know how to shoot. Maybe they were ex-military, like their dead boss Hector? If so, the man's partner would try to bring him back to safety. And three seconds later, that's exactly what happened.

The second man fired two long bursts toward Egan and then stepped out of cover to help his fallen comrade. Hunt was ready, and he didn't miss. His three-round burst punched holes in the man's chest, and he pitched backward. Hunt fired an extra burst into each body to make sure they would pose no further threat.

Hunt hurried outside. Egan was already next to Carter. He saw Abigail's SUV racing down the driveway and assumed either Egan or Dante had called her in. Leila ran to him, jumped up—almost knocking him over—and wrapped her arms around his neck. His daughter buried her face in his neck, and he felt her warm tears. His own eyes welled up. His mind whirled. So much had happened in the past two days. Hunt was exhausted, but he was afraid to move, unwilling to break the spell; but a second later, she did.

"We need to get Sophia, Dad," Leila said. "She's in a big house."

"I know where she is," Hunt said, letting his daughter down. "I'll get her."

Egan called out for him. "Pierce, get over here."

Carter had regained consciousness, but he was in pain. Dante gave him a shot of morphine from the trauma kit in Abigail's car. Abigail whispered in Hunt's ear, "He can't feel his legs."

Oh shit.

Hunt knelt next to Carter and took the man's hand. "You saved my life, Simon," he said, his voice breaking. "I . . . I . . ."

Carter smiled. "It's okay, brother. I'll be fine. Don't get that choked up."

"We'll get you some help, Simon. We're leaving."

Carter nodded weakly, and, with that, his eyes rolled up in their sockets as he passed out.

Hunt helped Dante and Egan carry Carter into the back seat of the Range Rover. Apart from a few scratches and dents where Egan's and Hunt's bullets had ricocheted off, the SUV was fine and wouldn't draw unwanted attention.

"Here's what's gonna happen," Hunt started. "Abigail, you and Dante will take the Range Rover and drive straight to the airport with Leila and Simon."

"Got it," Abigail replied.

"I'll call Anna to let her know you're coming," Hunt said. Then he turned to Egan. "You and I, Cole, we have unfinished business to attend to."

CHAPTER SIXTY-SEVEN

San Miguel de Allende, Mexico

Egan didn't remember the last time he was so nervous. Hunt's plan was sound but extremely dangerous. It could work, but the chances were they'd both be dead within the next five minutes. Egan wasn't afraid of dying, but he was frightened to leave Katherine behind and to never see the baby that was growing inside her. Still, like Hunt, he had to see this through.

"Here we go," he said, loud enough for Hunt to hear him. "We're there."

Egan made a left into the Black Tosca's driveway and stopped at the front gate. Two uniformed guards came out of the guardhouse. These two were poorly trained rent-a-cops. Egan wasn't even sure they knew who they were working for. The Black Tosca had hired them simply to keep the appearance of normality. Her real security detail was inside the gates, albeit a bit smaller since they'd killed a bunch of them at Óliver Sáez's house. One of the security guards gestured for Egan to pop open the hood. He did. The other guard, equipped with a long-handled mirror, swept the underside of the SUV in search of explosives. Egan was then asked to open the trunk. That he couldn't do, since it was where Hunt was hidden under a large tarp. The security guard approached. Egan pressed a button, and his window came down.

"I'm here to see the Black Tosca," he said.

"Wrong address," the guard said.

"Tell her Mr. Granger is here with a special package."

Clearly, the name didn't ring a bell with him. He was definitely not a cartel member. "I need to see the interior of the vehicle," the guard said.

"No, you don't," Egan replied. "Your employer will feed you to the fish if you open this trunk."

The guard looked confused but retreated inside the guardhouse. When he came back a minute later, his attitude had changed drastically. He was much more deferential toward Egan, and he apologized profusely.

"I'm so sorry, Mr. Granger. Mr. Nicolás will be down shortly to escort you to the residence."

Egan closed the window. "You got that, Pierce?"

"I did. I want a clean and quick in-and-out."

"Any special rules of engagement you'd like to share before we start?"

"Yeah, don't shoot Sophia. Everybody else is fair play."

Show time.

———

Hunt stretched his legs, trying to work the cramps out of them. He adjusted the tarp Egan had thrown over him to prevent him from being seen through the side windows of the Honda CR-V. He kept his Glock 22—to which he had added an Osprey suppressor—close to his chest, with his right hand wrapped around its grip and his finger on the frame. Hunt wanted to be ready for any surprises. He didn't know much about Nicolás, but Egan had told him the guy was a former Mexican navy commando, the Black Tosca's bodyguard, and a certified psycho.

On the bright side, Leila was safe, and that thought brought a huge smile to his face. Carter's predicament, though, wiped it off. Hunt felt enormous guilt for what had happened. But at the same time, he was furious at Carter for saving his life, as he might have destroyed his own in the process.

Abigail's words rang in his head. *He can't feel his legs.*

Hunt forced himself to get his mind back on the business at hand. He'd have plenty of time later to reflect—and torture himself—about what happened.

"Nicolás is coming," Egan called through gritted teeth. "Get ready."

———

Egan watched as Nicolás walked toward the SUV. Tall, broad-shouldered, with a slim waist, black hair, and brown skin. The guy was good-looking. Egan gave him that. What Egan didn't like, though, was Nicolás's walk. It was confident and assured. *Not good.*

As Nicolás came closer, Egan noticed a pistol tucked in the man's waistband. Egan lowered his window, thinking Nicolás would want to talk to him, but the man climbed into the passenger's seat and pointed his pistol at Egan.

"Put your hands on the steering wheel," Nicolás instructed. "Palms out, fingers spread, and lay them down easy. No sudden movements."

Egan did as he was told.

"Are you armed?"

Egan's eyes moved to the glove box. "In there."

Nicolás didn't bother checking. "Anything on you?"

"Glock 22. Left shoulder holster."

"That's it?"

Egan nodded. It was. *But I have Pierce Hunt in the back.*

"Use your right hand, and slowly reach into your jacket. Don't think you can draw quicker than I can shoot. It would be your last mistake, Mr. Granger."

Nicolás extended his hand, and Egan gave him his Glock. Nicolás handed it to the security guard waiting outside the SUV.

"Why are you here?"

"I have a gift for the Black Tosca."

Nicolás cocked his head to the side. "A gift? What kind of gift?"

"Behind you, in the black garbage bag."

Nicolás's eyes briefly moved to the back seat. "What is it?"

"A severed head," Egan replied truthfully.

Nicolás's face beamed with pleasure. A faint smile lurked at the corners of his lips. "I'm sure she'll love it," he said, lowering his weapon. "Drive forward, Mr. Granger. The Black Tosca is looking forward to seeing you."

Egan started the engine and put the transmission into drive. The front gate closed behind him the moment the SUV had gone through. Egan followed the winding driveway up the gentle slope for about a quarter mile until he reached the Black Tosca's magnificent colonial house. Two guards waited for them outside the main entrance. These men weren't rent-a-cops. Their demeanor, the relaxed-but-alert way they were standing, was a dead giveaway that they were Hector's men and former members of the Mexican military.

"I would have thought there'd be more than two guards," Egan said for Hunt's benefit.

"We're heading west to the coast tomorrow," Nicolás said. "Most guys are already there, preparing the compound for her arrival."

"Where's Hector? I'm sure he'd like to see the gift too," Egan said. "He gave me the contract."

"Hector and his crew will join us shortly, Mr. Granger," Nicolás said. "Please follow me."

Egan grabbed the black garbage bag from the rear seat and climbed out of the SUV. One of the guards opened the front door for them. The interior of the house was spectacular. Nothing about the elegant exterior prepared Egan for the sheer opulence within. It almost looked staged.

It was just too damn perfect—crystal chandeliers on the ceilings, heavy red velvet drapes on the larger-than-life windows, and bronze statues filling every corner. As he followed Nicolás deeper into the house, Egan noticed that all the rooms flowed into each other and were all meticulously decorated in authentic Mexican fashion with exquisite, high-end furniture. Nicolás led him down a long hall, their footsteps echoing on the marble floor. They made a right at the end of the hallway and entered a huge library dominated by a wide, curving staircase that spiraled up to the next level. The Black Tosca, magnificently dressed in a long, very tight red dress that didn't leave much to the imagination, was seated in a plush, green leather armchair.

"Hello, Cole," she said, lifting her eyes from her mobile phone. "How nice of you to stop by." She pointed at the armchair in front of her. "Come on—don't be shy. Have a seat."

She turned her attention to Nicolás. "I'll be fine," she said, dismissing him. When Nicolás didn't move, she whooshed him off with a wave of her hand. Once he was gone, the Black Tosca leaned forward. She delicately touched his knee and squeezed, and then she said, a half smile on her full lips, "I'm told you brought a gift?"

———

Hunt started counting the moment he heard Egan slam the door. When he reached six hundred, he pulled back the tarp, transitioned from his back to his belly and then to his knees, and slowly raised his head until he could see out the SUV's windows. Through the front windshield, he spotted one of the guards. Egan had mentioned two guards. Where was the other one? Hunt angled his head left to right. There was no sign of him.

Egan had been inside the house for ten minutes now. It was time for Hunt to make his move. He waited until the guard's attention was away from the SUV before climbing over the rear seat. He confirmed the SUV's doors were unlocked. With his eyes on the guard, Hunt raised his left hand and grabbed the door handle. In his right, his suppressed Glock was ready to go. Hunt threw the door open—not powerfully enough for it to bounce back—and raised his pistol to eye level. The guard, who had probably caught the movement in his peripheral vision, moved his hand to the inside of his jacket. The guard gave Hunt the same surprised, stunned look a six-year-old child gives his parents after they tell him Santa Claus doesn't exist. Hunt squeezed the trigger, burying a bullet in the guard's heart. The Oyster silencer jumped half an inch, and Hunt fired his second round the moment his sights were on the guard's head. The bullet tore away the right side of the man's face, spun him around, and dropped him on the polished marble of the entryway. From there, Hunt moved rapidly. He scanned around for the missing guard one last time and then entered the house, dragging the dead guard behind him.

CHAPTER SIXTY-EIGHT

San Miguel de Allende, Mexico

The Black Tosca accepted the plastic bag. She untied it but recoiled immediately, taken aback by the pungent smell emanating from the bag. She closed it without looking inside.

"Whose head is this?" she asked, holding the bag in one hand.

"Pierce Hunt's."

"Is it really?" she asked, wondering why he hadn't simply texted a picture to her. But she was glad to see him. It had been quite a while since their last "encounter."

"How's Katherine these days?" she asked, even though she couldn't care less.

For a fleeting moment, she saw something dark flare in his eyes, but it was gone the next instant. Had he fallen for Katherine? A surprisingly strong jolt of jealousy rushed through her. *How dare he?*

She felt as if she was being robbed. She, and she alone, was allowed to do whatever she wanted with whomever she wanted to do it with. Her expression hardened. She was about to shout something but remembered she needed "Mr. Granger" in Florida for the foreseeable future. So she bit her lip, almost drawing blood, and promised herself she'd find a way to hurt him in a way that wouldn't compromise the work he did for her.

Nicolás appeared silently behind Egan, a baseball bat in his trembling hands. His teeth were clenched, giving his usually soft and beautiful face a hard, set facade, and his eyes were wild with anger. She didn't know what this was about, but Nicolás had never failed her, in life or in bed. This must be important.

Then Egan lunged at her.

———

Egan sensed someone approaching behind him. The Black Tosca betrayed and confirmed the person's presence by moving her eyes above Egan's head. Egan planted his feet on the ground and propelled himself forward. The baseball bat that smashed across his back slammed Egan onto the swanky carpet of the library. The bat struck again, this time landing directly at the back of his neck. Lights exploded behind his eyes. He tried to turn to his side and use his forearm to protect his head against the next blow, but he failed. He blacked out when the next blow connected behind his left ear.

———

"Stop! Stop!" the Black Tosca yelled.

Like an obedient child, Nicolás stopped midstrike. Cole Egan was convulsing on the floor, his legs kicking and thrashing. *Brain damage. No longer useful.* These were the first two thoughts that popped into the Black Tosca's head. Then she looked at Nicolás and asked, "What have you done, you fool?"

"Hector's dead, and so are the men who went along to Óliver Sáez's with him. He might not be alone."

Nicolás picked up the black garbage bag and emptied its contents onto the floor. Two dead mice fell from the bag, followed by Hector's head, which rolled past the carpet and onto the hardwood floor. The

Black Tosca's knees buckled at the sight, and she had to grab onto Nicolás's arm to remain standing. She began to feel violently ill, and a moment later, she threw up in short, violent spasms. When she was done, she wiped her mouth with her forearm. She looked around her but was too stunned to move. Then a weird feeling engulfed her, and, oblivious to her surroundings, she made her way to the bar area of the library and poured herself a large quantity of single malt. She drank half the glass. Nicolás was next to her, and she saw that his lips were moving, but she couldn't understand anything he said. It all sounded like gibberish to her. Nicolás moved to her face, forcing her to meet his gaze.

"Valentina! Valentina! We must go!"

She pushed his hands aside and screamed, emptying her lungs in a guttural cry of pure agony.

"Valentina, we have to go," Nicolás repeated.

To her horror, her eyes filled with tears, but they never fell. It was as if her body was telling her she had no right to be sad, that she didn't deserve the relief they promised.

Nicolás grabbed her by the arm, but she broke free. "No," she told him. "We finish this."

She looked over at Egan. He had stopped twitching. He lay motionless on her carpet between the two armchairs. "Carry him downstairs, Nicolás. We'll add his name to tonight's main event. With luck, his Katherine will be watching."

CHAPTER SIXTY-NINE

San Miguel de Allende, Mexico

Egan came to with a splitting headache. His temples throbbed with each beat of his heart. He was naked and covered in sweat. At his feet, Nicolás was in the process of tying his ankles to a straight wooden chair. His hands were already behind his back, secured together. Two large industrial centrifugal fans attached to the ceiling hummed loudly.

He moved his eyes around in search of Hunt. He was relieved when he didn't find him. Egan tried to say something to Nicolás, but, for some reason, he couldn't. He opened his mouth again but had to close it. It was as if he didn't know the words. Saliva escaped from the corner of his mouth and slowly drooled down his chin. The saliva then formed a thin, glistening thread that swung back and forth over his chest and abdomen.

"So you woke up," the Black Tosca said. "We weren't sure you would, to be honest. But I'm glad you did. I really am."

Egan's eyes followed Nicolás, who was walking back toward him with two jerry cans, one in each hand. Egan panicked. He knew what was in the jerry cans. Gasoline. Behind him, someone cried for help.

Sophia.

"You can scream as loud as you want, honey," Nicolás told her. "Nobody will hear you."

"Nicolás," the Black Tosca said, "please turn our traitorous Mr. Granger's chair around so that he, too, can watch."

Nicolás put the jerry cans down and turned Egan's chair around. "How's the head?" he asked. When Egan didn't reply, Nicolás looked at him strangely. "Can't talk?"

Five feet in front of him, Sophia was tied to a bed frame. She was still screaming, but she had almost no voice left. Her legs and arms were tied so tightly that she hadn't enough room to move even an inch. Egan thought he heard a pinging.

Nicolás's face materialized in front of Egan. The man grinned. "He's gone in there," he said to the Black Tosca, circling the top of his index finger around his ear. "I'm not even sure he'll understand what's going on."

The Black Tosca joined Nicolás, and they both examined Egan.

"Last time I saw you naked, you were happy to see me," the Black Tosca said, looking at his manhood. "I guess that changed too."

Egan cringed inside, not because of what she had just told him but because of how powerless he felt. The feelings of embarrassment and frustration were overwhelming, his despair total.

Where the fuck are you, Pierce?

"We're ready," Nicolás said, pulling down a ski mask to hide his features.

"How many viewers?"

"Fifty thousand and climbing fast. And we aren't even live yet!"

"Start streaming."

Nicolás walked to a small desk where a laptop was set up. He typed for a minute and said, "We're live." He waved at the camera before walking to Sophia, jerry can in hand. For the first time, Egan noted the four GoPros set up around the room. Nicolás looked at Egan with a sadistic smile as he unscrewed the lid off one of the jerry cans. "I'll start with her," Nicolás told him. "But you're next."

Nicolás gently poured gasoline over Sophia, as if he was watering a flower. Egan's frustration reached a new height, but he must have been hit on the skull harder than he had originally thought because he couldn't even summon enough strength to move his head around. Sophia had stopped moving too, but, unfortunately for her, she was still alive. Egan could see her chest heaving up and down. For her sake, he wished she were dead.

Nicolás walked back to the laptop and announced proudly that they had reached seventy-five thousand live viewers. Then, as promised, Nicolás came to him and poured gasoline over his head. Egan felt the liquid run down behind his neck and ears and over his back and chest. The smell was awful, and the vapor burned his lungs. He closed his eyes and held his breath for as long as he could. Visions of his past appeared before him. His first vacation at the beach. His first kiss. When he received his Airborne wings and Ranger tab. Gaza. *Fucking Gaza.* Mr. Granger. The murders. All those murders. Katherine. His eyes became moist at the thought of Katherine. She deserved better than him. He hoped she'd never learn the truth about him, about the monster he really was. She would be a good mother. She'd know what to do.

Cole Egan let himself slide into darkness.

CHAPTER SEVENTY

San Miguel de Allende, Mexico

Hunt had been inside the house for three minutes, and he was getting irritated. He was worried that something had gone horribly wrong. Would it have been better to get into the house sooner?

Hunt cursed.

Egan had insisted that Hunt give him ten minutes with the Black Tosca. He'd sworn he'd be able to not only pinpoint Sophia's location inside the humongous estate but also neutralize Nicolás. Hunt would simply need to take care of the two guards and make sure no other bad guys came in. That was the plan anyway.

The house was silent, and Hunt kept getting lost. It took him longer than he wanted to clear the first floor, and he only discovered the library wing by chance. He wanted to move faster, but it wouldn't serve anyone any good if he ended up dead because he hadn't cleared a corner correctly. Clearing a house room by room was a complex operation and very stressful. Hunt wiped his brow to keep the sweat from stinging his eyes.

The library was enormous but somehow maintained a cozy feel. There was a bar area, a couple of reading tables with plenty of chairs for a large family to sit together, and four oversized green leather chairs next to a bulky fireplace. A wide, curvy staircase dominated the center of the library. He was cautiously advancing toward the staircase when he saw Hector's head.

As he got closer, he realized that the staircase wasn't only spiraling up to the next level; there was a basement too. Hunt stopped, listening for any hint that would help him locate either Egan or Sophia. The first thing his senses picked up was the smell. And it was a smell he recognized.

Gasoline.

This was no time to be timid or cautious. He busted his ass down the stairs, his Glock leading the way. When he hit the bottom step, he stopped to peek down the hallway. From where he stood, Hunt could only see one door. Unfortunately, it was made of reinforced steel.

As he drew closer to the door, the stench grew worse. A red light started blinking, and there was some sort of electronic locking system attached to the door. When he was within ten feet of the door, he heard something in the background. A low humming, like a big electric fan. Then he heard something else and stopped walking. He heard it again, but by the time his brain realized what it was, it was too late. He had fallen into the deadliest trap an operator could fall into—tunnel vision.

Two rounds slammed high into his back, sinking into his vest and forcing him forward into the reinforced steel door. Hunt turned around and dropped to his knees just as the man fired again. The zip of bullets cracked above his head and pinged against the reinforced door a millisecond later, just as Hunt leveled his Glock and returned fire, a tight, three-round grouping into the man's center of mass. The cartel member fell backward but fired another round that went wide. Hunt got back to his feet, hurt and dazed, but kept his Glock trained on his assailant. The man gave a barely audible moan. He tried to get up, but Hunt dropped his left foot into his sternum. The man was wearing a bulletproof vest under his suit. Hunt aimed the Glock at the man's head.

"What's the code?" Hunt asked.

The man was quick—Hunt gave him that. He tried to stick the knife that had appeared almost magically in his right hand into Hunt's left leg. Hunt fired one round, and the man's elbow exploded. Before he could yell in pain, Hunt dropped his left knee onto the man's chest and jammed his Osprey silencer deep into his wide-open mouth.

"You done?"

The man blinked several times. "Do you need a code to access the door at the end of the hallway?" Hunt said.

A nod.

"Do you know what it is?"

Another nod. Hunt removed the silencer from the man's mouth.

"You have a family?"

"Yes. Three girls and a dog. I have a dog!" the man said, as if that were going to save his life.

"Your boss kidnapped my daughter and her friend," Hunt explained, his voice a rasp in the darkened hallway. "Tell me the code, and your family will live a long and happy life. They'll never see me. But give me the wrong one, or simply refuse to tell me what it is, and I'll fucking kill every one of them."

The man was crying now. He was under no illusions about his own life. The only decision to make was whether he wanted his family to survive. For most men, it was an easy decision, but, for this one, it seemed a little more complicated. Hunt supposed the man was considering whom he was most afraid of—the guy in front of him with a gun pointed at his head, or the Black Tosca.

"One, three, one, four."

"Only four digits?" Hunt asked, but he already knew the man was telling the truth.

The man nodded.

Hunt was about to shoot him twice in the head but changed his mind at the last second. There was no point in killing the man. Instead, Hunt brought the butt of his pistol down on the man's head, knocking him unconscious, then secured the man's hands behind his back. Hunt inserted a fresh magazine into his Glock and moved quickly down the hallway.

The humming was much louder now, but Hunt couldn't hear anything else. He punched in the four-digit code. There was a deep, metallic clunk and a sucking sound. Hunt pushed down on the door handle and shoved the door open.

CHAPTER SEVENTY-ONE

San Miguel de Allende, Mexico

A couple of loud pinging sounds, like metal on metal, rang inside the room and jerked Egan awake. He opened his eyes. Nicolás was standing next to him, holding a lighter. He had heard the sound too, and his face registered surprise. He pulled his pistol from his waistband and aimed it at the door.

"Get behind me, Valentina."

Once she was next to him, Nicolás told her, "I have a revolver in an ankle holster. Take it."

"Set them on fire, Nicolás," she urged him. "Do it now!"

Nicolás didn't question her order.

Egan knew what was coming and accepted it. If this was the price to pay to atone for his sins, he was ready.

Hunt barged into the room, gun drawn.

Thank God, Egan thought, as the lighter landed on his lap. At least Katherine and the baby would be saved. Hunt would liberate them from the Black Tosca's grasp. *Thank you, my friend. Thank you.*

The flames started to lick his skin.

———

Hunt rushed into the room and instantly moved to his left, away from the door. In a flash, his eyes took in the whole scene. To his right, Egan was tied to a chair, naked, his body wet with gasoline. In front of him stood the Black Tosca. She was holding a small handgun, but it wasn't aimed at him yet. Towering next to her, and in the process of throwing a lighter in Egan's direction, was a man wearing a ski mask. *Nicolás?* To Hunt's left, Sophia Garcia was tied to a bed, wearing only gasoline-soaked underwear.

Then, as his eyes returned to his right, he saw something that gripped his heart with icy fingers. Egan was on fire. Before Hunt could react, the Black Tosca fired twice, and, at a distance of thirty feet, she'd be hard-pressed to miss with both shots. She didn't. The first small-caliber bullet caught Hunt high in the left shoulder, and the other one embedded itself in the wall five inches above Hunt's head. But the Black Tosca wasn't Hunt's priority. His priority was the man with the ski mask. He had pulled another lighter from his pocket and was about to lob it at Sophia. Hunt pulled the trigger twice in quick succession. His rounds tore into the masked man's upper body, propelling him back against the wall just as the Black Tosca emptied the last four rounds of her revolver into Hunt.

———

A high-pitched shrieking rushed out of Egan's gaping mouth. In a flash, the flames devoured their way through the gasoline. Then it was his flesh. He howled as the fire engulfed him.

———

The next round the Black Tosca fired missed Hunt, but the two after that smacked into his chest, thudding against his body armor and driving him back. The last round grazed his right side and doubled him over in a firestorm of agony. His Glock slipped from his fingers, and Hunt fell to one knee. Egan screamed, which made Hunt look up just in time to see the Black Tosca lunge, her eyes filled with murderous rage. Hunt was ready for her and grabbed her by the throat. Using her own momentum, he lifted her above his head. He released her midflight and sent her crashing into a work desk on which a laptop was set up. The work desk split in two on impact.

Hunt turned his attention back to his friend. Egan let out a horrendous, desperate scream. Hunt's heart plummeted. His friend had become a human torch. Hunt tried to pick up his pistol, but his right arm didn't respond the way he wanted it to. The stabbing pain in his shoulder was getting worse. He used his left hand to pick up the Glock and, as tears rolled down his cheeks, shot his friend in the head, ending his misery. Remorse immediately filled his heart. Dread crammed his mind, but he had to push through.

Sophia.

She was still alive, but her eyes were staring blankly at the ceiling. He walked back to the Black Tosca, who was slowly getting up, and punched her in the face. Blood spattered in every direction. She was barely conscious when Hunt grabbed her hair and pinned her against the wall. Her eyes widened with fear. He pressed the silencer against her belly and fired twice.

Pffft. Pffft.

A soft cry escaped her lips, and her hands moved to her stomach. There was an expression of pure disbelief on her face, which pleased Hunt. He let go of her hair, and she slowly slid down the wall. Next, he used his knife to saw through Sophia's restraints. He was about to take her in his arms when he heard a rasping sound coming from the masked man. Hunt had seen him go down in a mist of blood and had wrongly assumed he had killed the man. The man's pistol was out of reach, but Hunt kicked it away anyway. He pulled the man's mask off his face.

"Hello, Nicolás," Hunt said.

The man just blinked; he didn't answer. His face was covered with sweat, and his pupils were unfixed. Hunt lifted the man's shirt. There were two neat holes three inches to the right of the man's heart. Blood flowed with the rising and falling of Nicolás's labored breath. He had minutes to live.

Hunt went back to Sophia and picked her up gently. His shoulder protested, and it took Hunt every ounce of control he had not to scream. Sophia opened her eyes.

"Sophia, I'm Leila's dad. My name's Pierce," Hunt said, introducing himself. "I'm here to help."

Sophia offered him a weak smile.

"You're safe now," Hunt continued. "I've got you. You'll be home soon. I promise."

As he stepped out of the room, he glanced once more at Cole Egan.

Sorry, brother. I failed you. You, on the other hand, held on to your promise to help me save my daughter. Thank you for your sacrifice, old friend. It wasn't in vain.

———

"Are you sure you can walk, Sophia?" Hunt asked in between grunts of pain. His hand slid over to his shoulder. It was soaked in blood. He needed medical attention. Soon.

"Yes, I'm fine," the teenager replied, shivering. "I can walk."

They were on the first floor, standing in the library. Hunt made sure Sophia had her back to Hector's severed head. She had had enough traumas for a lifetime.

Hunt grabbed a blanket from one of the armchairs. He wrapped it around her shoulders. Sophia hugged herself with it.

"Where's Leila?"

"She's fine. She's with Chris and your aunt Anna."

Sophia started crying. Hunt was lost for words. Comforting teenage girls wasn't one of his strengths. Hunt patted Sophia awkwardly on the shoulder and said, "We need to go, okay?"

"Please, I hate this fucking place."

Hunt didn't think it was the right time to discipline Sophia on her use of swear words, so he said, "Me too."

Hunt led the way, with Sophia following closely behind him. Hunt had his left arm extended in front of him, pistol in hand. His right arm was now hanging at his side, useless. They were thirty feet from the door when it blew inward with spectacular energy. The blast sent a hailstorm of wooden shards and rocks in all directions. One, with a thump, sank into Hunt's leg, above his right knee, as he and Sophia were propelled back through the air. Hunt landed on his back next to Sophia. He lay on the floor, stunned, as smoke and a contingent of black-clad men sporting rifles surged through the foyer. He crawled on top of Sophia to provide her with the protection his body armor offered.

"Policía! Policía!" the black-clad men yelled, but Pierce Hunt didn't hear them. He had already passed out.

EPILOGUE

Three months later
Miami Beach, Florida

"How have you been?" Hunt asked Anna.

"I don't know, Pierce," she said. She sounded exhausted. "It's been busy."

"Yeah, I'm sure," he replied, taking a small sip of his beer.

They were on a terrace on Ocean Drive, less than a mile from Graham Young's condominium.

What used to be Graham Young's condominium, Hunt thought. The DEA had seized all of BlueShade Rental's properties, and the FBI had arrested Graham Young for money laundering and drug trafficking, among other charges. He was now awaiting trial.

Sophia and Leila had their own table inside the restaurant, pigging out on deep-fried chicken wings and sugary sodas.

"It's nice to see you," Anna said, offering him a shy smile. "I'll never forget what you've done for Sophia. And for me. Thank you."

"I'm glad she's okay. We got lucky that Dante was able to get through to the Mexican authorities. To be honest, I'm surprised they responded at all."

"The live feed forced their hand. Someone tipped them off. They had no choice but to respond. I'm just glad they were able to cut it off before it turned morbid."

"As I said, we were lucky."

"Sophia was lucky to have you."

"And now she's lucky to have you."

Anna sighed. "It's harder than I thought, Pierce. I have no idea what I'm doing."

Hunt chuckled. "Me either. Welcome to the club."

Anna reached for her glass of cabernet. She swirled the wine around, sniffed it, and then tasted it.

"I'm so sorry about your brother, Anna," Hunt said. "I meant to call."

She looked down and rubbed her eyes. Tony Garcia had died due to complications during the surgery to remove the bullet lodged in his abdomen. The bullet had caused serious damage. The doctors had been unable to stop the internal bleeding.

"He passed out in the car on the way to the hospital," Anna said, her eyes wet with tears. "He never woke up."

She buried her head in her hands. Hunt leaned toward her and lifted her chin. A big, sloppy tear ran down her left cheek. Hunt wiped it away with his thumb.

God, she's beautiful, Hunt thought. "I'm sorry."

"You don't need to apologize to me, Pierce. Not anymore. Not after what you've done for Sophia." She reached up and pressed his hand against her face. She held his gaze. Then she asked, "What about you? You still have a job?"

McMaster had reached out to Tom Hauer—the acting administrator of the DEA—who in turn had called in pretty much all the IOUs he had in Washington, DC, to get Hunt off the hook regarding his actions within the United States. In exchange, Hunt had had to write an affidavit in which he'd admitted to all his wrongdoings. The documents had been signed and reviewed by a couple of bigwigs in Washington and ordered sealed by a federal judge. Hunt, though, had had to return his badge and gun to McMaster.

"Let's just say I no longer receive a paycheck every two weeks."

"How do you feel about that?"

"They say people change careers three or four times these days."

"So you're okay with this?"

"I guess."

The events in San Miguel de Allende had shaken him. Cole Egan haunted him every single night. Hunt knew he had done the right thing by his friend, but it didn't make him sleep better. Hunt was tired of the violence. In fact, he was sick of it. How long could he stay away, though? He had once sworn he'd never lose control again. Clearly, he had broken that self-made promise—first in Florida and then in Mexico. He had lived a life full of violence. Could he learn to live without it? He knew some people who couldn't. He prayed he wasn't like them. Only time would tell.

"Anything on your mind you'd like to talk about?" she asked, bringing her wineglass to her lips.

"There are so many things that I don't even know where to start."

"How are you and Leila doing?"

Hunt sighed. His relationship with his daughter was complicated.

"I need to have 'the talk' with her. You know? I still can't summon the courage to do it."

"Why?"

Hunt chuckled nervously, crossed his arms on his chest, and said, "Our relationship is so fragile that I'm afraid I'll ruin it all the moment I open my big mouth."

"Did you talk to your ex-wife about it?"

"She's more open-minded than I am, so I'm afraid we won't have the same discourse."

Hunt shook his head, exhaled, and looked up.

"What is it?" Anna asked.

"How would you react if you'd found a picture of your daughter's half-naked boyfriend on her cell phone?"

Anna cocked her head to one side. "It depends what half is naked."

Hunt smiled. "The top half."

"They're fifteen, Pierce. At some point, they'll start experimenting. You have to establish ground rules. Talk to Jasmine and Chris about it. Come up with a game plan, and talk to her. It's not rocket science."

"It is to me," Hunt said, scratching the back of his head.

"I think the important thing is for her to know that you'll be there, no matter what."

"I know that."

"Yeah, but does she?"

Anna was right, of course. He'd talk to Chris and Jasmine later today after dropping Leila back at their place.

"Thanks. I needed to hear that."

"You're welcome."

They sipped their drinks in a comfortable silence for a bit.

"Will you be looking for a job?" Anna asked after a few minutes.

"Simon and I were actually thinking about becoming private detectives."

Anna choked on her wine and coughed, red liquid coming out of her nose as she laughed out loud. Hunt noticed that her nose crinkled and the wrinkles around her eyes—not that she had lots of them—clustered when she laughed. It made her look even more attractive and real. He had fallen hard for this woman once before. He could fall again.

"Please tell me you're kidding."

Truth was, Hunt hadn't even started to consider what he was going to do with his life. His skill set wasn't the kind civilian employers needed in great numbers. Now that he thought about it, maybe being a private detective wouldn't be that bad. Part of Carter's immunity agreement with the Department of Justice was that he had to resign from the DEA. With the dismantling of the RRTs, Hunt knew Carter wouldn't have returned to the DEA anyway. He was upset the DEA hadn't offered his friend any kind of financial package, but Carter had been adamant.

"Don't fight this, Pierce. Please. I'm just happy I can walk again. I'm set, man. Trust me."

When Hunt had asked him to elaborate, Carter had replied, "Talk to Chris Moon."

Hunt had. And, once again, Moon had surprised him. Without anyone asking for it—even though Hunt was pretty sure it was Jasmine's idea—Moon had opened an account for the Carter family and deposited a cool million in it with a promise that he'd top it up if needed. He had done the same thing for Katherine Egan. As far as she and her father were concerned, Cole had been killed in action during a black CIA operation in Mexico to rescue American hostages.

"Hey," Anna said, bringing him back. "Where were you?"

"Did I miss something?"

"I was telling you my plan to close up the family business."

That was music to Hunt's ears.

"This makes me very happy, Anna. What are you gonna do?"

"I'm good with numbers and computers. I'll find something. I know it's gonna take time, but with Tasis's help, I think I can do it."

Hunt smiled, then asked, "Do you sometimes wonder about what could have been if we had met under different circumstances?"

Anna grinned and reached for his hands. "I do, but we already have our answer, don't we?"

Before he could reply, Leila and Sophia joined them. Hunt and Anna quickly withdrew their hands, looking a bit silly in the process when Hunt knocked over his beer with his elbow.

"I thought you guys wanted your own table so you could talk about your boyfriends," Anna said, winking at Hunt.

The girls looked at each other and giggled.

"What is it?" Hunt asked. "What's so funny?"

Leila said, "Seems to me like you're the ones who need privacy."

Hunt was saved from embarrassing himself further when his mobile phone rang. He looked at the call display but didn't recognize the number. He excused himself.

"Pierce Hunt," he said once he was away from the table.

"Tom Hauer, Pierce."

The acting administrator of the DEA was the last person Hunt expected to hear from. "What can I do for you, sir?"

Hunt looked back at Anna, who was in deep discussion with the two girls, and waved at her. She didn't wave back, but she smiled, and in doing so her eyes sparkled in the midafternoon light.

"I need your help."

That jolted Hunt back to full awareness. "My help? You fired me, remember?"

"Yes, but that's exactly why you're the perfect person for the job. Interested?"

ACKNOWLEDGMENTS

The first thank-you should go to you, my readers, for without you, this book would have remained an untold tale. Thank you for your time. Thank you for setting your life on pause and taking the plunge. I hope you enjoyed the ride. Thanks to all of you who joined my mailing list at simongervaisbooks.com. I love our exchanges, and I greatly appreciate your support.

This book benefitted from the hard work of many people. I truly believe that a novel's success is proportional to the quality of the team behind it, and I'm fortunate enough to work with the very best. Many thanks to the incredible editorial team at Thomas & Mercer. My deepest appreciation to Liz Pearsons, who took a leap of faith on my behalf. I'll always be grateful. Thanks to Grace Doyle, Sarah Shaw, Gabrielle Guarnero, and the rest of the team.

A sincere thank-you to Caitlin Alexander, whose keen eyes and feedback helped me make this a better book. Thanks, too, to my friend and *USA Today* bestselling author James Hankins. I owe you one. Thank you to my friends and *Wall Street Journal* bestselling authors Brian Andrews and Jeff Wilson for their support. Much gratitude to *NYT* bestselling authors Brad Taylor, Marc Cameron, Ted Bell, Lee Goldberg, Andrew Peterson, and Matthew Fitzsimmons for their kind words and encouragement. Thanks to Ryan Steck at the Real Book Spy for everything he does for the thriller writers community. Many thanks to my mom and dad for believing in me. It means a lot.

A special thanks to my remarkable literary agent, Eric Myers of Myers Literary Management. I appreciate everything you do for me.

I'm indebted to my wife, Lisane, who has been by my side from the very beginning of my literary adventure. Never did she waver in her support. I wouldn't be where I am today without her. She's my everything. A big thank-you to my two beautiful children, Florence and Gabriel, for their patience. I love you with all my heart. You make me a better person.

ABOUT THE AUTHOR

Photo © 2013 Esther Campeau

Simon Gervais was born in Montréal, Québec. He joined the Canadian military as an infantry officer and was commissioned as a second lieutenant in 1997. In 2001, he was recruited by the Royal Canadian Mounted Police and became a federal agent. His first posting was in Toronto, where he served as a drug investigator. During this time, he worked on many international drug-related cases in close collaboration with his American colleagues from the DEA. His career switched gears in 2004, and he was placed with a federal antiterrorism unit based in the Ottawa region. During the following years, he was deployed in several European and Middle Eastern countries. In 2009, he became a close-protection specialist tasked with guarding foreign heads of state visiting Canada. He served on the protection details of Queen Elizabeth II, US president Barack Obama, and Chinese president Hu Jintao, among others. Gervais lives in Ottawa with his wife and two children.